WORF HELD THE MACE ABOVE HIS HEAD . . .

. . . as transporter room three solidified around him.

"No!" he roared. He saw Picard standing to one side. "Captain, please!" he said. "The situation on the planet is desperate; I must return at once!"

Picard stared at him for a moment, then nodded at the transporter chief. Too slowly, transporter room three faded out and the crowded battlefield came once more into focus. . . .

Look for STAR TREK Fiction from Pocket Books

Star Trek: The Original Series

Star Trek: The Next Generation

Star Trek: Deep Space Nine

STAR TREK
THE NEXT GENERATION®

DEBTORS' PLANET

W. R. THOMPSON

POCKET BOOKS
New York   London   Toronto   Sydney   Tokyo   Singapore

An *Original* Publication of POCKET BOOKS

 POCKET BOOKS, a division of Simon & Schuster Inc.
1230 Avenue of the Americas, New York, NY 10020

This book is published by Pocket Books, a division of
Simon & Schuster Inc., under exclusive license from
Paramount Pictures.

ISBN: 0-671-88341-0

First Pocket Books printing May 1994

10 9 8 7 6 5 4 3 2 1

POCKET and colophon are registered trademarks of
Simon & Schuster Inc.

Printed in the U.S.A.

This is for my niece, Khela,
and my nephew, Matt

DEBTORS' PLANET

Chapter One

THE PROBE WENT sublight and scanned the space around it. The first readings matched the data in its memory banks: one yellow dwarf star, attended by a family of planets; nearest celestial landmark: Weber 512. The first planet was class J, dead and airless, unchanged since the last probe's visit. The second planet was class M, Earthlike, inhabited by primitives—

Data mismatch. High-intensity energy readings teased the drone's sensor array. Drawn by a curiosity as intense as that of its makers, the probe moved into the system. The mystery deepened as the distance lessened. The robot noted intense electromagnetic radiations, modulated into signals; neutrino sources pinpointed fission reactors; low-frequency radiations resolved into an electric power grid. Objects in low planetary orbits radiated more signals. The probe initiated a subspace transmission to its makers.

A spacewarp suddenly twisted in high orbit around the second planet. The drone located the starship and identified it as a Ferengi vessel. Logic dictated contact; the probe signaled the ship. *Greetings from the Vulcan Academy of Science. This craft is a robot probe on a routine survey. To access a full data readout, respond on subspace frequency J. A mutual exchange of data will prove beneficial.* Secrecy was illogical; cooperation was reasonable.

Ferengi are not Vulcans. The probe was about to repeat its greeting when the Ferengi ship fired its phasers and blasted the probe into atoms.

A container of live *gagh* in one hand, a bottle of prune juice in the other, Worf was on his way to Will Riker's quarters when Data stopped him in the corridor. "Lieutenant," the gold-skinned android said, "I understand that Commander Riker has invited you to observe a humorous cinema recording with him."

"That is correct," Worf said.

"Might I join you?" Data asked. "I would appreciate the opportunity to observe Commander Riker's reactions to comedy."

The Klingon security officer grimaced despite himself, a gesture that further wrinkled the ridges on his bare scalp. While he respected Data, the android's desire to become human annoyed him. It seemed to slight all the other races in the galaxy, including his own. "Commander Riker claims that the recording would appeal to the *Klingonese* sense of humor," he said, in what he hoped was a discouraging tone.

Discouragement was a mystery to Data. "I would still find his reactions informative."

Worf fought back a sigh. "You would have to ask Commander Riker."

"Certainly." The android followed Worf as he resumed walking down the corridor. "May I ask why you are bringing food to Commander Riker's quarters?"

"The commander suggested it," Worf said. "It involves an ancient Earth tradition."

Worf came to Riker's door and signaled. "Come," Riker's voice said, and the door slid away. Worf and Data entered the cabin, where the *Enterprise's* executive officer sprawled on a low, padded chair. A bowl of popcorn sat on the floor in easy reach. "Have a seat, Worf," he said.

"Thank you." Worf placed the *gagh* and juice on the floor next to an empty chair. "Commander Data has a request."

Data nodded as Riker looked up at him. "If you find it convenient, I would like to view this comedy."

"Well . . ." Riker fingered his neatly trimmed beard. "You might find the humor a bit—esoteric."

"Lieutenant Worf has cautioned me that the humor is directed at a Klingonese audience," Data said. "However, am I correct in assuming that you also find it humorous?"

"That's right," Riker said. His beard couldn't hide his smile. "But I'm looking at it from the Klingon viewpoint, too."

Data nodded. "Nevertheless, I believe I have enough understanding of humor to predict when and why you will laugh. I would like to test my understanding."

Riker shrugged. "Pull up a chair."

Worf had already taken his seat. Unlike Riker, he sat with an erect posture, which maintained his innate dignity; the chair seemed inadequate to support his muscular frame. "Sir," he said to Riker, "might I ask where you found a Klingonese comedy?" He knew of no such recordings. As did most Klingons, Worf considered humor an annoying alien custom.

"It's not Klingonese," Riker told him. "It's an action-adventure movie from Earth's late twentieth century. I'd thought it might supply some raw material for a holodeck adventure, but after I watched it—never mind. Computer, start projection."

The cabin lights dimmed. The chairs faced a blank wall, and an image appeared on it. A man in a blue uniform walked down the center of a dark, rain-slick urban street. As words appeared on the screen— *Missing Link 3: Vacation in Armageddon*—a second uniformed man joined him. They had just greeted one another when gunfire erupted from one of the buildings. The two men jumped behind a wheeled vehicle and shouted at one another. "They're trying to kill us, Link!"—"Yeah? They gotta try harder!" Their archaic accents made their words hard to understand.

Metal slugs pierced the vehicle, and the two men dashed away from it as its hydrocarbon fuel detonated. They continued shouting at one another as they ran. "They're going to kill us!"—"So let's kill them first!"—"Dammit, Link, you act like you're rabid!" —"Rabid? I was *born* rabid!"

The two men ran into a building, where men with massive rifles fired streams of bullets at them. The man called Link shot several of his enemies with his pistol. When he ran out of ammunition, he picked up a thick metal pipe. He waved it in front of himself, deflecting the bullets his last assailant fired at him. When that man used up his ammunition, Link struck him over the head with the pipe. Despite Link's massive musculature, it took him several blows to incapacitate the man.

Riker laughed at the scene, then glanced at Worf. "Admit it, Worf," he said. *"That* almost made you laugh."

Worf gave a noncommittal grunt. Riker had taken up the challenge of making the Klingon laugh, although so far he had not succeeded. *I wish him success,* Worf thought. *Humor is undignified, but understanding it might help me to deal with Alexander.*

4

His son was part human, and the boy's emotions and behavior often baffled his father. The sense of humor that Alexander had inherited from his half-human mother formed the greatest obstacle between father and son.

On the screen, the character Link put a bullet in his hand, pointed his fist at an enemy and squeezed until the bullet fired. Riker laughed, but Worf felt as mystified as Data.

"Offenhouse," Jean-Luc Picard mused. He leaned back in his ready-room chair and gazed at the message on the screen. The *Enterprise* was ordered to proceed to Starbase 144, where she would pick up Ambassador Offenhouse. The ambassador would supply further orders; the *Enterprise* would be at his disposal. By order of Admiral Singh, Starfleet Command, et cetera, et cetera.

"Offenhouse," Captain Picard repeated. Why did that name sound so familiar? "Computer, display the file on Ambassador Offenhouse."

The brisk contralto voice barely hesitated. "No such file is available."

"How very odd," Picard said, as much to himself as to the machine. "Computer, has there ever been a human named 'Offenhouse' aboard the *Enterprise?*"

"Affirmative," the computer answered. "Identity: Ralph Offenhouse, located stardate 41986.0 in cryonic suspension—"

"Enough." The memories came back now. The *Enterprise* had stumbled across a derelict Earth satellite that contained a number of humans in cryonic suspension. All of them had died in the late twentieth century, and they had been frozen in the hope that they could someday be revived and cured.

That day had come in the middle of the twenty-fourth century. Due to equipment malfunctions

5

aboard the antique spacecraft, only three of the passengers remained viable. They had been taken aboard the *Enterprise,* thawed out and restored to good health. Picard had not been present while this happened; he had been called away to an emergency conference at Starbase 718. Several starbases and outposts near the Romulan Neutral Zone had been destroyed, and suspicion had naturally fallen upon the Romulans. Picard had returned to his ship to investigate the situation . . . and to meet Ralph Offenhouse.

All in all, I prefer the Romulans, the captain thought as he gazed idly at the ready-room ceiling. Offenhouse had been by turns obnoxious, aggressive and self-centered, and Picard could readily imagine somebody back in the twentieth century freezing the man merely to be rid of him. After close to four centuries in suspension, his only concern had been with his financial situation. He had made long and loud demands to be put in contact with his bankers and breakers—no, brokers, that was the correct archaism. Offenhouse had been a financier, and he was blithely unaware of the changes the past centuries had seen.

To be fair, the man had proven useful during the *Enterprise's* confrontation with a Romulan warbird. The Romulan commander, Tebok, had blamed the Federation for the destruction of Romulan bases on the other side of the Neutral Zone. Offenhouse had listened to Tebok's threats and bluster—and somehow deduced that the Romulans were also mystified by the destruction.

That simple observation had allowed Picard to defuse a potential Federation-Romulan war. It had become clear that both sides were the victims of a third party, one with weapons of almost incredible power. The Romulans had seen that as well, and for all their belligerence they had proved too canny to fight the Federation when faced with a sudden unknown. It had turned out that the Borg were responsible for the destruction. . . .

Picard shook himself out of his reverie. He left the ready room and stepped onto the bridge. The primary team was off-duty at this time of the ship's "day"; the conn was crewed by Cadet Wesley Crusher and Ensign Shrev. A technician in antigrav boots stood on the ceiling, working at an open panel.

At his station, Wesley—currently on home leave from Starfleet Academy, and quite dapper in his cadet uniform—did his best to look alert for the captain. *Making amends,* Picard thought. Wesley had been involved in an incident at the Academy, in which one cadet was killed in a flying accident. The accident had come about owing to a gross violation of safety regulations, and Wesley had become enmeshed in a cover-up. He had made a mistake and he had been punished for it, but it was obvious that Wesley had not come to terms with his error, which had included lying to Picard.

The young Zhuik appeared to be dozing; her head was bent over her console—no, she had a look of concentration on her pinched green face. The wiry antennae that curved from her forehead waved back and forth as though reaching for the weak electromagnetic fields to which they were sensitive. "Try it again," the technician called to her.

Shrev's slender antennae quivered as she touched her controls. "Everything is perfect now, thank you." Her voice was polite and quiet, almost a whisper. Although humanoid, the Zhuik had evolved from arthropods—*a more diplomatic word than "insects,"* Picard thought—and much of their social behavior mimicked that of their hive-dwelling ancestors. Zhuik could be hot-tempered at times, but Picard had never heard of a rude Zhuik.

"Okay," the technician told Shrev. He closed the panel and walked across the ceiling toward the turbolift.

"Was there a problem, Ensign?" Picard asked.

"Only a minor power surge in the displays, sir," Shrev said. "Ensign Dayan has corrected it."

"Excellent," Picard said. "Cadet Crusher, how long will it take to reach Starbase 144 at warp six?"

Wesley keyed something into his panel. "Ten-point-four hours, sir."

Picard nodded. "Make it so." He turned toward the turbolift as Shrev laid in the new course.

Picard went to his quarters and lay down. He wondered if the ambassador had something to do with the Cardassian situation. The Federation had fought and won a limited war against the Cardassian Empire a dozen years ago, but the humanoid Cardassians had never fully accepted their defeat. They constantly maneuvered to gain a strategic advantage over the Federation, and several intelligence reports said that they were reinforcing their border with the Federation. The Cardassian War had been vicious enough, Picard reflected. With their pride stung by defeat, a second Cardassian war could be even more destructive.

You're tired, Jean-Luc, Picard told himself. Weariness always made him pessimistic. It was far more likely that the ambassador was on a routine assignment, something that could use the prestigious presence of Starfleet's flagship. A treaty negotiation, an inauguration, a new world entering the Federation—

The captain turned the lights off. *Offenhouse,* he thought as he drifted toward sleep. The name had to be a coincidence.

"Okay, Link, whadda we do now?"

"You die!" Riker suggested. He hurled popcorn at

the screen—a strange use for food, Data reflected, although Riker had described this behavior as a form of applause. Worf grunted in agreement as he ate more *gagh*. One of the wormlike *gagh* wriggled out of the jar and fell to the floor. Its eyespot sensed a light, and the creature squirmed toward it. Riker reached for it, but Worf caught it first and ate it.

"Sir—" Data reviewed the situation. The movie's central characters were in an awkward position. Trapped in a deep, narrow valley, they stood between a horde of drug-smuggling terrorists and a unit of killer cyborgs. Rabid vampire bats wheeled in the air above their heads. Giant rats—the product of a demented villain's genetic-engineering research— slithered out of meter-wide tunnels in the valley walls. A sign cautioned that the two humans stood in the center of a minefield. The foliage resembled poison ivy. It was about to rain. "Their optimum survival course is to destroy one of the rats, then—"

"No," Riker said. "You should never fight anything smarter than yourself." Data saw Worf smile at that, but he did not laugh.

"Hurry, Link!" the actor insisted. "We're in *biiiig* trouble!"

"What trouble?" Link roared. "Things have never been better!" He leveled his weapon—a massive rotary cannon that fired one hundred explosive shells per second—and blazed away at the stony ground. The shells touched off the mines, which threw clouds of rubble and shrapnel into the air. The shrapnel obliterated the bats. The multiple blasts stunned the rats, and while they staggered about in a daze the two actors surged up the valley slope. Riker threw more popcorn at the screen.

"This is all impossible," Data said. "The explosions would incapacitate the humans as well as the animals. In addition, the cannon would exhaust its ammunition after three seconds of firing. Furthermore, the recoil from such a weapon would propel its user through the air with an average acceleration of—"

"Data, Data!" Riker chuckled. "That's what makes it so funny! It's absurd."

The android looked to the Klingon. "Do you agree with this assessment, Lieutenant?"

"It is absurd," Worf rumbled. He took a handful of *gagh,* ate it, then passed the jar to Riker.

Data cocked his head inquisitively. "Perhaps I would understand if you defined the nature of the absurdity."

Riker took a handful of *gagh.* "It's funny because we know what real combat is like," he said, and popped the *gagh* into his mouth. "And this isn't it," he mumbled.

"Ah," Data said. One thing became clear. "Then you are laughing *at* the movie, not *with* it?"

Riker nodded at the distinction. "This movie wasn't meant as comedy," he said. On the screen, a massive explosion tore through the valley. The blast lifted Link and his sidekick into the air—to deposit them, unscratched, on the ground at the top of the valley. "But the people who created it knew nothing about war. Combat was never like this, even back in the twentieth century."

"But if it were," Worf said wistfully, "the twentieth century would have been a marvelous time."

Chapter Two

OFF-DUTY, lounging in his cabin with a Dixon Hill mystery novel, Picard seemed a man at peace with the universe. The universe, however, was not at peace with him. The intercom beeped just as Dixon Hill was about to apprehend Jack Larsen's killer. "Picard here."

"De Shay, sir, in transporter room three. The ambassador is ready to come aboard."

Picard glanced at his book. Dixon Hill had waited almost four centuries to catch Lefty Lefkowitz; he could wait a while longer. "I'm on my way," Picard said, putting the book aside.

A minute later Picard was in the transporter room, where Chief De Shay made a final adjustment to his controls. "Energize," Picard said. The transporter came to life, and Picard squelched a groan. If the man who had just materialized on the pad was not Ralph Offenhouse, then he was his twin brother. *And may a just and merciful God preserve the galaxy from two such men,* Picard thought. "Mister . . . Am-

11

bassador?" Picard asked, unable to control his disbelief.

"Yeah, that's me." Offenhouse stepped off the pad and shook Picard's hand. He was of average height and weight, middle-aged and pink-skinned, possessed of thick dark hair, and neither handsome nor unattractive. "Good to see you again, Picard. How's business?"

"Quite well, thank you," Picard said, and sighed. *What next?* he wondered. *Romulans? Cardassians? Tribbles?* "Admiral Singh informed me that you would deliver our orders. After you've settled in, I'll call a staff meeting."

"Good idea." A pair of suitcases materialized on a pad, and Offenhouse picked them up. "Are you going to let me have my old quarters?"

"If you like—"

"They'll do," Offenhouse said. "I'll see your staff in ten minutes." He left the transporter room.

Picard turned to the transporter chief. "Mr. De Shay," he asked, "did you have any difficulties when you beamed the ambassador aboard? Any power surges, or interdimensional shifts, or other anomalies?"

"No, sir," De Shay said. He scanned his instrument panel. "Everything went perfectly." He gave a helpless shrug which said that he remembered Offenhouse's last visit to the *Enterprise*. "Sorry, sir."

"I suppose it can't be helped," Picard said. "Carry on."

Picard went to the nearest turbolift and returned to the bridge. He recalled studying an incident aboard an earlier *Enterprise*. A transporter malfunction had swept the captain—either Pike or Kirk, Picard thought without much certainty—and several other crew members into a parallel universe, one in which the Federation was an insanely violent empire. Perhaps a similar accident had connected this universe with one in which the Federation was violently insane.

It was an appealing theory. It might even have been true.

True or not, Offenhouse appeared on schedule in the conference room. As he took his seat, Picard noted the reactions of his bridge crew. Worf and Riker looked at the man with distaste, while Deanna Troi's wide, dark eyes showed a mixture of curiosity and sympathy. Data's gaze, as always, was unreadable.

Offenhouse opened the meeting. "The *Enterprise* has been assigned to escort me to Megara, which is somewhere in the Perseus sector—what is it, uh, Info?"

"Data, sir," the android corrected. "Specifically, sir, Megara is the second planet of 329 Aurigae. It is a class-M planet, rated one on the industrial scale, with a population of four hundred million humanoids. It has no interstellar relations and is fully covered by the Prime Directive."

Offenhouse smiled at the android. "C-minus, Digit."

"Data, sir. I do not understand this term—cee-minus?"

"It's your grade," Offenhouse explained. "Your data is out of date, Data, by a decade or so. Right now Megara rates nine on the industrial scale."

"That's impossible," Riker said crossly.

"Glad to have your word for it, sonny," Offenhouse said. "A Vulcan robot probe scanned Megara last month. It may have been pre-industrial ten years ago, but now it's at the same technological level as Earth was a century ago. The probe picked up signs of high-intensity power sources, high-rate data transmissions, even something that may have been a warp drive."

"And this growth disturbs you," Troi said.

Offenhouse shrugged. "Me? Naw. But the Federation Council is having a fit. Especially because the probe detected a Ferengi ship in the area—and the Ferengi shot the probe down. My orders are to find out what the little twerps are doing on Megara."

"Why you?" Riker asked bluntly. "You're no diplomat."

Offenhouse nodded. "Who better to deal with the Ferengi?"

"You're an anachronism," Riker said. "Whatever knowledge and talents you may have"—*if any,* his tone implied—"are so outdated—"

"—that the Ferengi will skin me alive." Offenhouse looked at Riker in disdain. "You think I conned my way into this job, don't you?"

"Essentially, yes. You can't possibly know—"

Picard felt pained. "That will be enough, Number One. Mr. Ambassador, I was told that you would supply our orders."

"Yeah, I almost forgot." Offenhouse reached into a pocket—Picard felt a stab of envy; Starfleet safety regulations banned pockets from uniforms—and pulled out a computer card. He tossed it across the conference table to the captain. "Your orders are to do whatever I say will aid my mission."

Picard fingered the computer card. "I see. At warp seven, we can reach Megara in five days."

"Fine," Offenhouse said, and stood up. "I'm sure you can get me there without too much trouble. Well, I've spread enough cheer for one day, Picard. See you around the campus." He went to the door, then paused. "By the way—"

"I know," Picard said in a sour voice. "Everything discussed in this room is secret."

"Top secret," Offenhouse said smugly, and left.

Picard waited until the conference-room door had

slid shut behind Offenhouse before he spoke. "Comments?"

"This is a ruse," Riker said. "Nobody could seriously appoint *him* as an ambassador, not even to the Ferengi."

"I agree," Worf rumbled. "His presence conceals some other action."

"Yet the Federation does not play games with its diplomats," Picard said.

"That is correct," Data said. "Historically, efforts which use diplomatic personnel for clandestine purposes have often ended in disaster. The Federation is cognizant of this fact."

"So we must take the ambassador at face value," Picard said. He looked to Deanna Troi. "Counselor, you've been rather quiet."

"Ambassador Offenhouse is a complicated man," she said. "I don't believe he's fully adjusted to his presence in what is—to him—the distant future. Everyone he knew is long dead, but he's still alive, and very much alone. In a way, he's the sole survivor of an overwhelming disaster."

"And the only disaster is the simple passage of time," Picard said.

The Betazoid empath nodded. "There's more, Captain. He's distressed over his presence on board the *Enterprise.* I'll need to talk with him to pin this down, but he seems to think that we jeopardize his mission."

"Perhaps it is because Ambassador Offenhouse associates us with his revival," Data said. The android sounded hesitant; lacking emotions of his own, he was always unsure of himself when discussing their import. "However illogically, he may see us as the cause of his separation from the past."

Troi looked surprised. "That's exactly what I was thinking, Data. And his belief is dangerous. A man who *expects* to fail, *will* fail."

Riker snorted. "The ambassador himself is reason enough for his mission to fail."

"Captain," Data said, "I suggest we examine our orders."

Picard nodded. "Quite right, Mr. Data." He slid the data card into a reader slot. A holographic display appeared above the conference table. Much of it showed a planetary system, which expanded rapidly as the Vulcan probe made its approach. Letters and numerals streamed across the lower part of the display.

Picard noted that Data kept his gaze locked on to the readouts, while everyone else watched the images of the Megara system. That dichotomy between man and machine—well, biological and cybernetic life, Picard corrected himself, with a glance at Troi and Worf—always intrigued the captain. To humans, images were more easily understood than rows of numbers, while Data found it easier to detect patterns in endless ranks of numbers and letters.

It's not as though you could read that, *Jean-Luc,* Picard thought in self-amusement. The display data flickered by too quickly for the human eye to read; the captain settled back to watch the image. Megara expanded from a silvery star to a fat crescent. The illuminated part of the globe showed white clouds, blue oceans and a green swath of land. The nightside glittered with the lights of a half-dozen large cities.

A point of light gleamed near the planet. It expanded into a shape that reminded Picard of a horseshoe crab. "Ferengi battle cruiser," Worf muttered, as a phaser beam slashed out to envelope the probe. The holograph vanished.

A new image appeared: Admiral Singh. The dark man's turban and swirling mustachios gave him a fierce visage, and he seemed to glare at the camera. "Captain Picard," he said. "You are hereby informed that the Federation Council has placed *Enterprise* at the disposal of Ambassador Ralph Offenhouse. The council orders you to give him your full and unqualified cooperation."

Singh paused and softened. "Jean-Luc, I've met the ambassador, so I know how hard this will be. I'm told he's an expert on the Ferengi; he's studied everything we know about them, and Councillor Diem claims he's explained many of their incomprehensible actions. It would be tactless of me to describe this as an idiot-savant talent. Good luck; Singh out." The holograph flicked out.

Picard looked to Data. "Analysis?"

"The Megaran situation is precisely as the ambassador described it, sir," Data said. "It is clear that the Ferengi are helping the Megarans to advance their technology."

"But why?" Troi asked.

"That," Picard said, "is the question we must answer."

When the conference ended, Worf was the first to leave the room. He went straight to his post on the bridge and checked the weaponry. He did not fear a Ferengi battle cruiser, but he did respect its powers. In terms of hardware and energy, such a ship was an even match for the *Enterprise*. Fortunately, Federation crews had the edge in discipline and combat training.

Worf looked around the bridge. Data had gone to the science officer's post. The android was not an imaginative soldier, but he had cybernetic reflexes and a vast memory for tactical maneuvers. Wesley Crusher, on vacation from the Academy, and Shrev, the Zhuik, sat at the helm. Both were young, but both had seen combat—as bystanders, granted, but neither had lost their nerve under fire. Crusher was eager to prove himself, and it was said that Zhuik loved to fight.

Picard, Riker and Troi remained in the conference room. Troi hated battle, but her insights into enemy minds were always helpful. Picard was at heart a diplomat, but he did not dishonor himself when combat was the only choice. Riker—

Riker emerged from the conference room and stepped up behind Worf. "A Ferengi battle cruiser could supply us with a diverting afternoon," the human said.

Worf grunted in approval of Riker's spirit. Of all the ship's crew, Riker was the one most like him in temperament and inclinations. A year ago he had served as an exchange officer aboard the Imperial Battle Cruiser *Pagh,* and he had returned from that assignment with a deepened respect for Klingon ways. "I am more concerned with this *ambassador,*" Worf said quietly.

"Same here," Riker said. "He may be genuine, but something doesn't feel right. We'd better live back-to-back."

"Indeed." Among Klingons, *back-to-back* was the watchword of friends going into combat: stay alert and protect one another. Despite the unknowns in this situation, Worf felt reassured by those words. He could rely on Riker.

Picard and Troi returned to the bridge. "Helm," Picard told Shrev, "set a course for Megara, warp factor seven."

"Course plotted and laid in," Shrev said in her silken whisper. *Enterprise'*s warp drive came to life.

Five days to Megara, Worf thought. That would give him ample time to drill for action against the Ferengi.

Wesley went back to his stateroom as soon as he got off duty. *Something's going to happen,* he thought as he sat down at the computer. The new passenger and

Worf's repeated combat drills said as much, but nobody would say exactly what was going on. That was too much for his curiosity.

It didn't take him long to dig information out of the computer. There was a transmission from Starfleet Command, and although it was security-coded, Wesley had little trouble in breaking its protection. The transmission was a grab bag of information: a personnel file on Ambassador Offenhouse, data from a Vulcan probe, and the usual bureaucratic messages that authorized the *Enterprise* to carry out its mission. It looked like parts of the message had been deleted. Wesley didn't doubt that the erased parts would have told him exactly what was happening. Well, he mused, you couldn't have *everything*.

Wesley started reading. The probe data took his attention first. The most interesting thing here was the information on Weber 512, a gravitational anomaly about one light-year from the Megaran system. Weber 512 was a binary system, a pair of neutron stars that orbited one another at an average separation of about two hundred kilometers. Each member of the pair was as massive as Earth's sun, and their whirligig orbit caused them to generate some intense gravitational waves. The pair also had a powerful, complicated magnetic field, one which stirred up the interstellar hydrogen into a maelstrom of radiation as the pair spun through its orbit dozens of times every second. The system was more interesting than a simple pulsar, and Wesley hoped he would get the chance to study it when the *Enterprise* reached Megara—

"Caught you," he muttered to himself. Weber 512 wouldn't have anything to do with Megara. He was letting his fascination with science distract him from the real subject of his investigation.

He delved back into the probe data. The probe had

been destroyed by a Ferengi ship, which was the sort of thing you'd expect from the Ferengi. Before its destruction, the probe had made a partial scan of the Megaran system and found that Megara was a typical class-M planet, rated nine on the industrial scale.

Puzzled, Wesley checked the navigational summary. It said that Megara only rated one on the industrial scale. He didn't know what to make of that. It was unusual to see this big a discrepancy in the statistics, especially when the data was collected by Vulcans. He couldn't imagine what had caused the error.

As he mulled that over he noticed activity on the computer. Somebody else was accessing the probe data . . . somebody who had circumvented the security blocks. It looked like he wasn't the only curious person on the ship.

Solid gold, coated in diamond, the phaser bespoke Enforcer Durok's wealth. He smiled as he strapped it to his waist. Among Ferengi, power and wealth were one and the same. To display wealth was to display power, and command respect.

Durok picked up his neural lash and slung its thick blue coil over his shoulder. The Megarans understood the lash better than the phaser. Perhaps it was because a phaser either killed instantly or inflicted swift unconsciousness, while the lash delivered unlimited amounts of raw pain. Pain was the right coin in dealing with recalcitrant Megarans.

Durok left his cabin and went to *Dividend*'s transporter room. Technician Glupet stood at the control console. "I'm to set you down in Metari Leeg," he told Durok.

"I know that," Durok snapped. He took a map unit from the wall locker, switched it on and snarled at it. Only one red mark showed on it, but that was enough. "What trouble is there?"

Glupet grunted. "The debtors carved up Director Sumash."

Durok growled. Sumash had been an instructor, teaching the smartest—well, the least stupid of the natives how to run their new industries. That was a necessary part of the Daimon's plan; the Daimon Chudak hadn't hired enough Ferengi to administer all of Megara. Sumash's death would delay the project, and *that* would delay Durok's profits. "Sumash always was an idiot," Durok said.

"Well, he's a dead idiot," Glupet said. "Some of the Prophet-boys netted him. At least they didn't take his share of the profits away from us."

"I'm surprised Sumash didn't lose the money to them." Durok stepped onto the transporter stage. He resented Sumash for his carelessness, which meant that Durok had to expose himself to the natives. A man that witless deserved his fate. Even so, the debtors had to be taught that a Ferengi's person was inviolable. "Where does the city's security boss live?" Durok asked. "Put me in that place."

"Yes, sir." In the moment before Glupet pushed the control slides, Durok noted dry bloodstains on the pad under his feet. Carved, he thought, as with metal wedges. The debtors were savages.

Durok materialized on a sidewalk, in a district jammed with crude brick buildings. The air reeked of ozone, ill-managed sewage, sweaty Megaran bodies. Natives scurried away from Durok as he uncoiled his lash. *Get close enough for pain,* he thought, *and I'll teach you to let harm befall your benefactors!*

None obeyed his wish; the debtors had learned to avoid a Ferengi in a vengeful rage. Durok stomped into the police building, driving Megarans out of the way with his lash. When the security boss emerged from his office to gape at the commotion, Durok coiled the lash over his shoulder and jabbed a finger at him. "You!" the enforcer snapped. "You were supposed to keep Sumash alive. Why didn't you do your job?"

"M-my job I have done," the man stammered. "Into a crowd alone Sumash insisted on walking, to me he would not listen—"

"Enough!" Durok said curtly. He rested a hand on his phaser's heavy golden butt. "Your job was to keep him alive, you oversized hairball. People who can't do their jobs don't need their work permits. Give."

The man's brown face turned gray as blood drained from it. He fell to his knees and began begging: he had tried, how would he feed his family without work, his children would starve—

Irked by his wheedling, Durok drew his phaser and stunned the man. He sprawled on his back, and as a dozen other Megarans gaped in the hallway Durok went to the man, rifled his coverall pockets and found the man's work permit. The electronic card's identification light pulsed green and red as Durok tossed it on the floor. He readjusted his phaser and vaporized it with a single shot.

Durok recognized one of the Megarans in the hall. "You!" he said to the muscular-looking woman. "You're this idiot's assistant?" The woman nodded dumbly. "Well, you're the security boss now. Do a better job than this lazy debtor."

Durok left the police building. He thought about returning to the safety of the *Dividend*—but for all its dangers, he thought suddenly, Megara had advantages that the ship lacked. "Durok to *Dividend*," he said to his communicator. "I'm going to spend a few hours inspecting the city."

"Understood," Communications Officer Nyenyor answered. The man snickered. "Have a good—*inspection.*"

Let him laugh, Durok thought as he deactivated

his communicator. *I'm after something better than laughs.*

Metari Leeg was a mixture of old and new. Radio antennae poked from thatch roofs; superconducting power cables were slung from wooden posts along the streets; artigrav vehicles floated along cobbled roads. The debtors might have shown gratitude for all the good the Ferengi had done them, but instead they repaid their debt with riots and murder.

I'll be safe enough today, Durok told himself as he walked down the street. Sumash's death would have released some of the tension the natives felt. The debtors might even feel eager to make amends, to preserve their own safety.

Still—carved, like a slab of meat. The thought made Durok shiver, and wonder if the Daimon Chudak truly knew what he was doing on Megara. Chudak's plan was simple and bold: turn Megara into an industrial world and exploit its production. The rewards would be great . . . and the payoff was now only months away.

Bold, but dangerous, Durok thought, *giving high technology to slaves . . . even if they agreed to indenture themselves in payment.* Once Megara was modernized, the debtors could arm themselves and repudiate their debt. Perhaps it was in bad taste to question the plans of one as wealthy as the Daimon Chudak, but at times like this Durok found it hard to quell his doubts. There was something mysterious about the Daimon's plans and behavior, as if he was keeping something hidden from his crew. Secrecy was a Daimon's privilege, and no doubt he was just hiding the full extent of his profits—but Durok still had qualms. Something just didn't *feel* right.

Durok stopped cold when he saw a building with the Prophet's symbol on it. The circle and jagged lines symbolized a planet shattered by a lightning bolt—a typical display of debtor ignorance, Durok thought in contempt. Lightning wasn't a world-splitting force. *Of course,* he reflected, *the symbol is easily drawn, and it's as simple as the Prophet's blather. And Glupet said the killers followed the Prophet. So—*

The phaser shattered the symbol, and the brick wall behind it, as readily as a lightning bolt. That left a message as simple and direct as the Prophet's ravings against the Ferengi. Durok smiled as he holstered his phaser.

The street opened onto a broad avenue, a main street lined with factories, warehouses and inns. The sidewalks were crowded with humanoids, and half of them were female. Invitingly tall, with flesh the warm brown color of expensive Vulcan amber, faces that exaggerated the most desirable characteristics of a woman—delicate teeth, dainty ears, smooth forehead —and packaged in clothes that kept the goods, so to speak, tantalizingly hidden.

And all free, Durok thought with a gleeful chuckle, his doubts and fears forgotten. There was no need to pay a vendor for any of these feminine delights, no need to waste money on satisfying unpredictable feminine whims. They were fun, too; unlike Ferengi females, alien women would often talk for *hours* without harping on their own greedy wants. Durok locked his eyes onto the loveliest of the lovelies and set off in pursuit.

Durok would not have thought it possible, but something distracted him from his mission: the unmistakable bleep of a computer's data pulse. He should not have heard that here. There were no modern computers on Megara; not even a man as bold as the Daimon would trust the Megarans that far.

Yet there it was again. Drawing his phaser, Durok moved toward the source of the sound while Megarans ran to avoid him. The scooplike Ferengi ear was highly sensitive, a product of evolution in Ferengal's thin atmosphere, and Durok had no trouble locating the source. When he came to the brick wall of a building, he thumbed the phaser and blasted his way clear.

He coughed on brick dust as he stepped through the shattered wall. The room he entered held crude wooden furniture—and a computer, and subspace communications gear, and a holographic projector.

"Treachery," Durok growled, at once angered and pleased. One of his shipmates must have sold out to the debtors, an act that might endanger his own profits. He couldn't imagine how the Megarans could make betrayal profitable, but here was the evidence. On the bright side, the Daimon Chudak would reward Durok for uncovering this, and the traitor's share of the profits would be divided among the rest of the crew—

There was a snick and something stung the top of his bare scalp. Durok started to reach for the sting before his hand went limp. As his body grew numb, he tumbled to the wooden floor and lay slumped on his side. In seconds his paralysis grew so complete that he could not even move his eyes.

Two Megarans entered the room; he knew their number by their voices. His Universal Translator brought their words in flat, neuter tones. "We'll have to kill this one, too."

"Two dead aliens, so close, so soon. The other Ferengi will grow suspicious."

"No, they will only know two of their kind are dead."

"That will bring more reprisals."

"Reprisals will feed the hatred. We need that."

"It will also impede our progress."

"What else can we do? Should we let this beast tell its mates about us?"

"I command here, but you are correct."

Durok's phaser had fallen in front of his face, and his hand lay only centimeters from its golden handle. He struggled to grasp the phaser, willing his hand to cross the distance and take the weapon. His thumb twitched slightly, once, twice. More effort shoved his hand halfway toward the phaser.

A Megaran reached down and took the weapon. "A pretty toy."

"The handle is solid gold, very heavy."

"Club him to death with it."

Chapter Three

POLITENESS, Wesley told himself as he approached Shrev's quarters. Zhuik culture placed a lot of emphasis on good manners. Shrev might make allowances for human behavior, but a slip wouldn't help now.

Wesley came to Shrev's door and signaled. "May I ask who it is?" her quiet voice answered.

"Wesley Crusher. If it's convenient, I'd like to talk with you."

"Please enter." The door slid open.

Wesley stepped inside. The light was dim and orange, the twilight glow of Zhuik's sun. As his eyes adapted to the gloom, he saw Shrev slip into the quilted gray tunic most Zhuiks wore. He had a brief glimpse of the exoskeletal plates that covered her bare torso and upper arms. The chitinous green hexagons made Wesley think of a tile floor. Shrev was warm-blooded, but clearly not mammalian.

"Please, borrow a seat," Shrev said as she adjusted her garment. She took a brush and quickly straightened her shoulder-length blue hair. "Would you find brighter lighting more comfortable?"

27

"This is fine, thank you." The seat was a bare wooden stool, as austere as the rest of the room. The only decorations were a wall mosaic, whose flat gray hexagons echoed the pattern on Shrev's torso, and a set of sheathed daggers that hung by belts from wall pegs. The bed remained sealed in plastic, as though it had never been used. "I think we've both noticed that something odd is happening on the bridge," Wesley said.

"I would agree with that." Shrev sat on a stool and tilted it back until her shoulders rested against the bulkhead behind her. She bowed her head slightly, to better focus her wiry antennae on Wesley. He found something oddly intense about her scrutiny, as though she were staring at him. "I believe you are more familiar with the bridge personnel than I am," Shrev said.

Wesley nodded, then reminded himself that nodding wasn't a Zhuik gesture. "Yes. Something's up. Lieutenant Worf is running combat simulations against Ferengi ships. And—did you hear what Commander Riker said to Mr. Worf?"

" 'Back-to-back,' " Shrev said. "A phrase which Klingons use to describe survival in a desperate battle. But there is more. The ambassador delivered a computer message to the captain."

"I've looked at it." Wesley kept his voice low. It seemed polite, and Shrev's own quiet voice encouraged that. "The message wasn't private—or if there was a private part, it was deleted."

"I, too, have seen it," Shrev said. "A record of a planetary survey, ended by a Ferengi attack."

"And the data on Megara doesn't match the computer records," Wesley said.

"The Ferengi may have done something." Shrev hesitated. "May I ask a question which could seem rude?"

"Sure—uh, I mean, I won't take offense."

Shrev smiled; that seemed to be the one truly universal expression. "Why do you come to me with this? Others are more knowledgeable, and you have highly placed friends."

"I've got several reasons," Wesley said. "When I was on the computer, I noticed you were interested in this, too. We work pretty well on the bridge, and I figured we could work together here.

"For a second thing—" He sighed. "This is going to sound silly. If I ask the captain, or Mr. Riker, what's going on, they're likely to turn this into a research assignment." *And it's still hard to face the captain,* he thought, *after the way I lied to everyone. He may have forgiven me, but I haven't.*

"Instead you create your own assignment." There was humor in her silken voice. "Pardon me; I intend no mockery. You wish to work on your own, without pressure from our seniors."

"Right," Wesley said. "I thought you'd understand, because you haven't been out of the Academy all that long—" Did that sound rude? he wondered suddenly. "I don't mean that you're inexperienced. I mean that your memories are fresher."

"They are." Shrev rocked forward on her stool and rose to her feet. "Did you know that this matter is a secret?"

"Well—it can't be *too* secret," he said. "I mean, if you really want to keep a secret on the *Enterprise,* you don't put it in the computer where just anyone can find it."

"Anyone, that is, who finds a minor challenge in bypassing security blocks. As I do." Shrev began pacing back and forth, her hands folded behind her back. "Let us define the matter. We wish to understand the Megaran situation. The Federation sends a special ambassador, which suggests that more is at stake than Ferengi interference."

"It does." Wesley realized he had hardly given Offenhouse a thought. He had looked at statistics and probe readings, as though this were strictly a scientific problem.

"This ambassador must have special talents," Shrev said. "If we can identify them, we might understand the situation."

"I'll see what I can find out about Mr. Offenhouse," Wesley said. "A secret is one thing, but I don't think anyone will mind talking about the ambassador himself."

Shrev smiled as she paced. "No, especially as the ambassador annoys everyone who meets him."

Wesley hadn't noticed that. "I didn't know that Zhuiks can sense emotions. Uh, I don't doubt you, but I don't know as much as I'd like about your people."

Shrev laughed lightly. "You are the most delightful human I have ever met, Wesley." She waved a hand alongside one of her slim, quivering antennae. "We do not detect emotions, as would a Betazoid, but we can sense the electric fields which surround most living tissue. These are often indicative of emotions. I believe the captain, Mr. Riker and Mr. Worf were annoyed by their conference with the ambassador. He puzzled Counselor Troi. I cannot answer for Mr. Data."

"Nobody can," Wesley said. "Mr. Data doesn't have emotions. But that means he notices things other people miss. I'll see what he has to say."

"And the others, as well," Shrev said. "If they speak of the ambassador they may disparage him, but we can take that into account. While you do this, I shall see what I can learn of the Ferengi presence in this quadrant."

"Okay," Wesley said, and stood up. "I'll let you know as soon as I learn anything."

Out in the corridor, Wesley went to the nearest computer station. "Where's Ambassador Offenhouse?" he asked, thinking the direct approach might work.

"The ambassador is in a turbolift," the computer answered. "He is en route to the Ten-Forward lounge."

Then so am I, Wesley told himself. He decided to walk. It was ship's evening, and the lights were dimmed in simulated night: a good time to think.

I screwed up, he thought, thinking of the accident. Five one-seat training spacecraft, flying a tight formation in a rehearsal for the Academy's commencement exercise. The team's cadet leader had wanted to do something spectacular, and he had persuaded Wesley and the other team members to try a simple maneuver, one which would mingle their trainers' exhausts and ignite the plasma into a glorious rosette. The maneuver was dangerous and against regulations, but Wesley had agreed to try it.

It had failed. The trainers had collided during a practice run near Saturn, and Joshua Albert, one of the cadet pilots, one of Wesley's best friends, had died. There had been a board of inquiry—and the team's leader had convinced Wesley and the other survivors to lie about the accident, to protect the team. That had failed, too. The lie had grown too complicated to withstand investigation, but Wesley had told the truth only after Captain Picard had threatened to reveal it himself. His punishment, the loss of a year's academic credit, had seemed trivial in comparison to what he had done.

Why didn't I show a little backbone? Wesley asked himself. *I should have said the maneuver was too dangerous . . . should have owned up to what I did, should never have lied to everyone.* That disgrace was as hard to bear as the death of a friend. He didn't know how he would ever cleanse himself of it.

The Ten-Forward lounge was half full when Riker, Worf and Data entered it. "Evening, gents," Guinan said from behind her bar. As always, the dark woman seemed amused, as though she had caught the universe in the act of playing a subtle joke. "What will it be?"

"The usual, Guinan," Riker said. "All around."

The lounge's hostess nodded. "Coming right up."

Data turned to Riker as the three officers waited at the bar. "I remain uncertain about the cinematic recording we observed," the android said. "The putative hero, George Lincoln, was referred to as the 'missing link.' Am I correct in assuming that this refers to a hypothetical stage in the human evolutionary process?"

"That's right," Riker said. "It means the missing step between us and our prehuman ancestors."

Data nodded. "It is my understanding that such a reference, with its implication of inferior mental abilities, would offend a human being, yet the character reveled in this appellation."

"It figures that he would," Riker said. "Only an idiot would get into the fixes he did."

"But why did he enjoy this name?" Data asked.

"I guess the twentieth century didn't have a lot of respect for brains," Riker said. "Or for life, when you consider that people back then took movies like that seriously."

"But it was—diverting," Worf said.

And it almost made you laugh, my friend, Riker thought as he nodded. Someday Riker would break the control—or fill in the void—that kept Worf from laughing. He took that as a challenge. If he could make Worf laugh, it would mean he had a better understanding of the Klingon soul.

Guinan returned to them with a tray bearing three goblets. "Here you go," she said. "One Skagway Slide, one prune juice, and one Data Surprise."

Riker raised an eyebrow. "What's a Data Surprise?" he asked.

Guinan's smile broadened. "Anything that surprises Data." She watched as Data tasted his drink. "How about it, Data? Surprised?"

"I have not yet developed an understanding of that emotion," Data admitted. "However, as to the concoction, I believe the appropriate descriptive terms are sweet, heavy and dry, with sweet predominating. Am I correct in assuming that this drink would make a suitable after-dinner liqueur?"

"Very good," Guinan said in approval. "That's exactly how they use it on Argelius. We'll make a gourmet out of you yet, Data."

Worf grunted and sipped his prune juice. Riker tried not to smile as the purple liquid brought a pleased glow to the Klingon's face. *Someday,* Riker thought, *someone is going to work up the nerve to tell him why humans drink prune juice—but that someone won't be* me! Riker's own drink had the sledgehammer taste of fermented fruit juices; it was similar to the moonshine made by lumberjacks in his native Alaska. Even with synthehol to take the place of ethyl alcohol, it still tasted like a man's drink.

The lounge door slid open and Ambassador Offenhouse came in. There was something belligerent about the way the man walked up to the bar, but Guinan only smiled at him. "Hello, Mr. Ambassador," she said. "What's your pleasure?"

Offenhouse nodded at Worf. "I'll have what the big guy's having."

Guinan verged on laughter. "Coming right up."

Prune juice has a soothing effect on the Klingon soul, and Worf remained calm as Offenhouse looked at him. "Tell me something," the human said. "The Ferengi have been doing business with the Romulans and Klingons. Do you think either of them would sell that ship-cloaking gimmick to the Ferengi?"

"No," Worf said. "Do you fear a cloaked Ferengi ship?"

"Yes." Offenhouse accepted a glass of prune juice from Guinan. He started to raise it to his lips, then lowered it. *"Could* the Ferengi have a cloaked ship?"

"Perhaps we shall find out," Worf said.

"Why worry about that?" Riker asked him. Despite himself he couldn't take his eyes off Offenhouse's drink. He wanted to see the look on the man's face when he belted down a slug of prune juice.

"Why? It should be obvious," Offenhouse said. He stared into his drink. "What if the little SOBs have an ace up a sleeve? I'd hate to find out the hard way."

"Mr. Ambassador," Data said, "does this issue not fall under your definition of a top secret?"

"Yeah, it does," he said. "But I don't understand modern warfare, and I hate surprises. Worf, just *suppose,* for one wild minute, that some day you chance to meet a cloaked Ferengi battle-cruiser. What happens?"

"They die," Worf said, and tossed down half of his drink. It made him talkative. "No cloaking device is perfect. Against the *Enterprise* a cloaked ship has no defense but overconfidence."

Offenhouse rested an elbow on the bar. "So you can detect them?"

Worf shrugged. "It is not impossible."

"But it *is* difficult," the ambassador said.

"You could ask Commander La Forge about that," Riker said, hoping that the ambassador would take the hint and leave. "He's always looking for new ways to improve our sensors."

Offenhouse grunted. "Is he any good at that?"

"Geordi has earned several commendations for his innovative work in sensor technology," Data said. "His work on tachyonic heterodynes is especially well regarded."

The door opened again, and Riker saw Wesley Crusher come into Ten-Forward. He paused in the doorway and looked around, then steered himself toward Offenhouse. "Mr. Ambassador?" he asked as the man hoisted his glass. "I'm not interrupting, am I?"

"No." Offenhouse lowered his glass and peered at the youth. "Wesley Crusher, isn't it? What can I do for you?"

Wesley hesitated, then plunged ahead. "Well—I'm taking a history class at the Academy next term, and the course description says we're going to spend a week talking about the twentieth century. I thought I'd do better if I talked with someone who really was there when everything happened."

Offenhouse toyed with his glass of prune juice. "You sound like my boy did when he got into Annapolis."

Riker, a military man at heart, felt interested despite himself. "Annapolis was the American naval academy, wasn't it?"

"Right," Offenhouse said, and looked at Wesley. "Ask your questions, but you have to understand that I wasn't there for the entire century. I missed the last couple of years, and I'm a bit hazy on the early things, like the Wright Brothers and the invention of the crossbow."

Wesley nodded eagerly. "But you still must know a lot of things. Like—you were a businessman, weren't you?"

"Yep." Offenhouse looked down at his fingernails. "One of the best, in fact."

"What was business like?" Wesley asked. "The history texts aren't too clear on that."

"Things have changed a bit," Offenhouse admitted. "Okay, take my job. I was a financier, an investor— what you'd call a developmental analyst. I'd buy property—a factory, or an airline, or stock—at a low price, and sell it at a high price. The difference in prices was the profit—the extra money I made. I'd use that to make more investments, so I could make more profits."

Wesley seemed perplexed. "It sounds pretty circular," Wesley said. "Didn't you *do* anything?"

Offenhouse looked thoughtful as he twisted his glass around and around. "Yeah, I always did make a profit, and I'll tell you, I earned every single denarius of it."

"Mr. Ambassador," Data said, "the denarius was an ancient Roman coin which went out of use long before the twentieth century."

Offenhouse grunted. "I suppose you read that in some history book?"

Data nodded. "That is a correct assumption, sir."

Offenhouse gestured at Data with his drink. "Who are you going to believe, me or some historian? Remember, I was *there.*"

Data looked polite. "The historical record—"

"—ain't all it's cracked up to be," Offenhouse finished. "You wouldn't believe how many errors get into it. Like we used to say, it's the wieners who write the history books."

"I still don't understand what you *did,*" Wesley said impatiently.

"Basically, Wes," Riker said, "he did what the Ferengi do."

"That can't be right," Wesley said. "I mean, the

Federation wouldn't *let* anyone act like them. The Ferengi are liars and thieves."

Offenhouse's jovial air leached away. "I know," he said.

Wesley missed his sudden change. "They don't even make sense. Ask Captain Picard. He made our first contact with them, and the first thing the Ferengi did was to attack. They crippled his ship, the *Stargazer,* and—"

Offenhouse slammed his drink down onto the counter with a crack that drew startled looks from everyone in Ten-Forward. He stomped over to the intercom station, blind to the world around him. "Computer, where's Picard?"

"Captain Picard is in his quarters," the computer's brisk female voice answered. "He is to be disturbed only for ship's business."

"'Disturbed'?" Offenhouse let out a growl that impressed Worf. *"I'll* show him 'disturbed.' " He left the lounge.

Wesley looked from Worf to Riker to Data. "What did I say?" he asked plaintively.

Riker spread his hands helplessly. "Beats me, Wes, but you should say it more often." He watched Worf as the Klingon went to the intercom. Worf spoke quietly; Riker heard Picard's voice answer.

Data was looking at the door. "The ambassador's reactions are most unusual," he observed.

"Do you know what's bothering him?" Wesley asked.

"It's nothing we can discuss right now," Riker said firmly. "The ambassador insists on keeping a few secrets."

"Why?" Wesley asked. "Look, I know we're taking him to Megara. What's so secret about Megara?"

"You've checked the data on it, I suppose?" Riker asked.

"I've looked at the navigational summary," Wesley said. "It says Megara is primitive."

"We have more data than the summary," Riker said. "If you're interested, you *could* give me a report on the library information."

"I'll think about it," Wesley said. He turned and fled out the door.

Riker chuckled as Worf rejoined him and Data at the bar. "Nothing scares a cadet like the threat of an extra assignment."

Guinan had been listening quietly while she polished the bar with a rag. "Riker, you have a mean streak," she said.

Worf nodded at the hostess. "He *does* have many admirable qualities—for a human." He picked up Offenhouse's glass and drained it in a gulp.

Picard nodded at the reflection in his dresser mirror. Only his admiring smile spoiled the classic film-noir look that the fedora and trenchcoat gave him. If his hunch was right, dealing with Ralph Offenhouse was about to become much easier.

The cabin door slid open and Offenhouse strode into the room, uninvited. "Picard—" he began, and stopped cold. "What's with the costume?"

"I'm going to spend an hour on the holodeck," Picard said. "We can talk there—in private."

"All right," the man said grudgingly. He stepped into the corridor with Picard. "But why are you dressed like Humphrey Bogart?"

Picard needed a second to place the name; recognition was an unexpected benefit of his passion for old detective stories. "One of my favorite pastimes is to play the role of Dixon Hill," Picard said. "He's a fictional detective of the San Francisco of the Roosevelt era, and I simulate that world on the holodeck. You might find this amusing—I researched the background myself, but I have my doubts as to the accuracy of the settings."

"And you'd like me to spot the errors?" Offenhouse asked.

"If you would." In truth, Picard had done a good deal of his own historical research, and he doubted Offenhouse would find any glaring anachronisms. If anything, he should find himself at home in surroundings that approximated his own era.

"It'll be my pleasure," Offenhouse said with a smile. "Somehow you don't seem like the detective-novel type, Picard."

"Appearances are deceptive, aren't they?" Picard said. "I quite enjoy a good mystery. The beauty of the Hill novels is that they present all the clues one needs to solve the mystery, but the presentation is made in such a way that one can easily miss the clues. One never quite knows what is happening."

"I'd think you get enough of that in real life," the ambassador said. They entered the turbolift at the end of the corridor, and Picard ordered it to holodeck three. "By the way, Picard," Offenhouse said, "you might want to keep an eye on that Crusher kid. He knows something's in the wind."

Picard raised an eyebrow. "Does he, now?"

"Yeah. He was pumping me for information a few minutes ago, down in Ten-Forward."

"Wesley is an inquisitive and intelligent young man," Picard said. "He's also discreet. If he uncovers any secrets, he won't reveal them."

Offenhouse looked thoughtful. "If he's that smart, maybe we should bring him in on this."

"No, not yet. I'd like to see how far he can go on his own." The turbolift stopped and released them. Picard led Offenhouse to the holodeck entrance. "Computer, run Picard program number one. Set a date in March, nineteen thirty-six."

"Program engaged," the computer said, opening the door for them.

They stepped into a waiting room, where a blond secretary sat behind a desk, buffing her nails with an emery board. "No calls for ya, Mistah Hill," she said to Picard.

"Understood, Madeline," Picard said, manually opening the knobbed door to his office. "Mr. Offenhouse and I are not to be disturbed."

The office was dingy and run-down, but the chairs were comfortable. "Not too shabby," Offenhouse admitted as he seated himself. "Of course, your secretary should wear green lipstick and orange gloves, and most offices like this would have a cuckoo clock on the wall."

"I see," Picard said. He sat behind his desk, wrote a memo on the ambassador's suggestions, then opened a drawer and pulled out a gin bottle and two dirty glasses. He found himself slipping into the Hill persona almost without thought as he poured the drinks. "I think it's time we both came clean," he said as he offered a glass to Offenhouse. "I take it you don't want my services."

Offenhouse tasted the drink, shrugged and looked at Picard. "Damn straight. When Starfleet told me they were sending the *Enterprise* to Megara, I banged my fist on desks, screamed till I was blue in the face, threatened to resign—"

"Why?" Picard asked. "If you feel a personal animosity against me—"

"It isn't you, Picard, it's your *ship*. When Singh gave me this cock-and-bull story about how no other suitable ship was available—" Offenhouse looked at his glass in disgust, then put it on the desk. "Picard, a talk like this needs *real* booze, not this synthehol sissy-juice."

Picard put his own glass down. "Precisely what is wrong with my ship?"

"Civilians," Offenhouse said. He got up, went to the window and looked at the San Francisco skyline. The Golden Gate Bridge was a series of curves, as graceful as a Shinto shrine yet almost overwhelmed by the ugly lump of Alcatraz. To Picard, those neighboring structures had always brought home the extreme contradictions of the twentieth century, the good and evil that had so frequently lived side by side—and the inept way in which good had fought evil.

"Civilians," Offenhouse repeated. He turned away from the window with an expression that verged on pain. "Picard, this is a battleship—right?"

"If necessary, yes," the captain admitted.

"It's also an exploratory ship," Offenhouse said. "You're supposed to nose around in odd places and see what turns up."

Picard nodded at the man. "That's true."

"Combat and exploration—those are two good, fast ways to die."

"Indeed they are." Picard leaned back in his chair and rubbed his chin in thought. "You're asking what gives us the right to take civilians into harm's way."

"You catch on fast," the ambassador said. He stepped back to the desk and looked at the documents cluttering it. One was a local newspaper, the *Sun*. The paper crinkled as Offenhouse idly fingered the headlines. *Colored Wards May Vote For FDR This November,* one announced, while another warned *Germany To Reoccupy the Rhineland, Hitler Declares.*

"The risk is a necessary evil," Picard told him. "There *was* a time when Starfleet ships were primarily military vessels. We had a 'heroic age' of such captains as Garth, Pike, Kirk and Sulu—"

"That was a little after my time," Offenhouse said.

"—but it was a dangerous era," Picard went on. "Too often such captains took enormous risks with dubious benefits. They would violate the Prime Directive for reasons that seem trivial. Several times they almost plunged the Federation into war. They were sane, by all medical standards, yet still unbalanced."

"I read about that," Offenhouse said. He sat down and propped his feet on Picard's desk. He closed his eyes, but Picard saw nothing restful in his face. "Decker slugged it out with a doomsday machine, just for the hell of it. Garth tried to become the new Napoleon, Tracey committed genocide on Omega Three—you Starfleet captains sure are a distinguished lot."

"Some of us become carried away with our authority," Picard said. "And Starfleet tried numerous solutions to this problem. Civilian crews, female command staffs, crews which mixed races from scores of worlds, automated decision processes. Nothing worked. Then we realized that we were placing military men in military vessels, and cutting them off from the rest of the Federation. A few weeks in such a restricted environment will distort anyone's worldview."

Offenhouse opened one eye to look at Picard. "So they pack a ship with families just to keep you from getting careless?"

"That's one of several reasons for a civilian presence here," Picard said. He found the Cyclopean gaze unsettling, and was glad when Offenhouse closed the eye again. "Bitter experience has shown that this is necessary. When you have children underfoot you can't pretend that the universe is strictly a place of heroic battles, or forget that your actions have far-reaching consequences. You also live in a more balanced world, and that preserves one's own balance."

"And you're convinced this is right," Offenhouse said.

"No, sir, I am not," Picard admitted. "Even though this principle works, I do not know that the means justify the ends. But I do know that Starfleet will not replace the *Enterprise* on this assignment simply to calm your nerves. You will have to weigh your decisions as carefully as I must."

Offenhouse snorted. "I had that in mind anyway."

"The captains you named had good intentions, too," Picard said. "But let's discuss our intentions in regard to Megara. Why do you think this world is dangerous?"

"Aside from a trigger-happy Ferengi ship?" Offenhouse sighed. "Picard, I estimate the Ferengi have spent fifty billion credits on Megara. They're trying to hide what they're doing. I'm sure Dixon Hill has investigated people who've killed for a lot less."

"Put that way, I understand your concern." Picard opened his desk drawer and took out a flat steel rectangle. Its top made a snapping noise as he flipped it open, revealing a peculiar arrangement of a bit of twine, a vented metal cage and a tiny ridged wheel. "Fifty billion credits?"

"Yeah. That's based on the probe data. When you look at the budget, and Megara's location, this smells like a clandestine military operation."

"Except that the Ferengi are not overtly militaristic." Picard studied the rectangle. Its purpose eluded him—wait, he could smell a volatile hydrocarbon fuel soaking its wick. Thumbing the wheel created sparks, which ignited the wick. Perhaps the device was evidence from one of Hill's cases—it could be useful in starting a fire. "They only fight when they might win a profit," Picard said. His nose wrinkled at the device's acrid smoke.

"I know," the ambassador said. "And—" He sniffed the air. "And—I never meant to—that is, I don't see a profit in, in, I mean *around*—"

Awkwardly, Picard closed the cap on the rectangle, extinguishing its blue flame. "Mister Ambassador?" he asked in concern. Offenhouse had clenched his chair's armrests in a white-knuckled grip, as though desperate for something to anchor him to this world. "Are you all right?"

"Yeah . . . I just need a little sleep." Offenhouse chuckled as he stood up. "You'd think that after taking the big sleep I'd be wide awake for the rest of your—I mean *this* century."

"We can continue our talk later," Picard said.

"Yeah . . . we've got all the time in the world." Offenhouse gave Picard an absentminded wave as he went to the holodeck exit. It slid open, revealing the starship corridor beyond the illusory office. Picard saw a look of painful disappointment on Offenhouse's face as he stared at the hallway. "All the time in the world," he repeated sadly.

Chapter Four

ADMIRAL SINGH'S image vanished from the viewscreen. Picard sat in silence for a long moment, then stood up and went to his ready room's window. *We're on our own,* he thought as he looked at the drifting starfield.

The door hissed. "You wanted to see me, Captain?" Riker asked.

"Yes, Number One." One dim red star moved a bit more quickly than the others. Parallax, Picard thought idly; the red dwarf was probably within a few light-weeks of the *Enterprise,* and the ship's speed made it seem to race along.

Picard turned away from the window. "I've just spoken with Admiral Singh. The mission goes on."

Riker scowled. "With an unstable anachronism of an ambassador?"

"Ralph Offenhouse is not unstable," Picard said. "But he is troubled."

"Does anyone know what's 'troubling' him?" Riker asked.

Picard shook his head. "There's very little information available on the ambassador. As Admiral Singh just told me, his file *begins* with his death certificate. He was less than cooperative with his counselors, but they believe that he's quite capable of fulfilling his assignment, and that his work is the best therapy for his troubles. His talents more than outweigh his problems—and the historical record suggests that before his death he was a stable, even brilliant, man."

"By twentieth-century standards," Riker said.

Picard smiled slightly. "After speaking with him on the holodeck I find that he's more impressive than he lets on. For example, he knows that Wesley Crusher is investigating the Megaran situation."

"Is he?" Riker asked in obvious surprise.

"It would seem that Wesley asked some well-directed questions in Ten-Forward." Picard returned to his seat and gestured for his executive officer to join him. "Number One, both Dr. Crusher and Counselor Troi assure me that the ambassador is all right. However, I would like to know what made him so edgy today. What transpired in Ten-Forward?"

Riker stroked his beard. "Well . . . he asked Worf if Ferengi ships used a cloaking device, and if fighting them was a problem. That's when Wesley came in. He asked Offenhouse what sort of work he did, and the ambassador gave him a lot of double-talk. Then Wesley mentioned the *Stargazer* incident, and that's when Offenhouse called you. He seemed upset," Riker finished.

Picard nodded. "What was said about the *Stargazer?*"

"Only the basic facts," Riker said. "You commanded the ship, it was our first contact with the Ferengi, and they attacked without provocation."

That explains a great deal, Picard thought. *Or does*

it? It's almost too obvious. "Can you think of anything else?"

"Well—Offenhouse mentioned his son," Riker said. "I think Wesley reminded Offenhouse of him."

"Interesting," Picard mused. "Thank you, Number One."

Riker left the ready room, and Picard turned his attention to his computer console. After a few informative minutes, he called Deanna Troi.

Wesley spotted Shrev in the corridor outside holodeck two. She wore her gray tunic, and she had a knife belted to her waist. Wesley fought the urge to call her name as he walked up to her. He hadn't had the time to read up on Zhuik customs, but intuition told him that Shrev's people regarded loudness as rude.

She saw him approach. "Hello, Wesley," she said. Her head bowed slightly to focus her slender antennae on him. "You look as though you have news."

Wesley kept his voice low. "I do, Shrev. I talked with the ambassador a few hours ago. He said he's a developmental analyst—well, sort of."

"I do not understand this qualification," Shrev said.

"It's the nearest modern equivalent to his old profession," Wesley said. "I would have come back to you sooner, but I wanted to learn a little about the profession first."

The holodeck door opened and De Shay stepped out. He wore a soccer player's uniform, now muddy and grass-stained, and he grinned toothily as he juggled a soccer ball. He had a black eye. "Hi, Wes, Shrev," he said. "Hope I haven't kept anyone waiting."

"Not at all, sir," Shrev said. "I merely arrived a moment early."

"Did you—" Wesley cleared his throat and raised his voice to a normal level. "Did you have a good game, Mr. De Shay?"

"That I did," De Shay said cheerily. "We kicked the stuffings out of the bloody Brits, two-oh. There's never been a game like *that, mon amie.*" He strolled away, deftly bouncing the ball from wrist to heel to head.

Wesley glanced at the holodeck door; Shrev would be eager to get in there. "We could talk later, when you're done here," he suggested.

"I must go on duty in an hour." She paused and seemed to think. "You might consider joining me here, although I fear my relaxation might distress you."

Wesley hesitated. "Could I ask how you'll relax?"

She nodded once, obviously copying the human gesture. "I will walk through a city hive. Certain people will behave rudely and I shall kill them." Shrev patted her sheathed dagger.

Wesley decided that didn't sound any worse than some of the things Worf and Riker did on the holodeck. "I'd like to join you," Wesley said. "We can talk privately, and I might learn something about Zhuiks, too."

"May what you learn be useful." Shrev turned to the door control. "Shrev program one, if you please."

The door opened into an oval tunnel that curved up and to the right. By the glow of feeble orange lamps, Zhuiks streamed up and down its translucent length in utter silence. The hard, pinched green faces glanced at Wesley, then turned away. Many of them looked unconscious despite their open eyes. Zhuiks did not sleep, but from time to time their minds lapsed into a somnolent state; as with human sleepwalkers, their bodies remained in motion while their brains rested. Wesley noted that, like terrestrial hive insects, all of the people he saw here were female.

"I have researched the Ferengi, as I promised," Shrev said to Wesley. "I found only that they have never entered this sector before. It is far from their own space, and the distance would make trade unprofitable."

"But they're still here," Wesley whispered. Walking amid this alien horde made it easy for him to keep his voice low. He walked quickly behind Shrev; wherever they were going, they moved at a pace as rapid as that set by the other Zhuiks.

"And the ambassador is here because they are here," Shrev murmured. They went around a sharp bend in the tunnel. Here the curved floor sloped downhill, toward a Y-shaped junction, while more Zhuiks swirled around them. Wesley saw two Zhuiks standing in a cubbyhole, heads bowed to let their antennae brush against one another. "You mentioned that he is a developmental analyst. I must confess my inexcusable ignorance of this topic. Could I trouble you to enlighten me upon it?"

"I can't claim to be an expert," Wesley said, "but a developmental analyst studies how an economic system works and finds places where you can improve it. That covers a lot of territory: resources, factories, personnel, research and development, distribution, transport—all sorts of things."

"A man who understands such matters could infer much about a society from only a few observations," Shrev said. "Now we must consider—"

They had reached the tunnel junction. One Zhuik stepped out of the crowd and stood before Shrev. She glared at Wesley, then looked at Shrev. "Is there iron in your knife as well?" she asked quietly.

Shrev drew her knife. "You see that my knife is hardened copper. May I inquire who faces Shrev of Hive Zss'zhz?"

The woman brandished her own dagger. "I trust it

pleases you to know that I am Zhen of Hive Zss'zhz. It is my station in life to examine the eggs laid in our clutches, and reject those which are defective."

"And I was hatched to be a Starfleet officer, serving the Federation to which Zhuik belongs," Shrev whispered.

"Mutant tool of aliens," the woman murmured, and pounced on Shrev. The crowd pulled back to give the fighters room. Wesley stepped forward to help Shrev, then retreated against the curved tunnel wall. *It's what she wants,* he told himself as Shrev and the woman circled one another, knives drawn and heads down. The woman lunged forward. Shrev spun on her heels and slashed at her. Shrev's dagger cut into her chest, and she flashed out of holographic existence. Shrev slid her dagger into its sheath and turned away, suddenly oblivious of Wesley.

The crowd surged on, and Shrev was drawn into the flow of bodies. Wesley shook himself out of his surprise and hurried after her. When he caught up with her, he saw a glaze over her eyes, as though she walked in her sleep.

Her attention returned to Wesley. "Now we must consider matters which might interest a developmental analyst," she said, sounding as though nothing had happened. "We have the enormous growth of Megaran industry. It is clear that the Ferengi are involved in this."

"They must be importing a lot of high-tech gear to do this," Wesley said. He wanted to ask her what had sparked the fight, but this didn't seem the proper time for curiosity. "And advisors. That's expensive . . . and . . . time."

"What about time?" Shrev asked.

"The changes they've made on Megara must have taken *years,*" Wesley said. "But Ferengi don't make long-term investments like that. They go after quick profits. The quicker, the better."

"I know little of Ferengi," Shrev said. "Is it possible that they could make enormous profits by what they do here?"

"I don't know," Wesley said. "I guess that's one thing Mr. Offenhouse is supposed to learn. But Ferengi *never* act like this."

"Then we must refine what we know," Shrev said. There was a hole in the tunnel floor, with numerous bent copper rungs set in the walls. Zhuiks climbed up and down the rungs. Shrev went down the hole, and Wesley tried to descend as quickly as she did. It was invigorating, like working out in a gymnasium.

A Zhuik woman bowed to Shrev as she reached the ground. "May I trouble you for directions to the surface?" she whispered. Wesley clutched the rungs and watched Shrev draw her knife again.

Deanna Troi focused her attention on Ralph Offenhouse as she neared his quarters. He was awake and relaxed, and in a humorous mood. His rebound did not comfort the Betazoid empath. Mood swings were not uncommon in people with emotional troubles. His present good humor was not a healthy sign.

She signaled her presence at his door, and it opened at his invitation. The ambassador lay on his bed in a bathrobe, arms crossed behind his head as he watched a holographic recording of a popular stage show. "Have a seat," he told her, and chuckled at the show.

"Thank you," Troi said. "How are you—"

His raucous laugh cut her off. "Sorry," he said when his laughter had subsided. "But this show is a classic. See, it's the one where Mister Ed thinks he's ready for the glue factory, so he asks Wilbur to buy a little pony to keep him company and make him feel young again, only Wilbur accidentally buys a *Shetland* pony, and when Ed realizes the 'pony' is over twenty he suddenly understands he isn't so old after all, and it's as funny now as when I was a kid. Classic!"

"I see," Troi said, noting the way he rambled. "But, Mr. Ambassador, you couldn't possibly have seen this show as a child. It's 'Robot Rolls.'"

"Sure, that's what they *call* it," Offenhouse said with a knowing smirk. "But somebody just stole an old episode of 'Mister Ed,' changed the talking horse into a robotic aircar, and passed it off as new. You people may have replaced TV with staged plays, but popular entertainment hasn't changed a bit since I kicked the bucket."

"Then why are you watching it?" Troi asked.

"Why? Simple." Offenhouse went to the replicator. "Two vodka martinis, with olives," he said. The replicator produced a pair of conical glasses, and he carried one to Troi. "You were born into this century. I wasn't. I need to pick up the background, schlock and all. A good businessman does things like that."

"That's very sensible." Troi sipped her drink. *Thank goodness for synthehol,* she thought. Drinking was an important ritual in many cultures, and synthehol had many of alcohol's benefits without the damaging side effects. The intoxication faded swiftly, but for social purposes it was enough. "You've probably guessed that this isn't a social call. Captain Picard tells me that you were extremely uncomfortable on the holodeck earlier today—"

"—and now you want to help me count my marbles," Offenhouse said, as he sat down with his drink. "That shouldn't take long. One, two. Yeah, I still got 'em all."

She smiled. "Can you tell me what you felt on the holodeck?"

He sighed. "It *looked* like I was back in the real San Francisco—I spent a summer there when I was a boy. Frisco was different then, but there were still offices like the one Picard showed me, and my dad took me to some of them. I was okay at first, but I almost lost it when Picard started playing with that cigarette lighter. My dad's old Zippo made the same noise, and then there was the smell of lighter fluid . . ."

"And the past came rushing back," Troi said. Smells and sounds were potent memory stimuli. She wished the captain had consulted with her; she could have warned him that his effort to put Ralph Offenhouse at ease was risky.

Offenhouse nodded. "It was too much, Counselor. I felt like I was back home . . . like I could walk out of that office and—and—"

"And take care of some unfinished business?" Deanna asked. She could sense how the question exacerbated his underlying sense of guilt. "There's something you'd like to change, isn't there?"

He nodded. "That's the trouble with dropping dead in your tracks. You don't get a chance to wrap things up." He sighed. "I figure that in time I'll get used to being where I am. If that's all—"

Deanna shook her head. "I'd also like to ask you about the *Enterprise.*"

He shrugged. "Picard and I already had this talk. Your ship has a dumb design, but I can live with it."

"I don't mean this *Enterprise,*" Troi said. "I mean the American aircraft carrier."

Offenhouse was silent for a long moment. "My son's ship," he said at last.

"Captain Picard checked the historical records," Troi told him. "Peter Linde Offenhouse was a pilot aboard the *Enterprise* when she was blown up in the Sea of Japan."

"Two years after I died," Offenhouse said.

"Why is that the first thing that comes to your mind?" Troi asked.

"I don't know." He finished his drink, got up and called for two more.

To be polite, Troi finished her first drink and accepted a second. "Do you think you were better off dead?" Troi asked.

"Sometimes I think so," he said. "At least I wouldn't have to know that my only child died in a war that shouldn't have happened."

"The Battle of the Sea of Japan was *the* turning point of the Eugenics War," Troi said. She had never cared much for Earth history, but its darker aspects had the hypnotic fascination of a good horror story. "It destroyed much of Khan Singh's military force and marked the beginning of the end for his super-race. After that battle, the Great Khanate splintered into a dozen factions which started fighting one another—"

"—and eventually their leaders were hunted down like rats," Offenhouse finished. "I know. My boy died saving the human race from tyranny, and all that. He still died."

There was a long moment of silence, during which Troi sipped her drink and Offenhouse's emotions in equal measure. To him, the Eugenics War and a centuries-old death were fresh, raw wounds. He had been conscious for several years, and he still had not come to grips with his loss. Perhaps it was because his son had died childless. Genetic continuity, carrying on the family line and name, meant a great deal to beings all across the known galaxy. Failure of this sort often led to suicide, and yes, she could sense that option shadowing the man's thoughts.

Troi put her empty glass down on the carpet; that seemed as good a place as any for it. Her head buzzed as she concentrated on the man's emotions. She sensed a raw current of guilt now. *Survivor guilt,* she guessed. *He wonders why he lived when everyone else died.* "I'm supposed to offer words of wisdom," she said. "So let me tell you that being alive is better than being dead."

Offenhouse grunted. "Why is that? Remember that you're talking to a man who's tried both."

"Well, Mr. Ambassador, dying is suicidal, that is, it's certain death, it kills people all the time. If you die you won't be alive anymore. Your friends won't talk with you, you'll miss out on life and you won't be able to do anything. You, now . . ." She leveled a finger at him; it wobbled as though not quite certain which way to point. "You're a man who wants to correct a mistake. You can't do that if you're dead."

"Interesting point," he conceded. "Anything else?"

"No, I don't want to press you today," she said.

"Okay, Counselor," Offenhouse said. Troi watched as he procured a third round of drinks. No doubt about it, her words were getting through to him. Her empathic sense was working with a magnificent clarity today, and she could tell that one fact—the inability of the dead to change the world—now pervaded his consciousness.

Troi toasted Offenhouse, finished the drink and left his quarters. She headed for the bridge, where she would tell Jean-Luc that something she had said to Ralph had given him an added measure of stability. The ambassador had annoyed the captain, true, but he would feel pleased for the man. Like almost all the people Troi had ever met, the captain took pleasure in witnessing the good fortune of others. Perhaps that was one way to define decency.

Halfway to the turbolift, Deanna Troi noticed that the artificial gravity was oscillating badly. The deck wobbled under her feet as she went to the nearest comm panel. "Troi to La George, I mean Fordie, I mean—are you there?"

"Deanna?" Geordi La Forge sounded puzzled.

"There's trouble with the grabbing art, I mean the artigrav, on deck, uh, the deck where I am. Right here."

"Trouble?" the chief engineering officer asked. "Deanna, all my boards show nominal function."

"Oh, good, but the deck's having an awful time holding on to my feet." She giggled as she swayed into the bulkhead. "It's rather nice."

There were several recreation areas aboard the *Enterprise,* and each served identical food and drink. Despite this, Worf preferred to dine in the one on the engineering deck. It was located between the battle bridge and the torpedo bays. The armory, which contained the weapons used by away teams and his own security unit, was nearby. Sharp ears could hear the rush of coolant through the phaser banks. Somehow the ambience made the *rokeg* pie sweeter, the *k'truyg* tarter, the *gagh* livelier.

Worf entered the cafeteria with his son, Alexander. The replicator was delivering a roasted *scrag* haunch when Riker entered the cafeteria. "Are you going to complain if your superior officer joins you?" he asked Worf, in the rude manner affected by Klingon warriors.

"If you must," Worf grumbled. It pleased him to have this human around his son. Riker was a good influence; Alexander was a Klingon and needed those things which humans called "role models." Living among so many non-Klingons, the boy was exposed to such unwholesome concepts as etiquette and pacifism. Riker's only fault was that he bathed in water— almost every day, Worf suspected. The man's behavior wasn't totally Klingonese.

Riker ordered the same dinner as Worf and Alexander, and joined them at a table. He picked up his *scrag* with both hands and tore off a mouthful with his teeth. "Alexander," Riker said as he swallowed. "I saw your teacher today. She tells me there are no bullies in your class."

"I've been behaving myself," Alexander said.

"So has everyone else," Riker said. "She credits that to you."

"There has been trouble?" Worf asked, honored by the compliment Riker was paying his son. A good Klingon enforced discipline.

Alexander shrugged. "Well, I saw Rajiv hit Nonong, once."

"And?" Worf asked.

"I told Rajiv that it looked like—*fun.*" The boy grinned, showing a mouthful of jagged Klingonese teeth. "I was holding him upside down by his ankles when I said that."

Riker laughed in admiration. Alexander was small and delicate for his age, by both human and Klingon standards. *But my son,* Worf thought, *more than makes up for his delicacy with his determination. He will conquer worlds!*

"Sounds like you're doing well," Riker said, and shoveled some *rokeg* pie into his mouth.

"I like being around humans," Alexander said. He looked up at his father. "I'm *glad* we didn't annihilate them." Riker laughed, and Worf clapped his son on the shoulder in approval.

"Hey, Worf?" La Forge had entered the cafeteria. He sat down at the table, and looked away from the mug of squirming *gagh* on Riker's tray. "We may have a security problem."

Worf grunted. "Who needs to be killed?"

"It's not *that* bad," the engineer said. "But somebody smuggled some ethyl alcohol onto the ship. Now

Deanna Troi's in sickbay with a bad case of alcohol poisoning."

Riker looked amazed. "Deanna is *drunk?*"

"She was doing about two warp factors more than the ship when I caught up with her," La Forge said. "Dr. Crusher is detoxifying her, but she's in no shape to say what happened."

"She had a talk with Offenhouse a while ago," Riker said. He grimaced as he saw the connection. "Worf, do you think—"

"I do." The cafeteria walls seemed to shake with Worf's growl. "I must leave this to the captain. Diplomats *do* have privileges."

"Better luck next time, Worf," Riker said, and took some more *rokeg* pie. He washed it down with prune juice.

"Yes," Worf muttered. He looked to La Forge. "Commander, might we discuss a technical matter?"

"Sure, Worf," La Forge said.

"I have been considering the problem of detecting cloaked ships," the Klingon security officer said. "Our techniques have not improved in several months. It would be shameful if we failed to detect a cloaked ship."

"So you want to keep ahead of the competition," La Forge said. "What brings this on?"

Worf glanced at Alexander. Admit that he was concerned for his son's safety? Never. "It is just a thought."

"Well, it's an interesting thought," La Forge said. Even though the golden corrugations of his VISOR hid his eyes, Worf could see how the problem intrigued him. The human had a special interest in sensors, perhaps because of his dependence on artificial sight. "Right now our sensor technology pretty well pushes the limits. We'd have to look for something that current sensors aren't set up to detect.

58

Trouble is, we already scan for all the things cloaked ships emit."

Riker finished his pie and picked up the *scrag* haunch. "What *don't* we look for now?" he asked.

"Lots of things," La Forge said. "Quarks, gravitinos, photinos, neutrinos, gravity waves—things that will pass through a cloak, but either are neutralized by other systems, or aren't easy to look for, or aren't emitted by ordinary matter."

Alexander looked up from his *scrag.* He had demolished most of it while the adults spoke. "Can you *make* another ship emit them?"

A smile slowly spread across La Forge's face. "Alexander, you're one smart kid. Maybe I can." He stood up. "I'm going to check a few things in engineering."

"Can I watch?" Alexander looked up to his father. "I already did my homework."

"So long as you do not annoy Commander La Forge," Worf said. He was still speaking when Alexander got up, grabbed the rest of his pie and followed the engineer out of the room.

Riker chuckled. "He's quite a kid."

"Yes—even though he bathes." Worf dug into his *scrag.* "Commander, I have examined the archives for more ancient films. I have found one that might interest you."

"Another comedy?" Riker asked.

"It is similar to your comedy, but it is more— glorious," the Klingon decided. "There are frequent, honorable displays of hand-to-hand combat. The villains are obvious. The hero never speaks. It is called *Rambo V."*

"And you say it's glorious?" Riker asked.

Worf nodded. "Everyone dies."

"Sounds promising." Riker swallowed a half-chewed bite of *scrag.* "And I've found another comedy."

Worf feigned annoyance. "You are *determined* to make me laugh."

"Yeah, even if it kills me. . . ." His face went pale and his lips twitched as his voice trailed off.

Worf looked at Riker in alarm. "Are you well?"

"Yeah, I just—uhn!" Riker gasped, clutched at his stomach and doubled over.

Worf sprang to Riker's side and slapped his communicator badge. "Transporter Room, emergency beam to sickbay!" he commanded.

The rec area dissolved into the sickbay as the transporter came to life. "Doctor!" Worf roared. He picked up Riker and slung him onto a biobed. Across the compartment, Deanna Troi lay unconscious on another biobed.

Dr. Beverly Crusher hurried out of her office. "What is it?" she demanded.

"Commander Riker has been poisoned," Worf said. He tried to think of how it could be done—by reprogramming the replicator? And why? Was some underling attempting to advance his career by assassinating Riker? That was a common business aboard Klingon ships, but it was unknown in Starfleet. Meanwhile Riker was losing the battle to hide his pain. "There shall be vengeance," Worf vowed to him.

"Easy," the doctor said. She activated the biobed's instruments, glanced at the readouts, then peered into Riker's eyes and mouth. "You were having dinner," she said. "What were you eating?"

Worf thought. "*Rokeg, gagh, scrag—*"

"*Scrag,*" Dr. Crusher said. She produced a hypospray and injected Riker in the arm. "Ah, yes. The flesh of the killer *garbat,* marinated in its own blood and treated with ten different spices. The finest achievement of Klingonese culinary arts—and completely indigestible by human beings." The doctor produced a larger hypo and pumped something into Riker's midriff.

Worf looked down at Riker as the agony drained from his face. *"Scrag did this?"*

The doctor nodded and gazed at her patient. "Will Riker," she said firmly, "I *warned* you to avoid certain Klingonese foods. I gave you a list of items which the human digestive system cannot tolerate. Didn't *scrag* top the list?"

Riker let out his breath in a rattling gasp. "I forgot."

"And I warned you that certain Klingonese substances can be lethal," she continued. "You're fortunate that all you had *this* time was what, in medical parlance, we call a dingwally of a tummy ache."

"It was worth it," Riker rasped. He forced a skeletal grin as he looked at Worf. "Bring on the second course."

Chapter Five

KARDEL ANIT was hungry and tired. His eyelid grated over his eye whenever he blinked, which was often. His body moved more out of habit than anything else as he dragged his junk cart down the alley. It had rained that day, and the streets were muddy where they were not cobbled. His boots kept his feet dry, and his coverall protected him from the air's damp chill. The garb and armor of a Vo's soldier had never been so good as what he wore now. Twice while a soldier he had fallen ill in such weather, and once frost had taken three toes from his feet. Yet who honored a man who wore this shapeless gray garment?

There was a fresh pile of waste behind the rat-eyes' factory. Most of what the workers cast aside was worthless, but enough could be salvaged to make this business worthwhile. Anit found several large cans, a pry-bar, a stained tarpaulin made from something that seemed more like metal than cloth.

The factory's rear door slid open, and an oxless wagon rolled into the alley. The man who held the steering wheel seemed unaware of Anit's presence as the wagon rolled past. Despite exhaustion, Anit felt the old rage at that. Who was this man to ignore a soldier?

A whole man, Anit answered himself. He had tried to get a job in such a factory, but the rat-eyes and their lackeys had rejected him. What use was a man with one arm and one eye? It counted for nothing that Anit had been maimed in the service of the Vo Gatyn, who now ruled all of Megara. A man received no work permit, no place if he was no longer "useful," if he could not meet a "production quota." It was all such a man could do to keep breath and blood in himself and his family.

Anit stopped and looked through a window into the factory. He saw men operating machines. The machines caused metal blocks and pipes to float through the air. Men in clumsy heatsuits pushed them together, and welded them together with sticks that spewed flamelike light. Ten years ago such magical sights would have filled him with awe. Now he only felt envy for the workers, who were assured of having their next meal and of finding the money to pay off the unending demands of the tax collectors.

The junk dealer was pulling his cart through another alley when a man walked up to him. At first Anit thought the man was a thief—crime had spread like weeds since the arrival of the rat-eyes—but when he reached inside his coverall it was to draw out a sheet of paper. He held out the paper to Anit, who took it when he saw the symbol drawn on it: a world, split by a bolt of lightning. The sign of the Prophet Against the Dark. The other side was covered with print. Anit hid the paper inside his coverall and went home.

Anit lived in a two-room brick building with his wife and five children. *Six, soon,* he thought as he saw

Molokan in the front doorway. Heavily pregnant, she waddled out and looked inside the cart. She picked up one of the cans. "A good bucket this will make," she said.

"Yes," he said. They carried the junk into the building's front room. The shop was already filled with clutter, much of which Anit knew he would never sell. Still, one never knew what people would buy.

Their work finished, Anit and Molokan went into the rear room. Their two oldest children sat on the floor against one wall, diligently reading the books from the rat-eyes' school—an old-style school, he reminded himself, of the sort where students sat on benches for endless days while a teacher drilled them in their lessons. Mercifully, the rat-eyes did not subject children to the learning helmet. The other children lay curled in a corner, their backs warmed by the cooking fire in the pit as they slept.

Anit sat at the table. Wordlessly, Molokan placed a bowl of stew and a mug of ale in front of him, and he fed himself with movements that made him think of factory machines. The food was not good; it had the stale taste of food stored too long, but the merchants sold no fresh food here—only preserved food, carried in on railways and stored in iceboxes.

Anit looked at his oldest son. Vaton's "schoolbook," Anit realized, was one of the adventure books that the rat-eyes had banned; the boy read them because they were illegal. Such books told crude, impossible stories about worlds that somehow circled the stars, where people did nothing but kill, betray and rob one another. If there really were worlds among the stars, Anit could believe that star folk would behave so monstrously. He had seen the rat-eyes do worse, and force people to do far worse.

Molokan stood behind her husband as he ate. When they had been young, before the rat-eyes came, she had objected to his demands that she behave as a proper soldier's wife. No more did she call this simple gesture a humiliation. Through it, she too clung to the old times.

She had always been good, he remembered. She had kept him alive after the battle that had maimed him. She had refused to take the children and find a new husband, one who could provide her with better food and a decent home. Molokan was a peasant, but she knew more of loyalty than the Vo Gatyn.

When Anit finished his meal, he took the paper from inside his coverall and handed it to Molokan. "Read," he ordered. The rat-eyes had taught many people to read, forcing them to submit to a demonic ritual that involved wearing a metal cap and having needles stuck into one's flesh, but they had not required Anit to undergo the ordeal. They had judged him too worthless to teach.

Molokan read. "'Thus speaks the Prophet Against the Dark,'" she said in a voice hushed from the children's hearing. "'Tomorrow I shall defy the evil which comes from the sky, which has occupied Heaven itself, scraping the filth of its boots on the Paths of Paradise and spewing its foulness into the beards of our gods. Soon shall we take from the rat-eyes all which is ours, and more. That which they force upon us, we shall turn against them, and our children shall crusade against the demon outworlders in Heaven itself. Tomorrow at midnight you will see me in the holy places. Now burn this paper and witness a miracle.'"

Anit was too tired to make sense of the tangled words. "The Prophet Against the Dark here is coming?" he asked, as simply as a child might. He didn't know if outworlders were monsters or evil men; he only wanted to know that there was hope.

"The paper says among us she shall walk," Molokan said.

"Good," Anit said. "Now let us see the miracle of the paper."

Molokan waddled over to the cooking fire and fed the paper into the flames. The paper caught fire and burned with an abnormal brightness. As the flames consumed it, a ghost no bigger than a man's fist appeared above it. *The Prophet Against the Dark!* Anit thought. He dropped to his knees in awe as the robed image raised its hands in benediction before it faded.

Anit and Molokan gazed at the fire for a long moment. "Good it would be," Molokan said wistfully, "the Prophet herself to see, in a holy place speaking."

"That we shall not do," Anit said, resting his hand on her swollen belly. "From rat-eyes and brigands too great the danger is. Of parents our children we shall not deprive. Besides," he added, nodding at the fire, "the Prophet we have just seen."

"We have," Molokan said reluctantly. Anit knew that she wanted to see the Prophet, with a need stronger than hunger or thirst. There was a grove outside the city, where people had worshiped before the rat-eyes had outlawed religion. It would be good to go there and see the Prophet, even if it meant being killed by vengeful rat-eyes—

Anit shook his head as if to drive out that thought. The world had turned cruel since the rat-eyes had taken over. If he died, who would take care of Molokan and their children? Orphans starved in the streets, a shameful horror that no one would have tolerated in the old days.

Anit and Molokan made ready to sleep. They lay down on their cot, and Anit ordered Vaton to turn out the glassfire. In the darkness, Anit pulled the blanket over himself and his wife, and pillowed Molokan's head on the stump of his arm. She slept deeply—this pregnancy tired her more than had any other—but despite his own exhaustion Anit could not sleep. He pictured the Prophet striding into the city, leveling the factories with a glance of her eye, restoring the old times with a spoken word, sweeping away the rat-eyes with a gesture.

Picard was familiar with the aftereffects of alcoholic overindulgence—his family owned one of the finest vineyards and distilleries in France—but what he found in sickbay astonished him. Deanna Troi looked like the victim of a brutal transporter malfunction. Her skin had turned pasty, her hair lay in disarray on the biobed, and her wide dark eyes had grown blood-shot and sunken. "Fear not," Picard said with sympathetic humor, "Dr. Crusher assures me you shall survive."

Troi winced and groaned. "Don't remind me," she said.

"Courage," Picard said, and sighed. "The ambassador picked a fine time to get you drunk."

"It wasn't deliberate," Troi said, in a voice that was barely audible. "I didn't sense any malice in him—he didn't even realize he was offering me anything unusual. That's why I didn't know . . ."

"But he did override the replicator programming to create some rather potent grain alcohol," Picard said, "in defiance of Starfleet regulations."

"It seems to have been what he needed," Troi whispered. "And if he can override a safety program, then he's not quite the primitive bumpkin everyone feels he is."

"That isn't at all what I feel," Picard said.

"It isn't? Good. Maybe that means this hangover is

going away." Troi started to sit up, then slumped back as the biobed's electronic squeals protested her movement. "And maybe it isn't."

Picard sighed again. "I need to know the ambassador's mental state."

"He's fine now, although be careful about mentioning his son." Troi winced again, as though a bright light had flashed in her eyes. "I don't believe it. The *walls* have feelings." She groaned and squeezed her eyes shut. "At least *they're* in a good mood."

"Counselor—" Picard began patiently.

"You want to know more about Ralph," she said. "It might help if you brushed up on the Eugenics War."

Picard nodded. "I have already done so. And I won't deny I'm fascinated by military history." Barbaric though it was, there had been something direct and vigorous about twentieth-century combat—especially when brave men had hurled themselves and their fragile aircraft against the flying battlewagons of the Khanate, or fought laser cannons and electromagnetic shields with rifles and artillery—

Troi cringed at what he felt. "Captain, Ralph isn't a pacifist, but he hates war. The death of his only child hit him very hard. Somehow it's given him an enormous burden of guilt."

"I'll keep that in mind," Picard said. "Is there anything else?"

"Yes," Troi whispered. She reached up, grabbed his collar and pulled his face close to hers. "Please don't *feel* so loud."

The captain extricated himself from her grip and left the sickbay. Troi's condition suggested that the ambassador would be dead to the world, but when Picard signaled at Offenhouse's door the ambassador greeted him in a cheery voice. "C'mon in, Picard."

Picard entered the room. Offenhouse looked quite

healthy. His eyes were clear, his face pink and clean-shaven. "Mr. Ambassador," Picard said, his voice at once firm and cordial, "henceforth please refrain from getting my crew members drunk."

Offenhouse looked puzzled. "'Drunk'?" he repeated.

"Counselor Troi—"

"Oh!" He shook his head. "Sorry, Picard. I didn't think a couple of vodka martinis could get anyone plastered. But I'll tell you, she makes more sense drunk than a lot of people do sober."

"Does she?" Picard asked. He waved a hand to dismiss the point. "I've come here to discuss our mission."

"Fine. Have a seat." Offenhouse sprawled on the bed while the captain settled into a chair. "Our first problem is going to be exploring Megara without tipping off the Ferengi."

"That can't be done," Picard said. "Suspicion is the natural state of the Ferengi mind."

"Correct," Offenhouse said, "so we've got to misdirect their suspicions. I think we can manage that, because they're going to *want* to believe their operations are still secret."

"That will be tricky," Picard said. "The Ferengi are sharp."

"They're a bunch of piranhas. But think of me as a shark." Offenhouse grinned, showing teeth. "Picard, back when I was a poor but humble financier, I learned how *easy* it is to outsmart crooked businessmen like the Ferengi. I can handle 'em."

Picard leaned forward in his seat. "Mr. Ambassador, are you saying that Ferengi behave like twentieth-century businessmen?"

"*Crooked* twentieth-century businessmen," Offenhouse said smugly. "That's the secret of my success, Picard, the one factor that makes the Federation think

I'm a genius, or at least a, a"—he looked at the ceiling as he snapped his fingers several times—"what's that French term, the one that means 'wise fool'—"

"Idiot savant," Picard said in a weak voice.

"Right. Not that anyone says it to my face." He rolled off the bed and went to the replicator. "One cherry cola, with crushed ice." He removed a glass from the opening and eyed Picard. "Took me a long time to duplicate *this* drink. You ought to try it, Picard."

Picard looked at the glass. The brown fluid fizzed and sputtered nastily, as though it had just made a forcible escape from a chemistry lab. "Perhaps some other time," Picard said. "We were discussing your approach to the Ferengi."

"Business is business," Offenhouse told him as he sat down. "And crooks is crooks. Picard, it's been a century since anyone in the Federation has had to worry about competition and percentages and all the other things that make business the grandest game man ever invented. Okay, you've rationalized your economy to the point where you have no unemployment, poverty or depressions, but it means you don't understand cultures who *do.*"

"Our sociologists might beg to differ," Picard said. He watched in barely restrained horror as Offenhouse drank the hissing brown fluid in his glass. "They have an excellent understanding of these matters."

"The way your android understands emotions," Offenhouse said. "I've told them things their 'expertise' has missed, because they can't imagine what it *feels* like to be threatened with unemployment, or poverty, or—well, a lot of things. I've studied everything the Federation has learned about the Ferengi, and I've felt like I was reading about some long-lost friends.

"The point is, I understand the Ferengi and I can

handle those smarmy weasels. Right now my real question is how we're going to investigate Megara. I'm going down, of course, but I can't be everywhere. I'll need other people who can look around, learn things and tell me what's going on."

Picard smiled. "Curiosity, observation and intelligence are prerequisite qualities in Starfleet officers. And one of the reasons we have civilians on this ship is so that they may visit alien worlds and allow other people to meet Federation citizens. It's an important diplomatic function."

"Sounds like a great little icebreaker," Offenhouse agreed. He sucked at his drink, and despite its corrosive effervescence he seemed unharmed. "How much money will they spend on Megara? For souvenirs, and dining, and whatever."

"Modest amounts, I should say," Picard said. "By and large our people aren't acquisitive."

"Tell them to get the habit," the ambassador said. "They'll need it."

"Very well," Picard said. "Now, Mr. Ambassador, let's discuss the Megarans. They're caught up in the Ferengi's machinations; what do we do about them?"

"Aside from running the Ferengi out of town?" The ambassador shook his head. "It's a safe guess that the Ferengi have turned Megaran society on its head, but beyond that, I don't know what to expect or what we'll do to help them recover."

"Nor do I," Picard said, "but, assuming we're successful, we can't simply walk away from the situation."

Offenhouse's knuckles whitened as his hand tightened on his glass. "No, I *won't*," he said, almost to himself. "Not this time."

Wesley hesitated, then walked into the Ten-Forward lounge. Guinan was nowhere in sight; she was off-duty, and Data had taken her place behind the bar. Shrev sat in a corner, eating something that looked like a bowl of gummy yellow soup.

Data was polishing a glass with a clean cloth. He was out of uniform, and dressed in the archaic, red-and-white-striped costume of a soda jerk. "Hello, Wesley," the android said. "What is your pleasure?"

"Uh—a hot-fudge sundae, please," the youth said. "A big one, with everything, like Counselor Troi likes."

"With nonreplicated ingredients?" the android asked. "Counselor Troi claims that replication does not 'catch' the subtle flavors of 'real' ice cream and chocolate. I would suggest you attempt the experience."

"Uh . . ." Wesley had heard similar claims before. Frankly, he thought that nonreplicated food tasted funny—especially when you thought about where some of the ingredients came from. On the other hand, he didn't want to offend Data. "Sure, I'll try it."

"Coming right up."

"Thanks." Wesley watched the android's hands as they swiftly created the dessert. "Say, Data, why are you doing this?"

Data's head tilted inquisitively. "Did you not request that I construct a hot-fudge sundae?"

Wesley smiled. He sometimes wondered if Data misunderstood questions on purpose, to provoke a smile. "I mean, why are you working behind the bar?"

"Guinan recently informed me that bartenders obtain a unique perspective on human behavior," Data said. He piled whipped cream onto the scoops of ice cream, then added an assortment of toppings. "This comes primarily in the form of what she called 'confessions,' a process by which bar patrons unburden their problems to the bartender after a quite modest stimulus. For example, I would make the observation that you appear troubled, and you would expound upon whatever matter troubled you, which would soothe your emotional state." Data poured hot fudge over the dessert. "As it happens, you *do* appear troubled."

"No, I've just been studying a lot the past couple of days. Zhuik culture," he added.

"You might consult Ensign Shrev," Data suggested.

"I've already talked with her a few times," Wesley said. "She's the reason I'm studying."

"Ah. You are cultivating a friendship?" Data asked.

"I hope so. The problem is, I've been around nonhumans most of my life, but I guess I don't understand how different they are." Wesley took the sundae and a spoon from Data. Instead of eating, he toyed with the spoon. "I start to think of other species as just different-looking humans, and then I get surprised when they do something a human would never do."

"This is a common human feeling," Data noted. "Has Ensign Shrev done something that troubles you?"

"Yes—no." Wesley shook his head. "It's me. I shouldn't expect her to act human, not when what she does is normal for her."

"Then you wish to accept her as she is," Data said. His head tilted again, as though he was consulting some inner data-readout. "I believe the proper course would be for you to dine with her, which will present the opportunity for further learning. And as with most races, Zhuik prefer to dine with friends."

"Right. Thanks, Data." Wesley picked up the sundae and crossed the lounge to Shrev's table. Her soup, he saw, was more like honey or nectar, and the spoon was a spatula which she licked clean with a raspy

73

tongue as green as her face. The meal probably *was* nectar, he decided, given the fact that Zhuiks had evolved from insects similar to terrestrial bees.

Wesley remembered to lower his voice when he spoke to Shrev. He had found that the forced whisper made it easier to affect the extreme politeness that Zhuiks found normal. *It's almost like being an actor in an intense role,* he thought. *When I'm "in character," it's almost impossible not to be hyperpolite.* "Might I intrude upon you?" he asked.

"I would welcome your presence, Wesley." Shrev sniffed delicately. "Your meal has a pleasant aroma."

"As does yours, Shrev." He bent his head slightly and raised his eyes to look at her. Even though he had no antennae to focus on her, he had a hunch that this position would seem attentive; to Zhuiks, humans probably looked as though they were staring off into the space above someone's head.

She smiled. "You have studied our ways since we last met."

Wesley nodded. "It seemed polite, and I wanted to understand what I saw on the holodeck."

"What you saw *did* distress you," Shrev said in alarm.

"Only my ignorance distressed me," Wesley said. He had rehearsed that line carefully, and he was glad to see how it soothed Shrev. "But now I think I know why you did it. Among your people, behavior is closely linked to genetics. A mutation can reveal itself as a change in behavior."

"And we are far more vulnerable to mutation than most species," Shrev said. The Ten-Forward lounge had excellent acoustics, but Wesley still had to strain to hear Shrev over the dinner chatter of the other patrons. "Our genetic material lacks the stability inherent in yours. If we did not purge our hives of mutants, then within a few generations we would slide into decay and extinction. Hence we accept our killings."

But it's unusual for a Zhuik to kill a mutant even once in a lifetime, Wesley reflected. Zhuiks with obvious birth defects were killed in childhood, usually by their parents—a custom not unknown in some backward human cultures, as more than one text had reminded Wesley. Shrev had killed over a dozen of her people on the holodeck. "It also means that bad manners must upset you," Wesley said. "And you must find life among humans a continual display of rudeness."

"My reaction to bad manners is genetic," Shrev whispered. "But I can make allowances for non-Zhuiks. And I find it relaxing to deal with you. Your manners are impeccable."

"I'm glad to hear I'm learning, Shrev." Wesley remembered his sundae and took a bite. "And I'm glad you can work off the strain on the holodeck."

She smiled. "You are kind, and knowledgeable. The killing relaxes me; my people feel *zh'hs'hzs,* the . . . instinctive need to kill under certain conditions. Through it I also reassure myself that I still recognize good and bad manners, that I am a proper person. But did you recognize the rudeness in the people I killed?"

Not even once, he thought. "I was often puzzled, Shrev."

"Well." She took a lick of her nectar. "The woman who asked about iron was insulting my choice of friends. Our blood uses copper and yours uses iron, you see?"

Wesley hesitated. "Among humans, we seldom fight to the death over insults."

"But among humans, rudeness is not a genetic failing." Shrev took another spatula of nectar. "I hope I will not offend you with my frankness, but some of my people feel that aliens contaminate our culture, by expecting us to conform to their morals. While we give this topic much debate, the woman was rude to mention it so bluntly in front of an outlander."

"And as a proper lady, you could not allow her insult to pass unchallenged," Wesley whispered, lifting his words from one of the texts he'd studied. "Might I ask about the woman who requested directions to the surface?"

"She showed a lack of direction," Shrev told him. "Most of my people have an inborn knowledge of our hive's pathways, but a mutant does not know which way is up—"

Wesley laughed loudly. "Sorry, Shrev," he said, then lowered his voice again. "That's a human joke. When someone acts confused or stupid, we say they don't know which way is up."

"An interesting point." She smiled. "It would be rude of me to say that I am suddenly reminded of certain Academy instructors."

"I believe I could name them," Wesley said.

"Indeed?" With her eyes and antennae focused on him, Wesley found her smile sly. "I most especially recall Klarten, whom I shall not deny is an excellent instructor in personal combat."

Wesley winced, recalling Klarten's habit of taking anyone who erred in his class and demonstrating judo holds and throws with his or her body. Klarten maintained, loudly, that no cadet could fight worth beans. "He's good, all right," Wesley said.

"And you will be under his expert tutelage for three more years," Shrev said.

Wesley saw where she was leading the conversation; she obviously had a very human urge to get even with Klarten. "I would welcome the chance to surprise him," Wesley said. "And I saw your expertise on the holodeck. Could I impose on you to teach me how Zhuiks use the knife?"

Shrev smiled again. "That would please me no end, Wesley." Her meal was almost done; her spatula scraped the bottom of the bowl. "Well. I have thought on our last talk. As you said, what the Ferengi do is expensive and time-consuming, and not in keeping with their customs."

"I still can't explain that," Wesley said. "I must be missing something."

"Perhaps we have tasted the wrong flowers. The nectar we seek may be elsewhere." She licked at the spatula. "What if the Ferengi are working for someone else?"

"Yeah . . ." Wesley said. "They'll do anything for money. But who has a reason to develop a backwater planet like Megara?"

"That question I cannot answer."

"Same here—wait, maybe I'm going at this backward," Wesley said. He looked up at the lounge ceiling; he had kept his head bent forward so long that his neck had begun to stiffen. "Who can afford to do it?"

"There are many possibilities." Shrev put her spatula aside. "Romulans, Tholians, Cardassians, Orion pirates, Gorn, renegade Klingons."

"Megara has a good strategic position on the Federation's border," Wesley said, "and there are a lot of unclaimed planets in the sector. Any of those people would jump at the chance to have a base on Megara."

"That is logical," Shrev said. "Now we must search for facts to support or deny our logic."

Chapter Six

THE TERROR had faded years ago, but Odovil Pardi still felt nervous around the Ferengi. It did not help that Ri'vok was talking about problems with her operation. "Two shipments in the past sixday have contained octahedral crystalline patterns," the little man said. He sat behind Odovil's desk, forcing her to stand in her own office. "It made the metal worthless. It screwed up the production quotas at two different factories. You're all lazy and stupid here, not checking the quality of your product."

"Our best we do," Odovil said. Pride would not let her remain silent, although facing up to the alien made her queasy. She felt cold sweat inside her baggy gray coverall.

"Your debt-ridden best," Ri'vok sneered. "If I were you, I'd kick out the lazy overdrafts responsible for this problem. Take away their work permits; that's an order. *Then* you people will learn to do your best." He raised his hand, and for a moment Odovil thought he was reaching for the glowing blue whip coiled around his shoulder. However, he touched one of the orna-

78

ments pinned to his vest, and shimmered as he dematerialized.

Odovil sat at her desk and waited until she stopped shaking. Each time she saw one of the outworlders she was reminded of her education. She had been ordered to report to the mayoral hall in Kasten Darr, where she had gone into a small room. A man—a *real* man, not one of these wizened, rat-eyed horrors—had placed a glowing helmet over her head, and that was the last thing she had known for three days; the treatment had cast her into a feverish daze.

It had taken Odovil weeks to regain her health. As she recovered she had found that she could read, write, manipulate numbers and remember in precise detail everything she heard and saw . . . and that a nameless fear shadowed her mind, leaving her with an urge to hide in the corner of a small room. In time she learned that the Ferengi education-machine had ugly effects on certain people, and when she saw the madness that afflicted other people she felt she had been lucky. The Ferengi had not cared; when she was healthy again they had tested her and told her what job she would perform for them.

Eventually Odovil left the plastic hut that served as her office. The metal-processing plant, *her* plant, covered an area the size of a small town. Flying cargo bins brought ores from around the world. Smelters and separators extracted metals from the ores; processors and ovens turned pure metals and other substances into alloys; mills and forges cast the alloys into plates, beams and other shapes. Ozone and the smells of glowing metal filled the air.

The plant employed over two thousand people. Some of them nodded or tipped their caps to Odovil as she walked past them. Odovil pretended she didn't see them. The outworlder had suggested she discharge a couple of these people, *her* people, and the Ferengi

never joked about that. Twice before they had ordered
her to fire workers, once to end a strike and once to
punish a quota shortfall. Odovil had done as ordered;
managers who disobeyed such orders were fired themselves, along with many innocent people. Resistance
was hopeless.

Depriving a Megaran of his or her work permit was
a punishment more diabolic than execution. Without
a work permit one could not hold a job, rent a home,
even buy food . . . not legally. People without a work
permit were forced into the criminal underworld, or
to find precarious, menial work in the black market.
Others simply starved. And now she had to throw
some of her people into that living hell—

Haragan Til supervised the main processors. The
old man had grown up as a farmer on this land, and
when the outworlders had established the metal plant
they had drafted his family into its service. Odovil
found him in a control shack, discussing the day's
schedule with his assistant. "Crystals," Til said in
disgust, when Odovil told him about Ri'vok's com-
plaint. "Fluctuations in the initial cooling phase we
must have. At once to it I shall see." Til left the shack.

The assistant closed the door. "Trouble we have
had," he said. Odovil couldn't remember the young
man's name. "The rat-eyes three of our best people
took away. Two of them the magnetothermic ovens
supervised. We their replacements still are training."

"Of this nothing I heard," Odovil said petulantly.
She did not feel surprised at her ignorance. The plant
had an efficient bureaucracy, but it often filtered out
"minor" facts, such as the loss of a few workers. "Why
the rat-eyes these people did take?"

"Why the rat-eyes did not say," the man said. He
looked at the control shack's instrument panel and
spoke as he adjusted a knob. "Only this I know, that
they our best people have taken."

Odovil left the shack and walked back to her office. She reflected that it was typical of the outworlders to create a problem and then blame it on someone else. But perhaps this would give her an excuse not to fire anyone. The trouble had come about because the new workers were not fully trained. Firing them would force her to train new people, which could only create more problems. Of course, the outworlders might simply order her to fire somebody else—but she could try.

Her secretary was waiting for Odovil on the gravel path outside her office. "You from the Vo Gatyn a message have," the old woman said. Her short hair was as gray as her coverall. "On your desk the letter is."

Odovil nodded. "Other business there is?" she asked. Her secretary had an expectant look.

"No . . . only that, tonight in Kes Pa'kess a dance there will be. A relaxing night you might enjoy."

"No," Odovil said. The thought of going to a dance filled her with a dull horror. "No. Work I must, more trouble there is. Good people away the rat-eyes have taken."

"The oven operators and an expediter?" the secretary asked. "We replacements already have hired."

"Good enough they aren't," Odovil said. "The others back we need."

"Back they will not come," the old woman said.

"Something you know?" Odovil asked.

"Something from my cousin in Metari Leeg I have heard," she said. "A new school there the rat-eyes have built. People there the rat-eyes train, on their starship to work. And to Metari Leeg the rat-eyes these people took."

"Servants on their ship they need?" Odovil wondered. She couldn't imagine why the outworlders would train people to work in space.

"Perhaps a new way to make profits they have found," she said. "Many talented people for this training they collect, or so I hear."

Odovil nodded silently and walked into her office. Talented people. If the Ferengi decided that they wanted her for this training—no, she couldn't let herself think about that.

She sat down at her desk and saw the Vo's letter atop a pile of requisitions and memos. It was a square of parchment—one of the many luxuries the Ferengi gave the Vo Gatyn—and it summoned Odovil to a business meeting tonight at the Vo's castle, where it would be the Vo's pleasure to discuss new ways to increase the power and wealth of her domain.

Odovil tossed the parchment into the disposer. Everyone knew that the Vo Gatyn was a Ferengi puppet. Her "contract" with the outworlders was a sham that allowed them to do whatever they liked. At least one and probably several Ferengi would be there, snarling with threats and demands . . . along with a hideous swarm of people, loud, laughing, pressing, crowding . . .

Haragan Til came to the office an hour later, and found Odovil crouched under her desk, her head cradled in her hands.

Megara was expanding rapidly on the main viewer. "Thirty seconds to orbit," Riker said. "Mr. Worf, sound red alert."

"Aye, sir," the Klingon said happily. The general alarm wailed throughout the ship. "All decks report ready for combat," he said.

Picard looked to Offenhouse, who leaned against the helm next to Wesley Crusher. "Satisfied, Mr. Ambassador?"

"Lock on to the Ferengi ship as soon as you can,"

Offenhouse said. "Oh, yeah—Data, how much did that Vulcan probe cost?"

The android spoke without looking up from his station next to Wesley. "Five-point-seven-three-two million credits, Mr. Ambassador."

"Call it ten million," Offenhouse said. "Even figures always sound more impressive."

More impressive than what? Picard wondered, as Wesley brought the *Enterprise* out of warp drive. The maneuver was neatly executed, and the starship entered a standard orbit around Megara. Wesley could not keep the pride out of his voice as he spoke. "On station, Captain. Ferengi battle cruiser bearing zero-mark-zero, range one hundred kilometers."

"All weapons locked on target," Worf announced.

"Hail 'em," Offenhouse said.

The Ferengi bridge appeared on the main viewer, showing alarmed men preparing for battle. "Keep your shields down!" Offenhouse roared at the Ferengi. "Which one of you sleazy wimps is in charge of that tacky peddler's cart you have the chutzpah to call a starship?"

One of the Ferengi snarled at the viewer, displaying a mouthful of sharp, conical teeth. "I am the Daimon Chudak," he said. Picard had to give him credit for his self-control; he seemed utterly unafraid. "Who are *you* to annoy me?"

"Quit sniveling," Offenhouse snapped. "Tell me, spendthrift, did you really think you could get away with it?"

Chudak bared his teeth. "What are you blathering about, you earless wonder?"

Offenhouse took two steps toward the viewer, and Picard saw him clench his fists. "Don't play stupid, you don't have the brains for it. I'm talking about the probe you destroyed. If you want to get out of this alive, you half-credit leftover from a garbage auction, you're going to pay the Vulcan Academy of Science the ten million credits you cost them—"

"That probe was worth no more than one million!" Chudak said.

"—*and* you're not going to bother us!" Offenhouse leered at the viewer. "We know what's happening on Megara, you hole in the change purse of the galaxy. Did you think you could fool the Federation *forever?* We know how you tampered with the last probe. What are you hiding here? A dilithium mine? Kevas? Pergium? Whatever it is, you are *not* going to hog the profits."

Picard saw the Ferengi's sudden befuddlement. "Tampered—we have never—that is—"

"I should kill you now." Offenhouse crossed his arms over his chest. "Ten years ago, you service charge on the great checking account of life, you fed false data into a long-range probe—or did your claw-handed flunkies tamper with the records at Memory Alpha? Either way, you *almost* fooled us into thinking that Megara was a primitive world. We can *see* that it isn't—"

Chudak's image vanished. "The Ferengi have broken the channel," Worf said.

"Naturally," Offenhouse said, suddenly calm and composed. "They'll need a minute to confer. Picard, I'll bet two bits that they agree to pay off the Vulcans, now and in full."

"It's no bet," Picard said. Offenhouse's rough diplomatic style seemed effective . . . and it had been a pleasure to watch. "Is that important, Mr. Ambassador?"

Offenhouse nodded. "It'll help confirm a hunch I have."

"Which is?" Riker asked.

"That these Ferengi have an unlimited supply of

money," Offenhouse said. "*And* that the little tight-wads will cough up to hide whatever they're doing here. Counselor, are you picking up anything from the Ferengi?"

Deanna shook her head. "Betazoids can't sense Ferengi mentalities. Their four-lobed brains are unreadable to us."

"Assuming they have something *to* read," Worf muttered. Ferengi did not number among his favorite people. "The Ferengi are hailing us," he announced a moment later.

"Put 'em on," Offenhouse said.

Chudak's image returned to the main viewer. "We deny that this Vulcan probe was worth ten million credits," he grated.

Offenhouse's hostility roared back to life. "Have you priced interstellar probes lately? You should have read the sticker before you blew it away. Ten million credits, Chudak, or I'll personally give you a five-fingered dental treatment." He smacked a fist into a palm for emphasis.

Chudak growled under his breath. "For the sake of a profitable peace, I shall pay for our understandable error—but you may *not* visit Megara. *I* have an exclusive contract with its government."

Offenhouse shook his head in defiance. "The Federation doesn't recognize any such contract. Never has, never will."

"The Vo of Megara recognizes my contract," Chudak said. "You! Picard! Since when does a civilian run your ship?"

Offenhouse laughed loudly before Picard could speak. "The Federation isn't a *military* society, chump. The soldiers work for the civilians. Like me. Got that? And *I* work for a profit."

Chudak glared at him. "The Megarans will deny you the right to land!"

"What's the matter, Chudak?" Offenhouse snickered at his opponent. "Are you *afraid* I can offer them a better deal?"

"You?" Chudak scoffed. "You couldn't sell money to a debtor, you badly written penalty clause!"

"No? Then why are you so nervous?" Offenhouse let out a lewd chuckle. "Having a bad-hair day, are we?"

Chudak glowered on the screen, and Picard felt a twinge of empathy with the smooth-scalped Ferengi.

"Land," Chudak grated. "Land and be damned, you furry ceiling-scraper!" The channel broke.

"That was fun," Offenhouse said idly, his rage vanishing. "I doubt I lit a fire under the Ferengi temper, but with any luck *he* thinks *I'm* a hot-tempered jerk."

"Which may lead him to underestimate you," Picard said. The captain rubbed his chin in thought. "Mr. Ambassador, your insults show an impressive understanding of Ferengi idioms."

"It's nothing," Offenhouse said. "When you figure how important profit is to the Ferengi, it's obvious that calling someone a bad businessman or a debtor is a low blow."

Worf growled. "Monitoring a subspace transmission from the Ferengi ship," he said. "It is a bank draft for ten million credits, payable to the Vulcan Academy of Science."

Offenhouse chuckled. "There's nothing more fun than being generous with other people's money. Picard, call this 'Vo of Megara' and tell him we're paying a visit. Then arrange shore leave—officers only, though, and just a token number."

"Is there anything else?" Riker asked, in a polite tone that verged on sarcasm.

"Yeah, sonny, you can get me a survey of the industrial infrastructure down there," Offenhouse said. "Factories, mines, transport—all that jazz. I need something more detailed than the probe data. Picard, I'm going to borrow your ready room for a few minutes."

"By all means," Picard said quietly. He glanced at Wesley, who was almost visibly straining to hear everything that went on.

The engine room throbbed as it fed power to the shields and weapons. Like many a Starfleet engineer, La Forge wished that the bridge crew would reset themselves, calm down and end the alert. The alert placed no real strain on the ship's systems, but Geordi had better things to do than play nursemaid to some overcharged phasers.

"There, Geordi." Alexander had perched himself on a seat at a computer terminal. He pointed at a readout near the top of the master display. "You got a power drop in the secondary starboard intercooler."

"Thanks, Al." Geordi made an adjustment. Civilians weren't supposed to be in engineering during an alert, but Geordi was willing to bend that regulation. Alexander stayed out of the way—and if things went to hell in engineering, no place would be safe. Besides, Geordi liked having the kid around. When it came to having unique perspectives on the universe, kids were as good as aliens—witness Alexander's idea for detecting cloaked ships. Geordi wasn't sure why Worf's son wanted to hang around him—the kid didn't want to be an engineer—but he wasn't going to ask any questions.

Geordi scanned the master display again, then sat in the operator's chair and adjusted its back to a comfortable tilt. "Hurry up and wait," he said idly.

"Can you run the simulations now, Geordi?" Alexander asked.

"Wish I could, Al," Geordi said, "but we can't tie

up the main computer during an alert. Don't worry. I have a hunch your idea is going to work just fine. In fact, it should be able to detect more than just cloaked ships—we should be able to find ships that're hiding inside nebulae and other natural phenomena, which is a pretty common tactic. The galaxy is full of blivets where you can't ordinarily detect a ship."

"Oh." The boy kicked his feet idly against the deck, then looked up. "Hey, Geordi, how many Romulans does it take to change a light bulb?"

"Search me," Geordi said. "How many?"

"Two. One to do it, another to kill him and take the credit."

Geordi laughed with Alexander. *When I was a boy,* he recalled, *we told that one about the Klingons. Aw, what the hell.* "How many Ferengi does it take to change a light bulb?" Geordi asked him.

"Ferengi never give change!" He giggled. "How many humans does it take to change a light bulb —uh—"

Geordi's VISOR picked up a sharp change in Alexander's facial skin; he was blushing in embarrassment. Still, it was a fair joke. "A light bulb?" Geordi asked, sounding ignorant. "What's a light bulb?" Alexander laughed, and Geordi heard a couple of his engineers chuckle as well.

The intercom piped for attention. "All hands, secure from red alert. Mr. La Forge, report to the conference room."

"Time to go," Geordi told Alexander. The boy hopped off his chair and followed Geordi to the turbolift. "Bridge," Geordi told the lift.

"Deck twelve," Alexander said, and looked up at the human engineer. "Geordi? Father liked that joke about not annihilating humans. You got any more like that?"

"Not offhand—wait, try this on him. Humans are okay, even if they *like* tribbles."

"Dumb," Alexander said with a smile. "Father will like it. So will Commander Riker. Thanks, Geordi." The lift stopped and Alexander got off.

Maybe he and Will Riker were swapped at birth, Geordi thought as the turbolift started again. Worf, to judge from the bytes of gossip that floated around the ship, didn't think his son acted Klingonese enough, and that was a source of tension between father and son. The boy could be rambunctious as all hell by human standards, but evidently Klingons had higher standards.

The turbolift stopped, and Geordi crossed the bridge to the conference room. The usual group was present: Picard, Riker, Troi, Worf, Data and Dr. Crusher. Ambassador Offenhouse was there as well. Geordi sat down between Crusher and Troi.

Geordi looked at his shipmates. His VISOR could detect the subtle changes that emotions generated in body-electric fields and skin temperatures, and while he couldn't read their meaning with anything like Deanna Troi's precision, he could often make a good guess as to what people felt. Everyone in the conference room seemed alert, but in a good mood; emotions were *not* running high. That was a pleasant surprise, because scuttlebutt had it that the ambassador was a real pain in the—

Offenhouse rapped his knuckles on the table, opening the meeting. "I've just gone over my file on Daimon Chudak—the commander of that Ferengi ship," he added, with a glance at Geordi and Dr. Crusher. "What I've got adds to the mystery. Computer, show Chudak's file."

An image and a text file appeared on the room's viewscreen. Geordi narrowed his VISOR's bandwidth to accept only the "visible" spectrum, that of light with a wavelength between four thousand and seven thousand angstroms. The constant headache his VISOR gave him faded as the data flow decreased. The image showed a typical Ferengi male: scooplike ears, bald and bulging head, wrinkled nose and forehead and a seemingly endless supply of fanglike teeth.

"Daimon Chudak," Offenhouse said. "Age, thirty-seven standard years. Personal fortune, two billion credits—good, but not outstandingly wealthy."

Geordi broadened his VISOR's bandwidth again, and his vision returned to normal. Pain returned with it; the circuits were now feeding in all the data his nervous system could handle, and the overload created a tension headache. Almost automatically, he slipped into the pain-suppressing discipline that a Vulcan healer had taught him when he was a boy. The pain meant nothing in comparison to seeing the electric fields and thermal patterns and magnetic fluxes that permeated the universe.

"Two billion credits," Riker said. "Does that include the value of his ship?"

"Yeah," the ambassador said. "Chudak made all his money himself; his family is poor—you'll notice that he doesn't have a Ferengi caste-tattoo on his forehead."

"That sounds like quite a handicap in Ferengi society," Deanna Troi said.

"Not really," Offenhouse said. "The Ferengi are more impressed by business acumen than ancestry. This just shows that he's sharp and aggressive, in addition to being handsome"—Geordi heard no irony in Offenhouse's voice—"and courageous. There's also evidence that he's skirted Ferengi law on a few occasions."

"You describe a pirate," Worf rumbled. Geordi thought he heard admiration in the Klingon's voice.

"Chudak's behavior on Megara is not piratical," Data said, looking to the ambassador. "Our sensor scans have confirmed the probe data. Within the past ten years the Ferengi have created an extensive industrial infrastructure on Megara, one which employs essentially all of the native population. A pirate would have neither the time nor the inclination to create such a technological society."

"Weird," Geordi said. "But maybe Chudak is using Megara as a slave world. They build things dirt-cheap, and he sells them at a profit."

"That's plausible," Picard mused. "Can we tell what the local industries are manufacturing?"

"No, sir," Data said. "Electronic interference in the factories makes a detailed scan of the surface impossible. However, there is no evidence that anything is being exported from Megara."

"Everything is staying here?" Geordi asked in disbelief. "I thought the point of business was to sell what you make."

"It is, and that brings me to another problem," Offenhouse said. "I can't explain where Chudak got the fifty billion credits he'd need to finance this operation. It didn't come from Ferengal; Federation Intelligence has a window into their financial system, and we know Chudak hasn't collected any money from his homeworld."

"He could still be holding Megara as a slave world," Riker said. "A Ferengi battle cruiser could force an entire world to work for free."

"But that wouldn't pay for everything Chudak would have to import," Geordi argued. "Construction equipment, replicators to build factory tools, blueprints—the Megarans could do a lot of work themselves, but not without a certain amount of 'seed' equipment."

"Exactly," Offenhouse said in an approving tone. "I

don't have enough information to solve that mystery yet, so let's get on to the next bit. Picard, did you wangle some invitations?"

The captain smiled. "The Vo Gatyn will see the two of us tonight. We're invited to a dinner on her private estate."

"Good, I always did like to eat out," Offenhouse said. "What about sending down some tourists?"

"We have permission to land twenty people in Gatyn's capital city," Picard said. "Kes Pa'kess, as it's called, is large and heavily industrialized. The arrangements should suit your purposes, Mr. Ambassador."

"They do," Offenhouse said. "I'll want to talk with our people before they go down. One last thing." He looked at Geordi. "Mr. La Forge, isn't it?"

Geordi nodded. "Yes, Mr. Ambassador?"

"We'll need some coins," he said. "Something made out of pure gold. Also belt pouches to carry them. Can you program the replicators for that?"

"No problem," Geordi said, "but are you sure you want pure gold? It's one of the softest metals around. Your coins will get scratched up in no time."

"Especially when somebody bites 'em," Offenhouse said as he stood up. "Picard, let's choose our tourists, then get ready for dinner."

The captain and the ambassador left the conference room. "I never thought I'd hear anyone call a Ferengi 'handsome,'" Riker said to Worf.

"Perhaps he's been studying them too long," Beverly Crusher suggested. "Some humans get that way, you know."

Geordi managed not to laugh at Riker's sudden, multispectral flush. Worf took umbrage at the joke, however; the Klingon's bioelectric field rippled in the angry display that always reminded Geordi of shields going up. "Say, Worf," Geordi said quickly, "I should be ready to test the new anticloaking sensor in a few hours."

Worf growled as though draining the charge from his temper. "The theory is sound?" he asked.

"I've still got a few simulations to run," Geordi said. Troi smiled as she sensed his exaggeration, but she kept quiet. "But, yeah, the theory looks good. And it should work on more things than cloaked ships. If everything works out, we'll be able to detect any operating reactor. It could give us quite an advantage."

"Until somebody figures out a way to counteract it," Riker said.

"Somebody always does, sooner or later," Geordi said, unperturbed. "That's what makes this game so much fun. Anyway, Worf, if it works I'll mention Alexander's contribution in my report."

"That is considerate," Worf growled, with all the politeness he could muster.

"Hey, he earned it," Geordi said as he stood up. "I'll let you know when I'm ready to test it."

Geordi left the conference room. *Coins,* he thought as he went to the turbolift. Except for a few special purposes, the Federation hadn't used physical currency in decades; replicator technology made counterfeiting too easy. Geordi decided he could fake it easily enough. After all, the Megarans had no idea of what might pass for money in the Federation. That was probably why Offenhouse had insisted on pure gold— on many planets it was the metal itself, and not the symbols stamped on a coin, that gave money its value.

"Geordi, wait up," Beverly Crusher called as he stepped into the turbolift. He held the lift door for her. "I want to ask you something."

"Sure, Beverly. Engineering," he told the lift.

The doctor smoothed her hair, and he saw static charges dance its length, playing hide-and-seek with her fingers. "Geordi, have you noticed anything odd about Will Riker lately?"

He chuckled. "Is this the same man who eats live *gagh?*"

"Several Earth cultures eat live insects," Beverly reminded him. "But I'm afraid Will may be going a little—over the top, if you know what I mean, with his admiration for the Klingons."

"Everybody needs a hobby," Geordi said. "But Will knows when to stop. Remember when Worf broke his back?"

"Yes. Will kept him from committing suicide, even though that's the Klingon way." The doctor shook her head. "I just have doubts about a man who courts food poisoning." The elevator stopped and opened into the main engineering compartment. "By the way, Geordi, I have a new report on optic-nerve implants. The Vulcans have made some remarkable advances. Stop by sickbay and we'll discuss it."

"I will, when I get the time." He hastened out of the lift and the door shut behind him.

As he always did when he entered engineering, Geordi looked around the high bay. Everything was as it should have been. Tight, intense glows wrapped themselves around power conduits. Structural-support fields limned the ship's framework. Computer chips winked and shimmered in cybernetic thought.

Normal eyesight would be nice, Geordi thought. He'd always wondered what a rainbow looked like; he could settle for himself the friendly debate over whether Deanna Troi, Beverly Crusher or Guinan was the most beautiful woman aboard the *Enterprise.* And yet—

Geordi stepped up to the main warp drive. Dormant now, the mechanism throbbed with the thoroughbred dreams of a racing horse. To every other human on the ship, Geordi knew, the unit was an opaque slab of metal shielding, its life visible only through the cloudy window of sensor readings.

Give this up? Geordi sighed, and wondered what excuse he would give the doctor this time.

Chapter Seven

"HOLD THE KNIFE higher, if you please," Shrev whispered, and feinted at Wesley with her holoblade. Wesley slipped back quickly—*I'm getting awfully good at retreating!* he thought sardonically—and parried her snakelike thrust at him. Then—

Skreee! Shrev's blade squealed in triumph, signaling a fatal strike. Wesley looked down at himself and saw the holographic projection that simulated a fatal wound; Shrev had caught him in the heart.

"Excellent," Shrev said, while the spectators in the gymnasium chuckled. She thumbed the hilt of her practice knife, and the holographic blade vanished. "I took a full minute to kill you this time."

"A minute?" Wesley picked up a towel from a wall rack and wiped sweat from his face. He was short of breath. "It seemed longer."

"A minute is very long in a fight," she agreed. "It is enough time for a friend to see your plight and aid you. Against an experienced fighter, as I claim to be, such survival shows amazing talent."

"Thanks, Shrev." The praise took some of the sting

out of the crowd's chuckles, and from his own record. Shrev had killed him a dozen times in the past hour, and he had barely managed to deliver a hypothetical scratch to her left arm. "I have an excellent teacher."

"We both do well here," she said. She returned the practice knives to their locker.

The intercom called for attention. "Cadet Crusher, report to the captain's ready room," the ship's computer said.

Shrev looked at him. "This is an interesting request," she said. "Could he be considering you for a landing party?"

"It could be," Wesley said. He had told her what he had heard on the bridge. "In that case, would you be interested in going if the opportunity arises?"

"Absolutely," Shrev said. "And now it would be polite for you to hurry, true?"

Wesley took the turbolift to the ready room. He was not eager to see Picard. The captain had been not unsympathetic about his disgrace, but the man was also a reminder of what had happened. Breaking a safety regulation, seeing a friend die because of that, then lying to cover it up—

Well, he told himself, *I can't pretend it didn't happen.*

Picard was alone in his ready room when Wesley entered it. He sat down at a gesture from the captain. "Cadet Crusher," Picard said, "how would you like to play tourist on Megara?"

"I'd like that, sir," Wesley said.

"I had hoped so," Picard said. "Tell me, how much do you know about Megara?"

The captain's neutral words seemed to hang in the air, while Wesley wondered how much the man knew. *This is no time to play games,* he realized. "I've seen the Vulcan probe data and other files, sir, but I can't figure out what's going on down there."

97

"That's a feeling with which I'm familiar," Picard said. "Very well. I'm going to assign you to the away team. I can't tell you what to look for, but any observations you make may be of value. Now, I do not anticipate any risk, but I expect you to exercise discretion. The Ferengi could see too much curiosity as an unwarranted intrusion."

"Understood, sir," Wesley said. "I won't stick my nose where it doesn't belong." Wesley paused. "Uh, Captain? Would it be all right if Ensign Shrev went with me?"

Picard raised an eyebrow. "Do you think she could contribute to your mission, Cadet?"

Wesley nodded vigorously. "Yes, sir. We've been discussing the situation, and she has some ideas."

"Make it so," Picard said, and smiled. "I believe this is the first time a cadet has picked his own commanding officer. Now there is something else I would like to discuss, Cadet."

Wesley braced himself. *The incident,* he thought. "Yes, sir."

Picard sighed. "I don't require Counselor Troi's talents to know that you've been uneasy in my presence. You're still troubled by what you did at the Academy, and my presence jogs your conscience."

"Yes, sir," Wesley said awkwardly. "I just feel . . . it's like—I don't know."

"You feel as though you'll never come to terms with what you did," Picard said. He nodded at the model starship in his office: the *Stargazer.* "I felt the same way after I lost the *Stargazer.*"

"Sir?" That puzzled Wesley. "That isn't the same thing. You didn't destroy the *Stargazer;* the Ferengi did."

"I blame myself for the way I handled events at Zeta Maxia," Picard said. "A better captain might have found a way to avoid trouble. It does not matter if I

am wrong or right; the point is that I still believe that I
erred . . . somehow. That I am responsible for all the
lives I lost.

"But you learn to accommodate yourself to such an
experience. You find that it becomes a part of you,
that it exerts a certain influence on your judgments.
High as the price is, it can make you a better person
and a better officer."

"I think I understand, sir," Wesley said. "You mean
it stops being like a weight on your back, and starts
being like a sibyl."

"Something like that," Picard said with a smile.
The sibyls had been ancient prophetesses, and accord-
ing to legend they had given advice to the early
Romans—advice that sometimes came at great cost.
"I see you've been studying Latin."

"I've taken a course in it, sir," Wesley said, recalling
that Latin was one of Picard's many interests.

"It's a remarkably useful language," Picard said.
"The study of Latin forces us to remember that not
too long ago we humans were as 'primitive' as many of
the races we encounter on new worlds. The works of
Cicero and Marcus Aurelius also show that
'primitives' can possess wisdom and genius without
our technological trappings."

"I hadn't thought of that, sir," Wesley said. "I guess
I've been too wrapped up in declensions and verb
conjugations to notice anything else."

"I was the same way when I began my study of
Latin." Picard spoke to the intercom. "Have Ambassador Offenhouse and Ensign Shrev report to me.
The ambassador will have a few things to say, I'm
sure."

"Yes, sir," Wesley said. He felt relieved that he had
faced the captain and the world had not ended.

Offenhouse stepped into the ready room a moment
later. "What's up, kid?" he asked as he seated himself.

"I'm sending Cadet Crusher and Ensign Shrev to Megara," Picard said.

The ambassador's face turned hard. "No. Not him. It's too dangerous."

"That's not my assessment of the situation, Mr. Ambassador," Picard said. "Our relations with the Ferengi have been largely peaceful, and I am confident of Cadet Crusher's ability to handle this assignment without incident."

The two men stared at one another for a moment before Offenhouse relented. "All right," he said, and looked to Wesley. "You've been snooping around this problem. Got any ideas about what the Ferengi are up to?"

"Ensign Shrev thinks they're working for a third party, sir," Wesley said. For a moment he had been afraid that Offenhouse would have his way. Wesley wanted to visit Megara, both to satisfy his curiosity and to show the captain that he would not disappoint him again. "What they're doing down there doesn't make sense by Ferengi standards, unless somebody else is paying them to do it."

Offenhouse nodded thoughtfully. "Could be," he admitted. "That just beggars the question, though— who hired them, and why? Does this Shrev have any ideas about that?"

"Not yet, sir, except that they're probably hostile to the Federation," Wesley said. "Megara has a good strategic location."

"Maybe not," Offenhouse said, more to himself than to Wesley. "It *could* be some kind of trading post . . . somebody outside the Federation, looking to do business with us while getting a head start on the competition. Or a research base, for somebody who wants to study *us* without attracting our attention."

"Those are interesting possibilities," Picard said, as Shrev entered the ready room. At Picard's gesture she sat down next to Wesley. "Mr. Ambassador, I believe we're ready to begin the briefing."

The leather pouch of gold coins tugged at Shrev's hip. "There's plenty more where that came from," De Shay said, "so call me if you use it up."

"Thank you, sir, I shall," Shrev said. It was hard to imagine spending so much gold—De Shay said there were two hundred coins in the bag, which weighed two kilos—but her orders from the ambassador were quite specific. Given the endurance of her people, she might need more gold to fulfill those orders.

Wesley fastened a pouch to his waist and stepped onto the transporter stage with Shrev. He nodded to her, and she took that as a sign of readiness. "Energize, please," she said to De Shay.

The transporter room faded into a bleak street. The sky was covered with clouds, but Shrev's sensitive eyes found the sun easily enough. Light polarization let her establish directions; north was *that* way, so the breeze came out of the west. Gravity was a bit lighter than that aboard the *Enterprise,* but not drastically so. Electric cables crisscrossed above the street, and cargo vehicles—some of them so primitive that they used wheels instead of suspensors—moved along the street. Nothing in the air smelled very good.

There were humanoids here, male and female, and with few exceptions they dressed alike in baggy coveralls. They walked on either side of the street, leaving its muddy center to the clumsy vehicles. They were basically human, Shrev thought, noting a general similarity to Wesley. Her antennae superimposed their own information on what her eyes saw, highlighting the gray faces and bodies with the shimmering traces of body-electric fields.

Wesley was looking around. "I wish I had a tricorder," he said.

"A tricorder? Why? We are but humble tourists," Shrev reminded him. She smiled. "Even though we have an exhausting task ahead of us."

"Huh?" the human asked. "I don't understand that, Shrev."

"Did not the ambassador tell us to shop till we drop? If I comprehend that—"

Wesley laughed, then caught himself. "My apologies, Shrev, I don't mean to suggest that you're wrong. From the way his words rhymed, I think the ambassador was joking. That sounds like a humorous way of telling us to spend a lot of money."

"Ah." Shrev had heard about rhymes, but she hadn't known that humans used them in casual conversation. "We must still spend money. Do you see any suitable places for this?"

"Well . . ." Wesley looked up and down the street. "I don't know, Shrev. This place is dreary."

"It looks impoverished to me as well." She pointed down the street, where her antennae sensed a crowd. "People swarm that way; let us see which flowers draw them."

The street opened into a square. As the two aliens crossed it, Shrev noted how the natives regarded them. The Megarans walked clear of their visitors, and watched them out the corners of their eyes. None of them spoke within earshot of Shrev or Wesley. She wondered if the Megarans had any unusual senses that they might focus on the visitors. "Wesley," she said, "you mentioned dreariness. Could these people lack your color vision?"

"My—oh." He looked around, then shook his head. "No, I don't think they're what we call colorblind, Shrev. I see colors here, but not many of them. Most of the clothes here are drab, either gray or dull blue. It reminds me of a prison, or a labor camp."

"As though the Ferengi keep them as slaves?" she wondered.

"Maybe. I've never heard of a world where people *like* to dress this way." He hesitated. "Although they might see their garments as attractive. I don't wish to seem offensive, but to the limited human eye your tunic appears gray and drab."

"Your point is well taken," Shrev said, idly fingering her tunic. "This material contains special metallic threads. Although invisible to your eyes and mine, they reflect certain radiations to which my antennae are sensitive. Yet I must note that the Megarans appear to have only senses equal to yours."

"It is puzzling," Wesley agreed. He pointed. "There's a store."

The store was one of a dozen brick structures that lined one side of the square. It had glass windows, which displayed a strange assortment of goods. Shrev saw a dozen musical instruments, including a double-flute similar to her people's *merredivy,* and a set of metal wind chimes. Other items were pretty, if useless; she smiled at the thought of trying to slip that tasseled bonnet over her antennae. And what good were earrings to a person whose earholes were surrounded by concentric chitinous ridges?

She and Wesley went into the shop. It was lit by a single incandescent light bulb in the ceiling, and divided into a maze by long wooden tables. The room was perhaps ten meters on a side, with a drape-covered door in the rear. After a few seconds, a youngish man came into the shop. He wore a patch over one eye, and his pinned-up coverall sleeve emphasized his lack of a right arm.

His good eye scanned his customers. "Yes?" he asked, his tone flattened by the Universal Translator.

Shrev picked up a twelve-stringed musical instrument, a device with a long neck and a bowl-shaped body. "Please excuse a foolish question," she said, "but is this work of art for sale?"

He made a grunting noise which the translator ignored. "If you the price have, for sale it is."

"I am uncertain of how to settle the price. Perhaps you would aid me?" Shrev handed him a coin from her pouch. "If this can serve as money, how many would you request?"

The man's one eye bulged as he fingered the coin. He bit it, grinned suddenly, then forced down his grin. "Six," he said, holding up a hand and displaying all his digits.

"The price delights me," Shrev said, paying him. He slid the coins into a pocket. Wesley found a packet of small iron tools, an octant and a massive spiked club. He gave the man thirty coins.

Wesley hefted the club. "I'm giving this to a warrior friend," he said—loudly, Shrev thought. "He'll want to know if it's been used in battle."

"Many times," the shopkeeper said. "When the Vo Gatyn, with cobwebs may her name grow tangled, the Vo Darvit fought, Anrom himself into combat on Ardev ground this mace carried. Before that . . ."

Shrev drifted away from Wesley and the man while they discussed combat—it seemed a universal constant that males enjoyed talking about different ways to butcher one another. The man made her uncomfortable. Among her people, anyone so badly maimed would seek to die, to avoid the disgrace of resembling a mutant. She reminded herself that many races had different views. Humans, for example, saw crippling injuries and deformities as a challenge to their ingenuity; the ship's chief engineer was living proof of that.

Shrev looked at trinkets until a wide metal plate caught her eye and antenna. The plate's surface showed that it had been beaten with a hammer, and something—impurities in the metal, some trick of polarized light, something—made it look like a flower impossibly rich in nectar. It looked even richer than the wall mosaic in her quarters, and it shimmered like the quilted fabric of her tunic. It was all she could do to keep from tasting the metal.

It might almost be a sending from the All-Mother, she thought. She knew that was rank superstition, yet such icons were important in every Zhuik religion, a symbol of wealth and plenty. It was a remarkable coincidence to find such an object here.

Shrev carried it back to the shopkeeper, who still chatted with Wesley. The cadet glanced at her and smiled. "My friend would be pleased to spend more money, Mr. Anit," he said.

"For that?" The man seemed disbelieving.

"I find it beautiful," Shrev said. "Have you more like it?"

"No," he said. "Its maker by the rat-eyes was taken away."

"'Rat-eyes'?" Wesley repeated. "Oh, you mean *them.*" He held a hand out, as if indicating something barely waist-high.

Shrev realized he meant the Ferengi. Something about the man changed, and Shrev noticed a sudden flicker to his body-electric fields, a sign of apprehension. "The rat-eyes are a problem on many worlds, I sorrow to say," Shrev told the man. "But let us not speak of them when I hold something of beauty."

"Er, yes," the shopkeeper said. His one hand rubbed his chin as he stared at the plate. "A beauty to you that old plate truly is?"

"To me, yes." She smiled at him. "I do not see it as you might. You may have noticed that I am not like my good friend, or like your own estimable self."

"We're from out of town," Wesley added.

The man laughed, although it sounded forced. "For

you, only one of those—credits, you said? One credit only I ask."

Shrev paid gladly. "If you can obtain more objects in this style, I shall happily buy them," she said, and looked around the shop. "You seem to have a talent for acquiring diverse items."

The man hesitated. "Yes . . . well . . . for a soldier to keep soul and body together these days, dealing in junk the only way left is. Honor to the rat-eyes nothing means," he added.

"You need say no more," Shrev said. "We know too much of—" She duplicated Wesley's waist-high gesture. "But they are no matter. Would you know of another shop that might sell more art in this style?"

"A poser that question is." His hand caressed his chin again. "About a shop that something might have I can tell you. Out of the square to the north go, and on your right at the second street turn. Down three doors on your shady side go, and there an open-air shop with utensils you'll find."

Shrev and Wesley said their good-byes and returned to the bustling square. "The universal translator needs *work,*" the human said.

"Work it needs," Shrev agreed, and chuckled with Wesley. They walked toward the square's northern side. "Did you learn much from the man?"

"Yeah. The local ruler, the Vo Gatyn, is a green."

"That sounds bad, but I fear I don't understand the meaning," Shrev said.

Wesley hesitated as though trying to frame his reply. "My apologies for expecting you to know an obscure detail of our history. A 'green' is a human who serves a nonhuman conqueror. During our Eugenics War, a British colonel named Green turned traitor and helped the Khans invade Australia."

"So you use his name this way," Shrev said. She knew a little about Earth's Eugenics War, which had started after a clique of scientists used some crude genetic techniques to create a race of superior humans. The superiority had proved a dangerous trap when the new race had decided to enslave the old. "I take it that a 'green' serves willingly?"

"*Very* willingly," Wesley said. "Anyway, that's one reason I bought this mace. Anit—that's the shopkeeper's name—looked like an old soldier, and I figured I could get him to talk about the local wars. He told me that when the Ferengi showed up, they bribed a minor chief named Gatyn into helping them conquer the planet. They gave her modern weapons and transport, and she trounced everyone else. Now she's a puppet ruler."

"So the Ferengi do not exert direct rule," Shrev said.

"Correct," Wesley said. "Officially, Gatyn has hired the Ferengi to modernize her world. They even had this big public contract-signing ceremony to make it look right."

"So they pretend to work for their slave," Shrev noted as they came to the square's northern exit. The cobbled road was uneven from the wear of heavy traffic, and they made slow progress through the crowd of natives and vehicles. Several vehicles floated on artigrav units. "Wesley, you implied that you had more than one reason for buying that mace," Shrev said, seeing the hostile gaze of many people. "Do you expect to use it here?"

"No," he said. "It's a gift."

"Indeed? It seems a rather exotic gift."

Wesley nodded. "It's big, it's clumsy, it looks like a cactus with a thyroid problem. Worf will love it. Data will like the octant, and my mom will like these old surgeon's tools." He held up the bag.

"Just as my clan's hive-matriarch shall appreciate this." Shrev tapped the plate. "I perceive this plate as the heart of a nectar-rich flower. In my religion, that symbolizes—" How to translate *hzs'sz?* "—divine favor," she finished.

The phrase was inadequate, but Wesley appeared to understand. "Do you think we can find more like it?" he asked.

"We shall see," Shrev said. She turned her head several times as a lack of something registered on her mind. "Wesley, am I mistaken, or are there no children about?"

"I don't see any little Megarans, either," he said after a moment. "And I haven't, not since we beamed down."

"As if they were being kept hidden from aliens."

"Yeah," Wesley said. "There's something else odd, Shrev. I look a lot like the natives, but you stand out. You should attract a lot more interest than you have."

"Unless Zhuiks are common visitors here, which I doubt," she said. She looked around again. "People seem to avoid us."

"Not all of them," Wesley said. "We're being followed."

"Dieu merci," Picard muttered as the ambassador entered the transporter room. Offenhouse had dressed in a black dovecote jacket, pin-striped pants, and a stovepipe hat. A wide ribbon held a gold-plated Federation medallion on his chest. He carried a walking stick with a fist-sized diamond knob.

Offenhouse chuckled under Picard's scrutiny. "I know. You can dress 'em up, but you can't take 'em anywhere."

Picard cleared his throat. "That's hardly standard dress for modern diplomats, Mr. Ambassador."

"Look rich, be rich—that's an old Ferengi proverb. I'm out to impress Chudak." He twirled the walking stick. "And jam any bugs with this beauty. The medallion has a translator and a limited-spectrum tricorder built into it, too."

Picard nodded. "And what does the hat do?"

"It keeps my head dry when it rains." Offenhouse stepped onto the transporter stage with Picard, then scowled at the deck pads. "Say, Picard, did you ever see *The Fly?*"

"I don't believe so," Picard said, and gestured to the transporter technician. "What is it?"

"It's an old movie——"

The transporter's hum interrupted the ambassador's words. Picard and Offenhouse materialized in a courtyard surrounded by high stone walls.

"——that you'll have to watch sometime," Offenhouse concluded. He looked around the yard and scowled. "Charming."

"It's rather medieval," Picard agreed, surveying the castle's crenellations, posterns and allures. "And in excellent repair."

"Like it still holds off invaders and rioting peasants," Offenhouse said. He nudged Picard's elbow. "Company."

A tall, brown-skinned man in white and yellow robes emerged from a doorway in one stone wall. "Ambassador Offenhouse, Captain Picard," he said, executing a minuscule bow. "I am Verden, pagus to the Vo Gatyn. In the Great Hall to the Vo I will introduce you. You will dine, and to you later she will talk. With me you will come, please."

Picard and Offenhouse followed the Megaran through the wall. The ambassador's walking stick tapped the stone floor as they entered a hall. The chamber was crude and not very large, but Picard knew that it pressed the limits of stone blocks and wooden beams. Light came from luminescent panels set in the ceiling. They needed adjustment; the glare made it impossible for Picard to look at the ceiling.

There were long tables set against the main walls of the rectangular hall, and they were loaded with platters of wine and bowls of drinks. A score of people stood around the tables, serving themselves and eating. They were well dressed, but Picard saw a half-dozen servants in ill-fitting coveralls waiting in the corners of the hall. The only chair in sight was a throne at the far end of the room. A thin black woman with short gray hair sat on it. Aside from a red cloak and a gold circlet for a crown, she dressed simply, and Picard saw that she had both a knife and a sonic disrupter tucked into her waistband.

Offenhouse tipped his hat to her. "Vo Gatyn, I am Ralph Offenhouse, ambassador plenipotentiary and extraordinaire of the United Federation of Planets . . ." Picard stood silent during the droning protocol exchange. Offenhouse assured the woman of the Federation's good intentions and high principles; Gatyn spoke of her lawful authority over the entire Megaran people, as given to her by the Elder Gods and demonstrated through her honorable conquest of all opponents, done without aid of any but herself and her noble lieges.

What nonsense! Picard thought with a polite smile. Simple logistics made it impossible to conquer and hold an entire planet with medieval technology. Gatyn sounded as though she was trying to assure herself that she was the true ruler of Megara, and not a Ferengi tool.

The introduction ended and Verden led the two humans away from the throne. "When to speak to you she is ready, return I will," he said, and walked out of the hall.

Offenhouse grunted. "C'mon, Picard, let's chow down before Chudak shows up."

Picard nodded. "What do you expect from Chu-

110

dak?" he asked quietly. "Information on who's really in charge here?"

Offenhouse nodded back. "The more I think about it, the more I'm sure that Shrev and Peter were right about the Ferengi working for a third party. That means all this"—he nodded toward the Vo's throne, and the courtiers surrounding her—"is a sham, so lean back and enjoy the show."

Peter? the captain wondered. *His son? That's an odd slip of the tongue.*

Picard accompanied Offenhouse to one of the buffet tables. Beverly Crusher had assured him that it would be safe to eat Megaran foods; sensor analysis of the surface life had verified that the local proteins, carbohydrates and sundry other substances held no unpleasant surprises for the human metabolism. That had come as good news to the captain, who welcomed new gastronomic experiences.

Picard found himself reviewing his talk with Wesley. He wished he could have spoken at length with him, but that would have been unfair to the young man. Wesley needed guidance, yet too much of that would interfere with his ability to make his own decisions. *The Prime Directive as applied to personal relationships,* Picard mused. *I want to help Wesley, but too much 'help' would deny him the right to choose his own future. Have confidence in him, Jean-Luc. He will discover his own answers.*

The captain was spooning up a small plate of sautéed mushrooms when Chudak entered the hall. He wore black garments, tidy, well-tailored and trimmed in silver. *A Ferengi with taste,* Picard thought in surprise. Chudak had dressed in a style that emphasized his face and build, and his manner suggested he knew that, by his people's standards, he was quite handsome.

Chudak strode up to Offenhouse. "You're even uglier in person," Chudak snarled. "Who'd have thought?"

"Certainly not you." Offenhouse shook his head sadly. "I'm sorry to see that my competition is so shabby."

"And *I* regret having *no* competition!" A half-dozen Megarans gathered around; one handed Chudak a fresh glass of green punch. "Look at you! The gods made some heads perfect. The others, they hid beneath hair. Eh, Picard?"

"Hair is a marvelous substance," Picard said, stoutly resisting Chudak's effort to drive a wedge between him and Offenhouse.

Chudak looked disgruntled by Picard's indifference. "Try your song and dance, human," he told Offenhouse. "See if you can take away my clients."

The ambassador smiled and shook his head. "The Federation can beat whatever deal you made with these people, but I'm in no hurry to take them away from you, you overdraft on the great checking account of life."

"You duck the issue," Chudak growled. "I have sold these people things they would never get from the Federation, with its selfish talk about the 'Prime Directive' and 'noninterference.' *I* help them to build a modern world. *You* would have left them grubbing in the dirt, human."

"And you'll leave 'em the same way." Offenhouse turned his back on Chudak and scooped himself a mug of punch. "This is a poor planet, Chudak. How do they pay you?"

"As of now, they *don't,*" Chudak said. "I *invest* here. But when this planet is fully industrialized, I'll get a quarter of their industrial production. Power generators, warp units, computer systems—*everything,* fur-head, for the rest of my life."

"You should live so long," Offenhouse said quietly, and sipped his drink. Looking at the men and women who surrounded them, Picard saw that the ambassador's words reflected the Megarans' sentiments. If they served Chudak, they did not do so willingly.

Chudak clearly knew he was hated here. "Do you think I would ignore my own safety?" he asked Offenhouse.

"Yes, if somebody paid you enough," Offenhouse said. "Speaking of payment, how *are* you financing this project?"

Chudak growled angrily. "What business of yours is that?"

Offenhouse shrugged. "Just morbid curiosity."

Picard turned back to the table. He set his plate down and picked up something that looked like a glass of red wine. It was, but it tasted far too sweet for his palate.

Chudak was lying, Picard thought suddenly. Intuition told Picard that the Daimon did not expect to collect anything from the Megaran factories. The only thing genuine here was the hatred.

A young woman in a yellow dress appeared at Picard's side. Her dark face was round and pretty, and had character. Picard guessed that she was sixty or so—no, thirty; these people lacked the Federation's extensive health care. Age would show quickly on them. "Our vintage your palate finds pleasing?" she asked.

"I seldom taste one like it," Picard said truthfully. He made himself smile as he sniffed its bouquet. "I come from a family of vintners."

"As well, myself," the woman said. There was something hesitant about her manner, as though she was not quite certain that speaking with Picard was a good idea, and her eyes looked haunted. "As a girl our vines and vats I tended. But when the rat-eyes came, a metallurgist I became, and now for industry alloys I supply."

"An honorable and worthwhile business," Picard said, "but of course, one always remains in love with the vineyards."

"To them a swift return I wish," she said. "Odovil Pardi I am named."

The captain bowed politely. "Jean-Luc Picard, at your service."

Odovil smiled, showing a charming gap between her front teeth, and then lowered her voice. "Your friend, of the rat-eyes not living long he spoke. Something he knows?"

"Wishful thinking," Picard said. "My friend and Chudak are bitter enemies."

"'Enemies'? Yet from above the skies you have come," she said. "In the skies all evil dwells, or so it is said."

That sounds almost religious, the captain thought, *yet religions in which evil comes from the heavens are very rare. Or has their experience with the Ferengi convinced these people that 'alien' and 'evil' are synonymous?* "Good and evil can both come from the sky," Picard said. "Think of how rain can save or destroy a vineyard."

Odovil nodded, then glanced furtively around the hall. "Many here about the 'weather' are wondering."

"Perhaps it shall improve," Picard said, hoping that he understood her meaning. "May I ask about your steel production?"

"Good it is," she said, and launched herself into a description of alloying techniques, bulk moduli and tensile strengths. Picard wished that La Forge had been present to help make sense of what she said, but he knew enough about engineering technology to see that her foundries were producing tritanium—and with some sophisticated technology.

"Production every year quadruples," Odovil told him. "When first the rat-eyes came, equipment and plans for the foundries to us they gave. Now foundries by ourselves we make, and more. Every year more we learn."

Picard nodded at that. The Ferengi would have "seeded" Megara with equipment and advice—and almost certainly with an extensive educational system; ignorant peasants could not operate advanced technology—but the bulk of Megara's transformation would have been done by the natives themselves. Doing so would have required an enormous change in their lives; no one would call a slave world a paradise. "The changes must have been difficult," Picard suggested.

"Difficult and more," the woman agreed. "Much work, many deaths; now many poor there are, and lucky to do so well I am. Lucky . . ." Her voice grew distant, and Picard saw something cold in her eyes. That made him wonder how much the Ferengi had truly changed this world.

Gul Verden remained in his native costume as he went down to the intelligence room. He hated the garb, but changing would inconvenience him now.

And there are already enough inconveniences, he thought as his hand touched his face. The implanted sixth fingers, the surgery that had smoothed and colored his face and body to resemble these weaklings, the drug that gave his flesh their bland odor—and, above all, the years of isolation on this backwater planet. He was tired of the inconveniences.

But he would endure them. This assignment was not as satisfying as a fleet command, but it was important. Megara represented one of many moves in the maneuverings against the Federation, a pawn pushed across a chessboard to a strategic square. It would give the Cardassian Empire a slight advantage when the next war began, and enough such advantages would let the Empire win that war. Disguising himself as a native seemed as cowardly as it was humiliating, but it was necessary. There were times when the Cardassian monitors had to move among the Megarans, and the plan might fail if the Megarans learned that other aliens were involved here.

At least I am not hiding from warriors, Verden told himself, salvaging a scrap of pride. *And this wretched assignment is almost over. The factories are ready; the natives are trained and primed for their role. We need only give them a few proper nudges to complete the mission. We could be on our way home in a month.*

The job was not yet finished, however. Gatyn, the nominal ruler of this planet, had disobeyed Verden by granting the humans an audience. The woman had a contrary nature, and she had decided to exercise her independence this way. All was not lost; spying on the humans now might uncover something important.

Verden walked up to his second-in-command's station. "Report," he ordered.

"The human ambassador is speaking to the Ferengi, Gul Verden," Ubinew said. He had a spy-eye fixed on Chudak and the human ambassador, and a unit in his control console transcribed their words into a written summary. Verden read Offenhouse's questions to Chudak, which proved that the human was suspicious. Around the intelligence room, other officers monitored the humans in the city. The Federation presence strained their resources to the limits, but the team was coping with them. The visitors were talking and spending a lot of money, but otherwise doing no harm.

The visual scanner looked down from the Great Hall's ceiling, where it was hidden in the glare of electric bulbs. Verden studied Offenhouse's image on the console display, but he could read no information into the expression on the pink alien face. "Can't you get a mindscan on that ambassador?" he asked Ubinew.

"No. The coward has a jammer against active probes. It's all I can do to get voice and image."

Verden climbed the steps to the command platform and sat down. "Give me the order book," he told his aide.

Obediently, Bwolst handed the electronic padd to Verden. The chief-of-mission already knew the orders for this situation, but Ubinew and the others in the room had to *know* that Verden followed the orders of his own leaders. Otherwise Verden might lose their obedience.

Verden sifted through the padd's memory bank and found that the orders remained as he had recalled them. "How many humans are in the city?" he asked Hrakin.

The surveillance officer was prompt. "Eighteen humans, sir. I also report one Zhuik and one Vulcan in the city. This is in addition to the two humans in the Great Hall."

"Excellent!" Verden smiled in approval. "You obey well, Hrakin. Kill all the Federation people in the city. Take all the men you will need."

Hrakin hesitated. "Sir, leaving the complex may expose us to the starship's sensors."

That gave Verden pause. It was tempting to face up to the humans now—but one did not spring an ambush prematurely, and Megara was an enormous ambush. "We must risk it," he decided. "They will not be looking for us—and we can improve the odds of escaping detection. Have the 'Prophet' stir up riots. That should keep the ship too occupied to scan us."

"I obey," Hrakin said.

"Excellent," Verden said. The riots would help

persuade the Federation intruders that they were not welcome here. A little diplomatic prompting would seal the matter; their own Prime Directive would force the humans to withdraw.

But what if that doesn't work? Verden asked himself. More drastic measures might be required. He summoned a squad of guards—his own people, not the natives—and went with them to the Great Hall.

Chapter Eight

"LA FORGE TO BRIDGE," Geordi said. "Worf, I'm ready to test the detector now."

There was a momentary silence. "Proceed," Worf said.

"Okay, people," Geordi called to the engine-room crew. "By the numbers. Gravity-wave oscillator to oh-point-oh-one percent power."

The oscillator was a basic artigrav unit, stripped of its damping circuits and mounted near the primary power generator. Instead of producing a smooth and constant distortion in the curvature of space-time, the artigrav unit would now emit gravity waves at a frequency of twenty cycles per second.

The unit came to life. *And I'd hate to be around it at full power,* Geordi thought as he felt its pulsations. It came across as a waspish buzzing, too low-pitched to hear but potent enough to set his teeth on edge. The engineer's VISOR let him see how the oscillator's shell vibrated under the load. "How're the readings?" he called out.

"Steady," Ensign Gakor said from the computer terminal. He sniffed loudly; rare for a Tellarite, he had a sharp sense of humor. "And no circuits are burning —yet."

"That's always a good sign," Geordi said. He liked working with Gakor. Most people thought of Tellarites as quarrelsome, and it *was* true that they liked to argue. Tellarites made an art out of debate, and they could be as maddeningly logical as a Vulcan. That was a useful talent when you needed to work the bugs out of some new design. "Okay, give me the neutrino readings."

"No deviation," Gakor said in annoyance. He kicked the terminal with a hoof. The readouts remained rock-steady. *"Still* no deviation."

"Rats," Geordi muttered. He looked toward the reactor. His VISOR could detect neutrinos, but just barely; if the experiment was working, he couldn't see the expected difference in the neutrinos. "Oscillator off," he said, and the annoying buzz ended.

"What's wrong?" Alexander asked. He had been sitting quietly, watching the preparations for the test of "his" detector.

"I'm not sure, Al," Geordi said. He sat down, removed his VISOR and massaged the bridge of his nose. Sometimes a little temporary blindness helped Geordi think; it was as though the entire universe had ceased to exist, leaving him alone with his problem. "I'm following a long, thin chain of logic here. Maybe I missed a link in the chain."

Blind without his VISOR, he heard the boy shift around on his chair. "What's the chain?" Alexander asked.

"Well . . ." Geordi gestured toward the metal plating around the containment field. "We mix matter and antimatter in there. In theory, they interact perfectly and turn into pure energy. In practice, they don't. We get every kind of particle you could name in there."

"Which is why you have all the shielding," Alexander said.

"Right," Geordi said. "Anyway, we have a lot of neutrons in the soup. Free neutrons are unstable, with a half-life of thirteen minutes. Most of them are annihilated or absorbed before they can decay, but not all of them. *Those* neutrons decay into a proton, an electron and a certain kind of neutrino."

"And it's the neutrinos that slip through the cloaking device," Alexander said. "Hardly anything can stop them, because they don't usually interact with normal matter. But that makes them hard to detect, too."

Geordi nodded. The kid had definitely paid attention in his science class. "Ordinarily it's not worth looking for neutrinos. The universe is flooded with them, and detecting the neutrinos from a starship's main power plant is like looking for a candle flame at noon on Vulcan. So we change the rules a bit. The gravity waves from our oscillator *should* change the way the neutrons decay, by compressing space and adding a bit of energy to the process. We *should* get neutrinos that are twice as energetic as normal, which would make them easier to detect."

"Sort of like seeing a blowtorch at Vulcan high noon," Alexander suggested.

Gakor joined them as Geordi snapped his VISOR back over his eyes. "All of this assumes that we understand the physical theory," the Tellarite engineer said.

"*And* that I configured the detector right," Geordi said. He wondered what he was doing wrong. *Probably displaying my ignorance,* he thought ruefully. He wasn't a physicist, even though a starship engineer had to have a grasp of that field. This whole concept was based on the idea that one type of nuclear decay would act as he expected. The universe was stubbornly doing things as it saw fit. What had he overlooked?

Geordi looked at the matter-antimatter containment field, as if he could see the answer swirling in its energies. The gravity waves *should* add energy to the neutron decay, and the energy should turn up in the neutrinos. Of course, neutrinos were peculiar even by the laws of quantum physics. They had mass—about a tenth of an electron volt, according to the latest experiments—but they also moved at the speed of light. It was supposed to be impossible for an object with nonzero rest mass to travel at light-speed in Einsteinian space, but there it was. Most of the theoretical explanations centered on the relationship between matter and energy, suggesting that the mass somehow redefined itself as energy. . . .

"Gakor," Geordi said, "let's reconfigure the detector. We've been looking at energy levels; maybe we should look at mass instead. The extra energy could be showing up as increased neutrino mass."

Gakor's pink snout wrinkled thoughtfully. "Weighing neutrinos is not the easiest task. We'll need several hours to reconfigure."

"We've got the time," Geordi said. He remembered Alexander. "This is going to drag, Al, and I definitely *don't* want your dad telling me I kept you up late on a school night."

"Okay." Alexander hopped off the chair. "I've got to take a bath now anyway. Bye, Geordi."

A bath, Geordi thought. He knew that some kids liked to get their parents' attention by annoying them, but Alexander found some pretty weird ways to do that.

This was the seventh shop Shrev and Wesley had visited, and Shrev had already seen a pattern. First, each shop sold items that were useful, but not necessary to life. Next, each vendor had at least one physical problem, either a birth defect or an injury. When they left one shop, somebody—usually a young child—could be spotted running ahead of them to the next. Shrev decided there was a network of shopkeepers, linked by their deformities and determined to absorb all the gold they could from two free-spending aliens. The arrangement had its advantages; these people obviously let one another know that talking with the aliens would bring more money, and that aided Shrev and Wesley in their assignment.

This shop sold handmade cloth, and to judge from Wesley's comments it was attractive to the human eye. It looked drab to her, just as—or so she suspected—the light-polarizing material of her tunic looked dull and murky to Wesley. "Do you weave this yourself?" Wesley asked the shopkeeper, a young woman with very long hair.

"My sister and I this cloth make," she said, and sighed. "Better work we cannot find. The falling sickness we have, and for us the rat-eyes no place allow. Lucky we are that for cloth some money-paper a few people can spend."

"'Money-paper'?" Wesley asked. "I've never seen any of *that.* Maybe I could buy some from you?"

The woman found that agreeable, and Shrev stood by quietly as they bartered. *Excellent,* Shrev thought. Wesley asked questions that established the value of local money, in terms the ambassador might find useful. Shrev found it impossible to think in terms of wages and prices, but at last she saw something that told her everything that mattered. Wesley swapped a single gold coin for a double handful of paper, and the woman shed a tear of joy at the trade. With the exchange made, Wesley gathered up the bolts of cloth he'd purchased and they left the store.

" 'Falling sickness'?" Shrev asked. They were on a narrow, muddy street, empty of people. Her voice seemed oddly loud here.

"She probably meant epilepsy," Wesley said.

"Ah, a neural problem." Other questions begged for answers. "I have also noticed how these people taste their coins. I wonder if they can sense the flavor of metals."

Wesley looked puzzled. " 'Taste'? Oh. You couldn't know, but biting is a traditional test for gold—our teeth are harder than gold, so they can dent the coins if they're pure."

"Fascinating." Zhuik "teeth" were chitinous horse-shoe plates, suitable only for crushing certain flowers to extract their nectar. She looked at Wesley's burden —bolts of cloth, an ornate rug, a set of bronze candlesticks. Shrev was carrying an armload of scrolls and a plumed helmet. "Shall we send our purchases to the ship?"

"Good idea." They found a dry spot near a brick wall, set everything on the ground and signaled the *Enterprise*. "I'd hate to see cargo bay two right now," Wesley said.

Shrev laughed quietly. "Imagine how the captain will feel. I fear his ship will look like an Orion trader's hold. Should you not add that paper money to the collection?"

"No, I want to show that to Mr. Offenhouse." Wesley tucked the paper into his coin pouch, then watched as the transporter took away their booty. "He'll want to hear what that woman told me about the local money. Maybe he can make sense out of it."

"One may hope." Shrev glanced at the sky. The clouds had thinned, but the light was dimming as the sun neared the horizon. Night would not handicap her, but it would be a problem for Wesley. Lacking her ability to see in the infrared, he could not find his way in that thing which his people called the "dark." "Wesley, please let me know when the light grows inadequate for your eyes. We will leave then."

"We should have another hour of daylight," Wesley said. He looked up and down the street. "There's our tail again."

"Our followers?" Shrev followed his glance, and saw the two Megarans who had followed them ever since they had beamed down. The men had stayed several dozen meters away, and Shrev had finally decided that they were police spies. No doubt the Megarans, or their overlords, wanted to know everything their visitors did.

Shrev and Wesley walked away from the two men, toward a small square. The town was filled with such squares, connected by zigzag streets. As they drew closer, Shrev heard a loud voice, rising above an angry mutter of other voices. Whatever was said, the tangle of voices was too much for the Universal Translator.

"There's someone in a brown robe up there," Wesley said. He was fifteen centimeters taller than Shrev, which gave him a better view. "She looks like she's doing the talking," Wesley said. "And—that robe looks funny, but I can't put my finger on what's wrong with it."

"We will have to get closer—" Shrev stopped as two men came out of a side alley, five meters in front of them. For one astonished moment she refused to believe what her antennae told her. Then she touched the communicator badge pinned to her tunic. *"Enterprise, we would be most appreciative if you beamed us up now."*

Wesley was shocked out of his manners. "Shrev, what are you—" he began in a loud voice.

The two men charged at them, without even the briefest introduction. One drew a knife with a curved blade and lunged at Wesley. Shrev went after the man, twisted back as he turned to slash at her, came forward again and chopped at his forearm with the side of her hand.

The knife stung into her left side, slicing through her tunic and cracking an exoskeletal plate. The blade became wedged in the chitin, and Shrev fought to ignore the pain as the man tried to jerk his knife loose. She clutched her fists together and slammed them into the side of the man's head. He dropped his knife as the blow stunned him, and a second blow sent him to his knees. Shrev struck two more blows to his head, and with the last she heard the sharp crack of bone. The man crumpled in death, the side of his skull crushed.

Wesley was battling the second man. Shrev saw him reel backward from a jab to his chest. Shrev took a step toward him, then clutched at her side and felt lukewarm blood soaking her tunic. Then the transporter locked on to them. Within seconds she and Wesley were back on the ship.

Wesley caught her as she sagged to the deck. "Sickbay!" he shouted at De Shay.

The transporter flicked them into sickbay. As Wesley helped her onto a biobed, Shrev saw several other injured crew members undergoing emergency treatment. Dr. Crusher hurried over to them. "Wesley, are you all right?" she demanded.

"I'm fine, Mom," he said. "Shrev's been stabbed."

"I see," Dr. Crusher said. She scanned Shrev, then cut away her tunic and went to work. She spoke as she adjusted an anabolic protoplaser. "Shrev, there's a hole in your left cardial tube. Don't talk, save your strength."

"I *must* speak," Shrev said weakly. "Wesley, our attackers were Cardassians, surgically altered to resemble Megarans."

"Cardassians?" he said loudly, then dropped his voice. "Cardassians. Please don't misunderstand me, I mean no offense, but are you certain?"

"Quite," she said. The pain eased as the protoplaser accelerated the healing process. "The modifications may fool human eyes, but not my eyes. Or my antennae. The scars and distortions are quite visible in infrared, as are the *hz'zhivezh,* the . . . body-electric patterns unique to each species. Inform the captain at once, Cadet."

"Hold it," the doctor said. "Wesley, you're not going anywhere until—"

"I'm all right, Mom," he said, clearly nettled.

"Then what's that on your face?" Dr. Crusher spoke without looking up from her work. "Catsup? You always were a sloppy eater, but you're usually not *that* messy."

Wesley winced as he touched his forehead. "I still have to tell the captain," he said.

"You can't," Dr. Crusher said. "He's down on the surface. Dr. Par'mit'kon!"

The Saurian hurried into the sickbay. "Yes, Doctor?"

Dr. Crusher nodded at her son. "Bulldog this cowboy and make sure his head isn't any more cracked than normal. And somebody bring me a unit of Zhuik blood, type arrow-down-curl-left."

The reptilian doctor turned his lidless yellow eyes on Wesley. "Come with me, Cadet."

"Just let me report first," Wesley insisted. "Crusher to bridge . . ."

Shrev puzzled over the human exchange while Wesley spoke with Commander Riker. Among Zhuiks, a child never disputed her mother, and a mother placed her child's welfare above all else. Concern for family was a genetic necessity; without it, one was no better than a mutant—if not actually a mutant. Dr. Crusher might have concealed her emotion behind a certain rough humor, but why would she conceal it in the first place?

Don't complain, Shrev told herself. The human willingness to place public duty above family had meant lifesaving attention for her from the ship's best doctor, and an added measure of safety for the ship from Wesley. Knowing at once that the *Enterprise* faced Cardassians might mean the difference between life and death for the crew.

"Shrev," Dr. Crusher said after a moment, "you're a very lucky young lady. You can expect some discomfort for a few more hours, but you won't even have a scar."

"I thank you for your excellent work." The news that she would not bear a scar came as a relief. There were cultures that regarded scars as a sign of fighting prowess, but Zhuiks considered them too suggestive of genetic defects. "And I must congratulate you on your son. Wesley conducted himself well during our mission."

"Glad to hear it," she said with a smile. An orderly brought a transfusion unit, and Dr. Crusher slid its needle into a vein on Shrev's forearm. Green fluid flowed down the tube.

"Wesley is quite remarkable," Shrev said, puzzled by her offhand response to the compliment. "He is intelligent, observant and polite."

"'Polite'? My Wesley?" Dr. Crusher shook her head in mock surprise. "We really do live in an age of wonders."

"I can assure you that I am quite serious," Shrev said.

"I know." The doctor smiled again as she patted Shrev on the shoulder. "You'd better rest now, young lady. You're a good influence on my son and we can't let anything happen to you."

"Cardassians," Riker repeated thoughtfully. He sat in the captain's chair and looked at the scene on the main viewer. Smoke plumes trailed from several fires in the ramshackle city. Gatyn's fortress, ten kilometers away, remained untouched by the riot. "You're certain, Cadet?"

"Yes, sir," Wesley said. He still wore his civilian clothing, as well as a mediplast on his forehead. He looked a bit worse for wear, but his spirits seemed high. "They're surgically disguised, but not well enough to fool Ensign Shrev."

"Interesting," Riker said. *Cardassians,* he thought. The armistice had banned them from this sector. Their presence was an act of war, and if he didn't handle this right, the situation *would* turn into a war. "I wish I could think of a way to tell the captain without tipping off the Cardassians," he said.

"Perhaps you should bring the captain and the ambassador back," Deanna Troi suggested.

"I agree," Worf said. "These attacks were too coordinated to be unplanned."

"As if someone was trying to run us out of town," Riker said. At least the riots created a perfect excuse to get the captain out of there. *"Enterprise* to Picard."

"Go ahead, Number One," Picard answered.

"Sir, there are widespread disturbances in Kes Pa'kess," Riker said. "Our away teams were attacked."

"Casualties?" Picard asked.

"Several injuries, two of them serious," Riker said. "Lieutenant Broz has a concussion and Ensign Shrev took a knife in one of her cardial tubes. They're both out of danger."

"I see. Why weren't our people evacuated at the first sign of trouble?" Picard asked.

"The disturbances started simultaneously," Riker said. "Between the surprise and the load on the transporter system, we couldn't act fast enough. We'll know more when Commander Data finishes debriefing all the away teams. Sir, it might be a good idea if you return until the situation stabilizes. I think the situation bears discussion."

Offenhouse's voice broke in. "We're safe here, Riker. We'll come home after we chat with the Vo Gatyn. Bye, now."

Riker heard Worf growl as Offenhouse closed the channel. "You're right," Riker said to him. "We should beam them up at once."

Worf growled again.

Riker sighed. "I know. The ambassador is in charge."

Worf growled for a third time.

"I don't like it either," Riker agreed. He got out of the captain's chair and went to Worf's station. "If you were a Cardassian, how would you hide a ship?"

"Through indirection," Worf said promptly.

"The Ferengi ship?" Riker asked. He shook his head. "We've scanned it. There are plenty of Ferengi on board, but no Cardassians, and no place for them to hide."

"And I don't sense any Cardassians on it," Deanna added.

"Perhaps a ship arrives only to transfer personnel

and supplies," Worf said. "A planetary base does not *need* a ship."

"True . . . but I can't imagine the Cardassians doing without one. A ship is too useful."

"The Cardassians may have hidden a ship in this region," Worf suggested.

Riker stroked his beard thoughtfully. "Could be," he admitted. "The Cardassians make an art out of ambushes. Where's the best place in this system to hide a ship?"

Wesley had been listening quietly. "Commander, there's a binary neutron star in the area, where they could hide a whole fleet," he said. "The radiation is too intense for sensor readings. Computer, put Weber Five-Twelve on the main screen."

Riker looked at the distorted, static-hashed image that appeared on the screen. Two neutron stars whirled around one another, so close that gravity pulled them into teardrop shapes, while their magnetic fields churned the wisps of hydrogen around the stars into a glowing plasma. Gravity waves made the image ripple as though seen through sheets of running water.

Worf growled at the unsteady image. "Computer, overlay the image with radiation levels."

"Unable to comply," the computer stated. "Radiation levels are fluctuating too rapidly for reliable measurements."

"The probe data said that the levels are high," Wesley said, "but a ship with a good set of shields could take them almost indefinitely."

"And if a Cardassian ship is hiding anywhere, it's there," Riker said. *If,* he thought. If a Cardassian ship was hiding there, he could count on them to exploit Weber 512's natural cover to the fullest extent possible. He would have no way to detect it . . . unless . . .

"Riker to La Forge. How are you coming with that new detector?"

"We're almost ready for another test, Commander," the engineer answered.

"Give it priority," Riker ordered. "We may need it."

Chapter Nine

SOMEBODY WAS TRYING to impress the Federation visitors with their lack of importance. In the hour since Riker's call, Picard had seen a half-dozen people approach the throne to speak with the Vo Gatyn, and he was certain that all of them had entered the hall after the humans. Nevertheless, Picard and Offenhouse waited patiently for their audience with Megara's ruler.

Picard bent his head and spoke quietly to Offenhouse. "Exactly what do you hope to learn from Gatyn?"

"A lot," Offenhouse said. "I'd like to know just how tight a grip Chudak has here, what sort of orders he gives, maybe who gives *him* orders—things like that. Why? Getting bored?"

Picard shook his head. "I'm concerned with my crew's safety."

"Riker has things under control. Now cheer up and look at our pal. Chudak's twice as bored as we are."

That was true. The Ferengi Daimon stood by a table, drinking wine while he eyed a Megaran woman.

From time to time Picard had seen him talk with various female Megarans, but it was clear that they loathed his attentions. Even so, that did not deter him from the Ferengi habit of pestering non-Ferengi women. As always, Picard wondered what attracted Ferengi to alien women. Simple logic suggested that the Ferengi heart should quicken to the sight of a bald head, slashing teeth, soup-bowl ears.

The captain smiled at himself. *Ah, Jean-Luc,* he thought, *since when does logic count in affairs of the heart?*

Verden reentered the Great Hall, his white-and-yellow robes fluttering as he hastened to the throne. The pagus spoke briefly to his monarch, then gestured for the two humans to approach the throne. They did so; Picard nodded to the thin woman, while Offenhouse tipped his hat. "Your Majesty," Offenhouse said. "The Federation would like to discuss trade and business."

"Such discussions we don't wish," she said. "Go away."

"Perhaps Chudak doesn't wish it," Offenhouse said, "but we can offer you better terms than he does."

Gatyn looked impatient. "Spoken we have. Go. Verden."

Verden gestured sharply to the humans. "Come with me."

"Happy to oblige," Offenhouse said. He raised his walking stick to his hat brim in a salute, and then he and Picard followed Verden into a narrow side corridor.

Verden stopped under a glaring light in the stone ceiling. "Spoken the Vo has," he said. "You must leave."

"She didn't say to leave *now,*" Offenhouse said.

"To say this she did not need," Verden said. Even through the Universal Translator, his voice sounded cold. "To discuss business you wish? The rat-eyes you would throw out, their work you would do instead?"

"Absolutely," Offenhouse said. "We'd charge less. You'd make more money."

"Trust you we do not," Verden said. He leaned against the rough, dark wall. "Aliens you are, like the rat-eyes. To take and take their only wish is. Why should we think you from them differ?"

"What have you got to lose?" Picard asked. He felt puzzled; there was something odd about Verden's grammar, as if he didn't speak the same dialect as the other Megarans.

Verden looked him over. *"Everything* to lose we have," he said. "Our homes, our lives. For charity you do not come here; things to take you will find. Even more will we lose."

"Guess again," Offenhouse said. "We want to get rid of the rat-eyes. That's our profit. Now——"

"No profit for *you!"* Chudak said. Picard turned his head and saw the Ferengi emerge from the Great Hall. He held a phaser. "Trying to sell me out, Verden? Break our contract?"

"No, never," Verden said.

"I don't believe you!" the Ferengi grated. "I ought to kill you now, you debt-ridden, overpriced piece of native——"

A phaser whined and Chudak toppled to the stone floor. The door to the Great Hall slammed shut as a pair of men ran into the corridor. They were dressed like native servants, in rough gray coveralls, but they both carried hand phasers of non-Ferengi design.

Verden drew a phaser from inside his robe, then spoke to the guards. "Search the Federation spies and take them to a cell. I will get the interrogation drugs." He nudged Chudak's unconscious form with a booted toe. "And put this rubbish somewhere—comfortable."

Verden returned to the Great Hall as the two guards herded Picard and Offenhouse down the corridor. They went up a spiral staircase, and when they reached the end of a second hallway the guards searched them with a tricorder. Picard lost his communicator badge, while the ambassador was relieved of his cane, sash, and several items from his pockets. Then they were locked in a cell.

Picard inspected the cell at once. It was three meters square and two meters high, and quite solid. The door was locked on the outside with a primitive but effective iron contraption, while a small window in the back wall was blocked by thick iron bars. There was an electric light in the corridor, and its glow came through the cracks around the doorjamb. There was a heap of straw on the floor.

Offenhouse seemed unimpressed by the cell. "D'you think this dump is bugged?"

"Certainly with vermin," Picard said, "but if you mean are we being monitored, I think the answer is no."

"Really? Why not?"

"There's no point," Picard said. "An eavesdropper couldn't learn anything that a skilled interrogator couldn't discover—and whatever else Verden is, I imagine he's a skilled interrogator."

"Yeah," Offenhouse said. "He acts like the boss here. What do you think he is, Picard? A renegade human?"

"Perhaps," Picard said. "I noticed that he doesn't talk like a native. However, what matters now is that we're his prisoners."

"Good point," Offenhouse said. Picard saw his dim shape inspect the door. "What would Dixon Hill do in a fix like this?"

"He'd wait for his secretary to post bail," Picard said.

"Too bad you don't have a secretary," Offenhouse said. He went to the window, grasped a bar and tugged. "Any chance of Riker beaming us out of here before Verden comes back?"

"It's not likely," Picard said. "And all things considered, I doubt we'll survive the interrogation. We know too much; Verden's only question may be how to kill us without exposing himself."

"I was afraid you'd say that." Offenhouse removed his stovepipe hat and tore off its brim. He went to the window and rubbed the brim's edge against a bar. Picard heard a quiet rasping noise. "Funny thing about people," the ambassador said. "They'll get so wrapped up in looking for high-tech answers that they forget about low-tech approaches."

"I beg your pardon?" Picard said.

"Kidnapping is an old Ferengi business practice," Offenhouse said. "I figured that if Chudak grabbed us, he'd take our communicators and whatnot, but I didn't think he'd look for files or saws. After all, you'd expect Federation types to use modern equipment. Looks like that logic applies to Verden, too."

"Your hat brim is a *saw?*" Picard asked.

"Sealed in plastic for camouflage. Makes me glad I used to watch those James Bond movies. Now this"—he patted the stones—"is one of the castle's outer walls, so once we cut the bars there's nothing between us and freedom."

"Nothing other than Verden and his forces," Picard said. "Suppose we encounter them?"

"I've got a plan," Offenhouse said. He began sawing on a second bar. "If it makes you feel any better, why don't you go carve a phaser out of a bar of soap?"

Picard chuckled at that; Dixon Hill had used a similar ploy to escape from an abandoned warehouse. A moment later Offenhouse stopped sawing, grasped a bar with both hands and pulled. Picard joined him, and the soft iron bent under their efforts. After more cutting and pulling, the second bar curled out of the way, leaving an opening big enough to pass two men.

Picard climbed out first. The night was almost impossibly dark, but the stars gave just enough light to reveal the ground, four meters below the window. The edge of a forest was a dark swath, five hundred meters from the castle. Picard dropped to the ground, and a few seconds later Offenhouse followed him. "You mentioned a plan," Picard asked. "What is it?"

"We run like hell," Offenhouse told him.

"It works!" Geordi exclaimed. Gakor laughed and slapped the display panel in triumph. The rippling gravity waves were causing the neutron-decay process to emit neutrinos that weighed nine-tenths of an electron volt. While neutrinos came in several masses, none occurred in nature with that weight. The gimmick was working far better than the engineer could have hoped. "La Forge to bridge. Commander, we've got the bugs worked out of the detector. We'll be ready for a full-scale test in an hour."

"Understood," Riker answered. "Hurry it up."

Geordi looked at Gakor, who gave him a very human shrug. "You just can't please some people," the Tellarite said.

"Things must be heating up," Geordi said. He switched off the oscillator and its annoying vibrations ended. He and Gakor walked over to the oscillator. "I figure it'll be easier to mount this beast outside a shuttle-bay door."

"No, we should reconfigure the hull mooring plates," Gakor said, jumping on a chance to argue.

"We'll just have to reconfigure them again after we're done," Geordi said. "That's a lot of work for one test."

"But if the test works, we won't want to reconfigure," Gakor said. "And the mooring plates are already plugged into the computer. Adjustments will be easier than with this oscillator, and the mooring plates can emit more powerful gravity waves."

"The trouble is, Riker wants us to hurry," Geordi said. He tapped the oscillator's base with a toe. "Besides, I'd just love to boot this thing out the airlock."

Gakor laughed heartily. "At full power it would interfere with the ship's artigrav systems, even placed outside. The whole ship will feel that *grauko* buzz, and that won't make us popular."

Geordi threw up his hands. "You've convinced me. We'll use the mooring plates."

"That will be time-consuming," Gakor said, smoothly changing his side in the argument. "We're only after proof-of-principle now, and if we don't get it, we'll have wasted our time and effort."

Geordi laughed. "Gakor, if I said suicide was a bad idea, I honestly think you'd talk yourself into trying it."

"Me? Never," the Tellarite said. "But if *you* were to try it, it *would* improve my chances for promotion. . . ."

Laughing, the two engineers went to the computer station and set to work on the mooring plates. These were powerful artigrav generators, placed at strategic points around the ship's hull and used to anchor the *Enterprise* in spacedock. They weren't designed for any other purpose, and Geordi could see that they would need extensive modifications before they could serve as gravity-wave emitters. Cross-connections—new circuit modules—sensors and controls—"We've got our work cut out for us," he said happily.

"It should keep us out of trouble for a while," Gakor agreed. He called up a master circuit chart on the computer display and highlighted points around the ship's hull. "I think we'll do better if we work together."

"No, we can get this done faster if we work separately." Geordi smiled. "But first things first. La Forge to Alexander Roshenko."

A rasping, grating noise answered him. *Like father, like son*, Geordi thought, hearing the Klingonese snore. He could wait until tomorrow to tell the kid that the test had worked. "Let's get going," he told Gakor.

Something had happened to put the entire castle in an uproar. The Vo Gatyn had vanished into her battle hall, and servants and guards scurried everywhere. The guests were leaving quickly, getting out of harm's way.

Odovil felt calm amid the uproar, as though her meeting with Chudak had broken something within her—or thrust her into a state beyond terror. When she had entered the hall this evening, she had argued with the outworlder, telling him that she could not blame a couple of trainees for defective alloys. Chudak had agreed with her reasoning—and had ordered her to discharge four of her people tomorrow morning, as a warning against sloppy work. Grab the last four who come through the gate, Chudak had said, and take away their work permits; latecomers are usually the laziest workers anyway, and deserve to starve.

She was not going to do it. It was time to gamble. These outworlders were Chudak's enemy, and they might be the key to destroying him. Enlisting their aid might be a problem, but she thought she could do it. If she failed—no, she would not think about that. She would not fail.

Odovil was standing in the mouth of a corridor, watching the commotion in the Great Hall, when a corporal strode by her. "Stop," she said quietly, touching his elbow. "What trouble there is?"

"Prisoners of the tall outworlders the Vo made," the man said. "Treachery they planned, and now escaped they have."

She nodded. "And now you the outworlders hunt?"

"Yes," he said, tightening his sword belt. Ferengi night-goggles dangled around his neck. "This escape to you nothing is, worker."

Odovil almost smiled as she saw the speculative look in his eyes. She had seen that gleam before, in people who had their price. Bribery-eyes, she called it; corruption had become common since the Ferengi took over. Odovil began to toy with her bracelet. The small jewels and silver facets glittered in the Great Hall's light. "The outworlders you will catch," she said. "How I do not care. When you do, with them I would speak."

"Hard that would be," the corporal said. "Other guards will look, and the outworlders to the Vo at once we must bring." His eyes had fallen to her bracelet. The corporal lacked all subtlety, and in a moment Odovil had made her arrangements with him. The bracelet vanished into a pocket, and he hurried away.

Hoping that he would not keep the bribe and betray her, Odovil went down the corridor. Stairs took her into the castle's underrooms, and after a few moments she found the laundry room. Piles of clothing lay heaped near the sonic machinery. Odovil picked through them, ignoring the Vo Gatyn's finery and the tailored garments of her soldiers and personal servants. At last she found a gray coverall that would fit her. Odovil changed into it, hiding her own yellow dress amid the soiled garments after she had transferred her jewelry and possessions into her coverall pockets. She regretted losing the dress, which had cost her dearly, but it would only attract attention now.

The castle's remaining guards seemed nervously alert, and Odovil kept in the shadows as she slipped toward one of the posterns in the outer wall. The small gate was barred but not locked. She had a bit of luck, and found several glowmoss sticks resting in the brackets by the door. Odovil took them and snuck through the gate.

The night was black, with only the stars and the shimmer of the moss to light her way. She found the hunter's trail and followed it, hoping that the corporal had kept to their deal. It would be hours before she knew. With luck, the man had already captured the outworlders and was taking them to the yeoman's hut hidden in these woods . . . a hut that had been a popular place to meet one's boy, when she had been a girl.

Odovil laughed nervously as she recalled stories about the witches and bandits who lurked in forests. The thought of meeting such creatures did not frighten her now. None of them could be as dangerous as the Ferengi.

When Wesley entered the sickbay he found Data standing next to Shrev's biobed. "You are recovering, Shrev?" Wesley asked quietly.

"Yes, thank you," she answered, her voice firm by Zhuik standards. Her torn, bloodstained tunic had been replaced with a loose hospital smock. "And yourself?"

"Just a scratch," he said, gesturing at his forehead. Wesley glanced at the indicators above the Zhuik's head. He didn't know the proper ranges for Zhuiks, but all the pointers floated within their green zones, so she had to be all right. That filled him with relief. She had accompanied him to Megara at his request, and he felt responsible for what had happened. "I imagine

Commander Data has questions for us," he whispered, with a glance at the android.

"That is correct—" Data stopped, cocked his head, then spoke in a low voice that matched Wesley's and Shrev's. "We will begin this debriefing with an account of your experiences, Ensign."

"Yes, sir. We arrived in a street . . ."

Wesley listened patiently while Shrev spoke. From time to time Data asked him to describe the conversations he'd had with different Megarans. Data was efficient, Wesley noted, and ten minutes after the start of the debriefing his questions had brought them up to the fight. "Perhaps you should speak with Counselor Troi," Data said, when Shrev described the native's death at her hands. "Killing is always a traumatic event."

"It is," Shrev agreed, and Wesley saw how puzzled she looked. "But I must tell you, sir, it is too late for Counselor Troi to have words with my traumatized assailant."

Wesley strangled a laugh. "Shrev, I believe Commander Data is concerned with your feelings."

Her wiry antennae squirmed in obvious confusion. "Indeed? I thank you for your concern, Commander, but I am not troubled, even though the man I fought was unforgivably rude."

"He didn't give his name when he attacked her," Wesley told Data. Then he thought of something that had been nagging him. "That woman in the robe."

"What about her, Wesley?" Data asked.

Wesley fought to put what he knew into words. "I'm not sure what this means, sir, but the robe looked . . . bright, like there was a light shining on it."

"Perhaps a trick of the sunlight—" Data stopped. "No, the lighting conditions make that improbable. I will note this as another oddity. Wesley, you mentioned obtaining paper money, with the purpose of analyzing its information content. I would like to see this money."

"Yes, sir." Wesley was still in his civilian clothes, with the pouch belted to his waist. He opened it and gave Data the money.

The android flicked through the wad of paper in a matter of seconds. "Fascinating," Data said. "When viewed in the ultraviolet portion of the spectrum, it would appear that numerous printing processes were employed here, using many types of ink and paper. All but one type is of low quality."

That touched a memory from a book Wesley had read. "Counterfeiting?" he asked.

"That is the logical conclusion, Cadet," Data said. He returned the money to Wesley. "Assuming that the money with the best-quality paper and ink is genuine, then one-third of this money is counterfeit."

"That is a large proportion," Shrev said.

"That is correct, Ensign," Data said. He looked thoughtful. "This suggests an unusually high level of criminal activity on Megara. In addition, this amount of counterfeiting would seriously destabilize the Megaran economy."

"And things are already bad down there," Wesley said. "Most people are paid just enough to live. I've never seen anything like it," he added helplessly. "It's like somebody is *trying* to destroy these people."

"Neither the Ferengi nor the Cardassians are known for their charitable natures," Data said. "Yet if they *are* exploiting Megara, this behavior does appear counterproductive."

"Perhaps it is a side effect of whatever they plan," Shrev said. "Yet I also find it hard to imagine that this destruction serves a purpose."

Dr. Crusher approached the group. "Shrev, you've had enough excitement for now."

"I feel in excellent health, thanks to your ministrations," Shrev said.

"Flattery will get you nowhere," Dr. Crusher said. She ran a scanner up and down Shrev's left side. Her cardial tubes were muscular, multichambered cylinders that ran from above her hip to the base of her skull, and the knife wound had caused extensive damage to the pseudoheart's muscle tissue. "There's still a lot of swelling, but *if* you stay quiet I *may* let you leave in the morning."

"As you wish," Shrev said. Her eyes remained open, but the pointers on her biobed monitor drifted downward, and her antennae curled back against her head.

Dr. Crusher looked at the readings. "Good. Dormancy will help her heal."

"Is she all right?" Wesley asked.

His mother nodded. "She'll be fine. And you can stop whispering now; she can't hear you."

"Okay—" Wesley stopped, cleared his throat and raised his voice to a normal level. "Okay, Mom."

"I may wish to question Ensign Shrev tomorrow," Data said to Wesley, as they stepped away from Shrev's side. "I am still puzzled by certain facets of your experience, especially this brown-robed woman. Several other people saw such a person immediately before the trouble began."

"They sound like clergy," Dr. Crusher suggested.

"That is not the only possible deduction," Data said. "There are indications that hooded robes are a traditional form of Megaran dress, at least among the lower social classes. The garb may be affected by xenophobic agitators as a political statement."

"That makes sense," Wesley said, while wishing that Data's maker had given the android a clearer speech style. "But why are you puzzled?"

"None of our people observed the robed individuals at any time before the attacks," Data said. "Lieutenant Somek, whose Vulcan memory is quite reliable, saw nothing. It is as though the agitators appeared out of thin air."

Wesley shrugged. "Maybe they didn't put on the robes until just before they started making their speeches."

"That is possible," Data admitted. "If you will excuse me, I will report to Commander Riker now. Thank you for your cooperation, Cadet." Data left the sickbay.

At a gesture, Wesley followed his mother into her office. "It sounds like you and Shrev are getting along famously."

"I like her," Wesley said.

"Enough to talk like a Zhuik," she said. "She tells me you're very polite."

"It makes her more comfortable," Wesley said. "It doesn't hurt me to do that."

His mother arched an eyebrow. "No, it doesn't—as long as you remember she's not *entirely* humanoid, biologically speaking."

"I will," he said, feeling a bit embarrassed. Wesley had studied enough comparative biology to know why Zhuiks did not intermarry with other species. He was glad his mother hadn't launched into one of her no-nonsense lectures about the facts of life. "And I think Shrev will remember I'm not part-insect," he said, rallying his spirits.

The doctor laughed. "Touché. Seriously, though, be careful not to let your feelings pull you into an impossible situation."

"Don't worry," he said. Wesley walked out of sickbay. He knew there was no danger of falling in love with Shrev. Zhuik males were drones: small and short-lived, and with intelligences barely equal to that of a tree shrew. Biology aside, Wesley knew that the possibility of romantic love could never enter Shrev's mind.

Which was too bad.

It was all Gul Verden could do to tame his rage. *Anger is a tool,* he told himself. *Use it, do not let it use you.* He repeated the dictum over and over, as he had done as a child, until he felt in control of himself again.

Verden knew he had reason to feel anger over his mistakes. He had underestimated his opponents, which was always a blunder in the combat of life. He had relied too deeply on native equipment; stone walls and iron bars *should* have been enough to hold the humans. He had trusted the native guards, who had not noticed the escape until Verden had returned to the cell with the interrogation drugs. And yet— who could have expected the humans to fetch along a thrice-damned *saw?*

Ubinew was supervising the hunt at his station. Verden did not waste his time and concentration by demanding a report; he could read the indicators and displays for himself. Half of the castle's native guards were scouring the woods around Gatyn's castle. They wore Ferengi night-goggles, but Verden doubted they would find anything. The native troops had little experience with night-goggles, and the humans had a small but precious head start on their pursuers.

Verden sat down in the command seat. He wished that he had sent his own people out there, with their own equipment. That would have made short work of the hunt—but he had to consider the human starship. One sensor reading—or one prisoner—would tip off the humans to the Cardassian presence on this world. So far the risks Verden had run had been successful, but he refused to push his luck.

I must face the worst, he thought. The two humans knew that the Ferengi were not the only aliens on Megara. The ambassador had already been suspicious, and Chudak's interference had forced Verden to reveal too much. If they got back to their ship, they would report what they knew. So the two humans must be killed before they could return to their ship—no, that was no good. The Federation ship would investigate their deaths.

We must destroy the ship, Verden decided. That would require him to call the Fleet for help, a decision that did not please him. His pride demanded that he remain as the commander, and not subordinate himself to another person—

Abruptly Verden got out of his chair and left the intelligence room. He found himself alone in one of the bunker's narrow passageways, where he remained until his training and discipline had subdued his instincts. *Pride is unworthy,* he told himself in shame, as he repeated the mantras of his earliest lessons. *Selfishness is unworthy. I must think of others. Alone we are weak. Together we are strong. Are my legs weak because I stand upon them? It is better to share in victory than to stand alone in defeat . . .*

At last he could accept the humiliation of calling for help. There was a binary neutron star less than a light-year from the Megaran system, and its radiation fields concealed a powerful Liburnian-class warship. The ship waited there for the chance to ambush any enemy vessels that pried into the Megaran operation. A battle against a Galaxy-class starship was a gamble, but the alternative was certain discovery and failure.

Verden returned to the intelligence room, where he went to the communications officer. "Signal the *Fatal Arrow,*" he told Bwolst. "We shall require their presence to destroy the human ship. And have the 'Prophet' keep the city stirred up."

"I obey," the man said.

As do I, Verden thought. He went to Ubinew and stood behind him. Verden frowned as he saw how disorganized the search pattern had become. The native troops were no good at this. One group was so thoroughly lost in the woods that it was running away from the castle.

Chapter Ten

I NEVER KNEW *there were so many shades of black,* Picard thought wryly, as he and Offenhouse stumbled through the woods. There was just enough starlight to let him see a few dim shapes, but not enough to let him distinguish between inky shadows and fallen branches. The captain's only consolation was that the ambassador had tripped and fallen more times than he had.

Offenhouse stumbled, fell flat on his face and cursed. "Picard," he said quietly, "would you say we're lost?"

"Thoroughly," Picard answered.

"Then there's not much point in moving on, is there?" Offenhouse asked. "For all I know we're heading straight back toward Castle Dracula. I'd rather sit quiet and not attract attention."

"I see your point," Picard said. Carefully, he sat down and rested his back against a tree trunk. "We should try to think of a way to signal the *Enterprise.*"

"With what?" The vague shape that was the ambassador sat down by a tree. "Think their sensors will find us?"

"Possibly," Picard said. "The question is, will it occur to anyone to search outside the castle for us?"

Offenhouse chuckled. "I hope you're not suggesting we go back. You know, it isn't going to take our playmates long to start looking for us, and I'll bet they've got night-vision gear, or whatever you people use nowadays."

"We use something that we call night-vision gear," Picard said. "Of course—"

The ambassador hushed him. "Light," he whispered.

Picard craned his head and spotted a feeble green glow moving in the woods. *Not Ferengi,* he thought. Their equipment would not give itself away with any light. The same rule applied to Federation equipment.

The light grew closer, and Picard saw several human shapes among the trees. He saw more lights and realized that he and Offenhouse were surrounded. If they stayed absolutely still, the searchers might miss them—

The search was too efficient for that, and within moments a trio of men found them. One man carried a wooden staff, which was covered by a glowing green moss. A corner of the captain's mind noted how the Megarans used a bioluminescent plant as a nightlight. The feeble light glinted oddly on another man's bulging eyes—*No,* Picard realized, *he's wearing infrared goggles. That's a Ferengi design, too. Curiouser and curiouser.*

The other two men carried swords, and they gestured for Picard and Offenhouse to stand. One man tapped the ambassador's elbow with his swordpoint, making him raise his hands. "Do you affect *everybody* this way?" Picard asked Offenhouse in exasperation while three more armed men joined them.

The man with the staff hissed urgent words. Deprived of his translator, Picard could still guess his meaning: *Keep quiet. Come with us. Or else.* The captain knew better than to resist; he hoped the ambassador felt the same way.

What happened next made little sense. A knife flashed, and the man with the staff fell to the ground with a gurgling sigh. His killer hissed harsh words to the other men, and the soldiers answered with sullen mumbles. The killer picked up the erstwhile leader's staff.

The Megarans led the two humans away. The phosphorescent staff gave enough light to make walking easy, and they struck a brisk pace. Picard tried to estimate the distance they crossed by counting his steps. He gave up after the first five kilometers.

They had walked through the woods for several hours before they reached a low stone building. Their captors opened the door, guided Picard and Offenhouse inside and then closed the door on them. Picard heard a heavy bar rattle into place, locking the door.

Offenhouse sniffed loudly in the darkness. "I'd be careful where I sat down, Picard."

"Yes," Picard said. "I imagine that this place doubles as a stable."

"Or a goat pen." Offenhouse sighed. "Our pals don't act like they work for the Ferengi. What do you suppose they want?"

"I can't imagine." Picard moved along the walls, feeling them with his hands. "They are, or rather *were,* the Vo Gatyn's soldiers; that's how they knew we were out there, and that's where they got those goggles."

"And then they double-crossed their Vo," Offenhouse said.

"It would appear there's yet another player in the game." Picard found the door and probed it with his fingers. As he had expected, it was quite stout. He felt the low ceiling; the smooth texture told him it was slate. The stone would interfere with a sensor scan; given the general similarity between humans and Megarans, the *Enterprise* might mistake Picard and Offenhouse for natives.

Picard sighed. "This is embarrassing," he told Offenhouse. "Starship captains are not supposed to allow aliens to capture them."

"Really? I heard that it happens to starship captains all the time," Offenhouse said. "Beam down to a planet, get captured, escape—"

"—jeopardize your crew and mission with a rescue," Picard finished. "That sort of carelessness is considered bad form, Mr. Ambassador. As for getting captured *twice* in the same day—" Picard shook his head ruefully. "I may never live this down."

"Take it easy," Offenhouse said. "It's after midnight now. You've only been captured once today."

"So I have. That's a great comfort." Picard scraped at the floor with a foot until he decided it was reasonably clean. He squatted down. "Well, Mr. Ambassador, it would seem we have privacy and time in good measure. Shall we discuss the diplomatic situation?"

"Why? It's as bad as the air in here." Picard heard Offenhouse settle to the dirt floor. "One thing's obvious. Chudak thought Verden was a native."

"While Verden is quite clearly an alien," Picard said. "It would seem that Ensign Shrev's inference was correct. The Ferengi are working for an outside party."

"Who haven't told the Ferengi what their real plan

is," Offenhouse said. "Chudak is as much in the dark as we are."

"So it appears." The Ferengi were normally quite canny; Picard found it odd to think that someone could use them as a tool. "I wonder what game is being played on Megara."

"A dirty one," Offenhouse said promptly. "Verden's people wouldn't play games if they were on the up-and-up."

"I quite agree," the captain said. "I imagine that this is a military game, as you suggested. Aside from the secrecy, there is the enormous expense involved here."

"That fifty billion credits," Offenhouse said. "That's a big enough budget for a military operation. Maybe Verden's people hired the Ferengi as defense contractors. That still doesn't tell us what Verden is, though."

"Quite true." Picard's dark-adapted eyes noticed a dim glow coming from a small vent in the hut's ceiling. *Dawn,* he thought. By now Riker would be searching for him and the ambassador. "Speaking of military operations, Mr. Ambassador, you took quite a risk when we encountered Chudak's ship."

"I wouldn't say so," Offenhouse said. "Chudak shot down that probe, and he might have done the same with the *Enterprise*. We were safer this way."

"You still gambled with my ship," Picard said. "Military force is a dangerous tool, Mr. Ambassador. The threat of its use often provokes a violent reaction from one's adversaries, especially when that adversary feels surprised and insecure. Even when force seems justified, it has often dragged its user to his own destruction, and more than a few victors have found that they were worse off after 'winning' a bloody war than they were beforehand. Your own twentieth century offered ample proof of this—"

A crude, grating buzz interrupted the captain's words. He listened for a puzzled moment before he recognized the noise. As it grew louder Picard sighed wearily. Ralph Offenhouse had a snore that would have impressed a Klingon.

"Something's wrong," Riker said when the captain failed to answer his call. Picard hadn't checked in for hours. That wasn't unusual on a diplomatic mission, but after the riots it made Riker uneasy. Riker clasped his hands behind his back as he paced the deck. "Data, get a fix on the captain."

Wesley watched the android cross the bridge to the science officer's station. He worked the controls for a moment, then faced Riker. "Sir," he said, "I can locate neither the captain nor the ambassador. I am commencing a scan of the castle environs."

"I don't think we'll find them that way," Riker said.

"They may have been taken hostage," Worf said.

"That seems likely," Riker agreed. He stepped up to Worf's station and looked at his display. "Ferengi, Cardassians, riots, assaults and now an abduction," he said sourly. "To coin a phrase, Mr. Worf, things have never been better." The Klingon grunted thoughtfully at that.

Wesley gave Data a puzzled glance. "The words come from a twentieth-century motion picture," Data explained quietly. "In their proper context they describe an extremely dangerous situation."

Wesley nodded. He'd heard that Riker and Worf had developed an interest in ancient movies. Riker paced for another moment, then settled into the captain's chair and glowered at the main viewer. "Mr. Worf, let's start looking for the captain. Hail the Ferengi ship."

The Ferengi bridge appeared on the screen. Wesley

looked at the man in the center, and saw that it wasn't Chudak. "I want to speak to Chudak," Riker said.

"The Daimon isn't available," the man answered. "I'm Oshal, his second-in-command."

"Where's Chudak?" Riker demanded.

Oshal shrugged. "He's conducting business with the Vo Gatyn. If *your* business cannot wait, you must do it with me."

Wesley scanned the Ferengi ship as Riker closed the channel. "Commander Riker," he reported, "there aren't any humans on board the Ferengi ship, and they haven't used their transporter recently."

"But there is something odd beneath the castle," Data said. "There are anomalous energy readings, suggestive of a small, shielded installation."

"Can you be more specific?" Riker asked.

"No, sir," the android said. "The installation is masked by the castle above it, and by electronic interference from the surroundings. I have only a few extra energy traces."

"Well, at least we know where the Cardassians have their headquarters," Riker said. "It makes sense that they'd stick close to their puppet. But we can't get in there while their shields are up." Glancing over his shoulder, Wesley saw him tap his fist on his chair's armrest in controlled frustration.

"Sir," Data said, "might I suggest that we signal the Cardassians and open negotiations?"

"That is a bad idea," Worf rumbled.

"I agree," Riker said. "The Cardassian presence is an act of war. *Officially,* we don't know they're here —because the minute we *do* know, we're back at war."

"And Cardassians execute prisoners of war," Worf noted.

Riker nodded. "That would be hard on the captain

. . . and the ambassador," he added after a thoughtful pause.

Wesley looked at his instruments while Riker, Worf and Data discussed their options. The helm position had its own sensors, and while they weren't as sophisticated as the ones at the science station, they were still quite capable. Wesley focused them on the Megaran castle.

It was night down there, but the infrared imagers placed an adequate view of the castle on Wesley's display screen. On a hunch, Wesley narrowed the bandwidth, so the sensor would detect only objects within a few degrees of human and Megaran body temperature. The image on his screen turned to a score of white points on a black field. He stared at it for a minute, puzzled, then saw how the points were moving. "Commander Data?" he called. "Look at the infrared image. Something odd is happening outside the castle."

"Outside the castle?" Riker repeated.

"That is correct," Data said. Wesley heard the computer station bleep quietly as the android fed in commands. "There are a large number of individuals outside the castle walls. Their motions suggest they are searching for something."

"Such as escaped prisoners," Worf said. "Can the sensors differentiate between humans and Megarans?"

"Not from orbit," Data said. "The differences are too subtle for long-range observation."

Worf growled in discontent. "If the captain has escaped, we must move quickly."

"But not blindly," Riker said. He got up, went to Data's station and looked at the display. "Which one of those dots is the captain?"

Wesley thought of something. He turned his seat

around and looked at Riker. "Commander, maybe the Megarans could help."

To Wesley's relief he didn't laugh. "A little while ago these same Megarans attacked our people," Riker said.

"Not all of them were involved, sir," Wesley said. "I think we can trust one of the people I met down there, a shopkeeper named Anit."

"What could he do?" Riker asked.

"I'm not sure," Wesley admitted. "But he's an ex-soldier, and he knows the land and the people."

"This has possibilities," Worf said.

"It has more possibilities than sitting around," Riker agreed. "Mr. Worf, take an away team and look for the captain."

"Yes, sir," Worf said. "Commander Data, Cadet Crusher, follow me."

Wesley followed Data and Worf into the turbolift. "Tell me about this Anit," Worf said to Wesley as the lift took them to a transporter room.

"He's an ex-soldier," Wesley repeated, "about thirty years old. He needs money to take care of his family, so I think we could hire him even if he doesn't like aliens. He lost an arm and an eye in a battle, but he's sharp and he has a lot of connections."

" 'Connections'?" Data tilted his head. "Ah. You refer to acquaintances, associates, business partners—"

"Can we trust him?" Worf asked impatiently.

"I think so, sir," Wesley said, "but it might be a good idea if I spoke with him before he sees you."

"That is an excellent suggestion," Data said. "You might negate some of his xenophobic tendencies."

"It would help more if we brought along a lot of gold," Wesley suggested.

The turbolift stopped. The trio walked down a

corridor and entered the transporter room. While the technician on duty produced phasers, night-vision goggles and money pouches, Wesley retrieved the mace from cargo bay two. After it materialized on the transporter stage, he picked it up and handed it to Worf. "I told Anit I was buying it as a gift for a warrior," Wesley told the Klingon. "He'll be pleased to see you carrying it, sir."

Worf nodded as he hefted the mace. "Useful," he said in satisfaction. Wesley recognized that as the highest praise a Klingon could give a weapon. Worf used it to gesture at the transporter stage. "You will go first, Cadet," he said.

The coffee was vile. Tired as he was, Geordi chuckled when he recalled the trouble he'd had programming the replicator to make this slop. The replicator computer was designed to cater to its users' pleasures, and the machine had had trouble believing that anyone would *want* a drink that tasted like—like—

Pond scum? Geordi wondered. *Reactor coolant? Tribble squeezings?* Geordi had never managed to identify the coffee's precise flavor, but it fit an old Starfleet tradition. When engineers needed to work long hours, they punched themselves awake with bad coffee.

Well, human *engineers,* he conceded, looking at Gakor. The Tellarite engineer sat at the high bay's main computer station, his hands folded across his potbelly and his head tilted back as he caught a quick nap. Mercifully, Tellarites did not snore.

Geordi felt awake as he finished his coffee. "La Forge to bridge," he said. "We're ready to test the new detector now."

"Understood," Riker said. "Proceed."

Geordi woke Gakor. The Tellarite sat up and scanned the computer display. "All readings are normal," he told Geordi.

"Okay," Geordi said. "Computer, activate detection sequence."

"Activating," the computer said.

Geordi sat down. His whole body felt sore, and not just from lack of sleep. He and Gakor had crawled through what seemed endless kilometers of accessways and Jeffries tubes as they made the rounds of the mooring-point stations, adjusting circuits and changing modules. Geordi hoped that the test worked; he didn't want to have to repeat that tour and put everything back the way it had been.

Gakor laughed and slapped his clawlike hands on his knees. "It works!"

"Son of a gun," Geordi said, trying to sound surprised. The detector was getting a neutrino flux, exactly as predicted. "Engineering to bridge. Can you give me the location of the Ferengi ship?"

A woman's voice answered. "One-seven-two mark thirty-eight, range one hundred kilometers."

"That matches our readings," Geordi said as he looked at the computer display. "Say . . . we're getting a second reading, from a power source on the planet's surface."

Riker's voice spoke. "Is that at bearing two-zero mark one-oh-seven?"

"Yes, sir," Geordi said, studying the data. The neutrino flux was barely one percent that of the ship's output. "It's not powerful enough to be a spacecraft power plant, though. I'd say it's a primary generator for a fixed installation."

"That's what it is," Riker said. "Well done. Geordi, what sort of range does this detector have?"

"Not much," Geordi said reluctantly. He didn't

like to admit it, but the new detector wasn't going to live up to his expectations. "Ten, maybe fifteen light-hours. Maybe I can improve that a bit, but we're up against a fundamental limit here. We use gravity waves and they drop off by the inverse-square law."

"Damn," Riker muttered. "I was hoping we could use it to scan Weber 512."

"That's almost a light-year away," Geordi said. "Detecting an operating power plant at the edge of the Megaran system is the best I can do."

"We can still use it. Hook your detector into the sensor network, then tie it into the fire control system."

"Aye-aye, sir," Geordi said, as Riker closed the channel. He went back to the food replicator. It looked like he was going to need more coffee.

Chudak dreamed. He was happy; he had all the wealth a Ferengi could want, with more on the way. Even now the most beautiful woman in the galaxy was entering his bedroom to tell him of new profits. He leered at her as she approached his bed and leaned over him. Tall, delicate, and seductive, she smiled as she touched a hand to Chudak's shoulder—

Chudak grunted as Verden shook him awake. "You are well?" the pagus asked.

"Yes—" Chudak felt a tumult of emotion as the immediate past flooded back. The sleazy debtor had *shot* him—the pagus must have connections with somebody else, if he had a phaser—he was beset by treachery—

Chudak looked at Verden's hand as the pagus released his shoulder. Now that he examined it closely, he realized that the Megaran's sixth finger looked deformed. There was a ridge at its base, and its brown color was far too even. It was clearly artificial, which could mean only one thing. "You're a Cardassian," Chudak said.

"Correct."

Chudak growled. His private negotiations with the repulsive creatures had been maddening. They had demanded secrecy and assurances of secrecy at every step; they had not even allowed Chudak to tell his senior officers that the Cardassians were involved here. That secrecy had complicated the operation—and now *this*—

Chudak felt fear. He had always expected the Cardassians to double-cross him. He had made preparations, of course—and here he was in the one situation for which he had never prepared. Well, his only hope was to brazen it out. "Why wasn't I told your people would have agents here?" Chudak demanded.

"You do not need to know the reason," Verden said. "What matters is that I command here."

"My contract—" Chudak began.

"I now invoke paragraph twenty of your contract," Verden said. "I speak of the real contract, not the one you signed with Gatyn. And I remind you of paragraph twelve. Should the Federation learn of our presence, you forfeit any profits you might make."

The bed creaked as Chudak sat up in anger. "You would not *dare* break our contract!"

"I speak of keeping it," Verden said. He stepped away from the bed—a very good bed, Chudak noted, and placed in one of the castle's more splendid rooms. To an experienced negotiator such as Chudak, this attention to his comfort suggested that Verden did, indeed, want to maintain the contract. And now that the situation had changed a bit, perhaps

Chudak could put himself in a more advantageous position.

Chudak lay down again and pillowed the back of his head on his hands. "Let's speak of keeping the contract, Verden. Of course, having the *Enterprise* hovering above us makes secrecy difficult, and you know how difficulties increase my expenses—"

"You will do as I say," Verden said. "You will help me to destroy the *Enterprise.*"

Chudak grunted. "That's risky. My crew will demand hazard pay—"

Verden's face twitched in irritation, a sight that pleased Chudak. *That's one thing I have in common with that fur-headed Federation ambassador,* he thought in grudging respect. *Offenhouse may be two lobes short of a full brain, but we both know how to put an opponent off balance.* "I have no time to waste in negotiation," the Cardassian said. "Name your price."

"One billion credits," Chudak said.

"The destruction of a Federation starship is worth that price," Verden said. "We have a deal. This is what you will do. You will return to your ship. You will contact the *Enterprise* and soothe them."

"Soothe them?" Chudak repeated. "They're already suspicious. What's happened to Picard and Offenhouse?"

"You will tell them that the humans have escaped after offending the natives," Verden said. "You will negotiate a rescue and ransom, but you will see to it that the negotiations are long and unsuccessful. While you distract the humans, a warship will arrive and destroy the *Enterprise.*"

Chudak smiled in satisfaction. "Put that billion credits in writing and we have a deal. And—will that warship of yours arrive any time soon?"

Verden looked at him in suspicion. "You do not need to know."

Chudak laughed. "I'm only looking for a spare hour or so. This is the Vo Gatyn's bedroom, isn't it?"

"Correct," Verden said. "What of it?"

The Ferengi Daimon laughed again. "It seems a shame to kick such a beautiful lady out of her quarters. Send her in."

Chapter Eleven

SOME INSTINCT woke Anit in the time before the dawn. *Thieves,* he thought, reaching for his dagger. Since the arrival of the rat-eyes, the number of thieves and bandits in the world had grown like flies on a dung heap, and they were as bold and greedy as a tax collector. The outworlders had left their gold all across the city, and now the city's thieves would come looking for that gold.

Anit slid out of bed; Molokan muttered in her sleep but did not wake. Anit went to the opening between the building's two rooms and stood behind the blanket that covered the doorway. The gold was in the living room, buried under the floor; he would kill the burglars when they came through the doorway to look for it.

He heard noises in the shop. Yes, someone was stumbling around in the dark. Then—"Kardel Anit?" a flat, familiar voice asked.

One of the outworlders, Anit thought. He felt uncertain. The Prophet had warned against outworlders, and there was no reason to trust them—especially not when they came sneaking in in the middle of the night . . . yet their gold was good.

"Kardel Anit?" the voice repeated. "I need help."

Anit came to a decision. "Enter," he said while Molokan and several of the children stirred. He took a step back from the doorway and placed his hand on the glassfire's knob.

The outworlder entered the home-room. As he came through the doorway, Anit turned on the glassfire, and its glare blinded the alien. It was the pink one, not the green one, and he was alone. A money pouch hung at his side. "My help you asked," Anit said.

"Yes, sir." He glanced at Anit's dagger, then looked into Anit's eyes. "The rat-eyes have abducted my ship-leader."

Anit puzzled over the alien's words. Did he mean his ship-leader had taken the rat-eyes? No, surely he had the words reversed. "More speak," Anit said, while Molokan and the children gaped in fright at the outworlder.

The outworlder obeyed. "We don't know where ship-leader Picard is, or how to find him here. I hoped you might help us."

"Help I might," Anit said. In truth he had no idea of what he might do, but this was a chance to get more gold. "Much risk I would take. Much gold to me must you give."

The outworlder held out his pouch to Anit. "Is this enough?"

One-handed, Anit gestured to Molokan with his dagger. She took the bag, opened it and dug into it. "Gold," she said, wide-eyed. "Three klets it weighs. Three!"

That much gold would feed his family for a year. "A deal we have," Anit told the outworlder. He glanced at his family, then stepped through the doorway into his shop. The young outworlder followed him. "Alone do you come?"

"My friends are waiting for me to call them." The outworlder touched an ornament on his chest. "Officer Worf, Officer Data, he'll help us. Come on down."

Light shimmered and two outworlders appeared in the room. Anit took their arrival in stride. Everyone knew that the rat-eyes traveled like this, and he had lost his awe of miracles after the first dozen times he saw a glassfire dispel the night. His children claimed this was not a true miracle, but how could you trust the things they learned in the rat-eyes' school?

Anit studied the newcomers. One was gold instead of pink, and had yellow eyes. The other was the color of a person, but had a ridged, half-bald scalp. He carried the mace that Anit had sold the first outworlder. The three outworlders spoke rapidly among themselves, and then the pink one vanished in a shimmer of light. As he did so, Molokan waddled into the shop and stood blocking the door. She held a carving knife, and Anit knew she would use it if she thought the outworlders might harm the children.

The one with the mace looked at Anit. "How shall we find our ship-leader?"

Anit sighed; he'd been afraid someone would ask that. "Disguises you need," he said. He took them into the shop, where he picked through a heap of clothing. Within moments the three men were clad in alt-robes. Ferengi law banned the old garment, but with the city in a ferment after the riots that law would go unenforced. The hoods would hide those alien faces, and the long sleeves would hide their deformed five-fingered hands.

The one called Worf looked at Anit with wary eyes. "After we find our ship-leader," he said, "you will receive ten more bags of gold."

Anit felt his lips tighten. *A canny one this creature is,* he thought. He had planned to lead the outworlders on a long and harmless march outside the city, avoiding danger and running them around until they gave up. But this reward changed everything. It meant decent food for his family, warm clothes, heat in the winter.

And if he died, or if the outworlders betrayed him? Anit shrugged inwardly. His death would free Molokan to find a new husband, someone who could give her and the children a better life. Children and honorable women were still highly regarded by people, despite the rat-eyes' efforts to treat them like merchandise.

And now a soldier again I will be, he thought. *A mercenary for my family. Honorable a mercenary is not, but long gone my honor is.* "With me now you will come," Anit told the outworlders. He led them out the front door, into an empty square touched by the dawn's first gray light. Molokan did not risk bad luck by saying farewell; after all these years she remained a soldier's wife.

". . . stack of pancakes, smothered in maple syrup," the ambassador was saying. He sat on the hut's floor with his back against the stone wall. By Picard's estimate the sun had been up for an hour, and light came through chinks in the walls. "With bacon and orange juice. And a side order of toast, with—"

"Mr. Ambassador," Picard said, "if I may be frank, you were less annoying while you slept." While not racked with hunger pangs, the captain felt in distinct need of a meal.

Offenhouse chuckled. "Sorry, Picard, but being a pain in the butt takes constant practice, especially if I want to stay ahead of Chudak. Did you see how he acted with all those gals at the castle? It takes *talent* to get turned down by so many women, so fast."

"He excelled at that," Picard agreed, glad that Offenhouse had turned the subject away from food. He sat down alongside the door. "I have always wondered why Ferengi males are so fascinated by non-Ferengi women. They seem rather mismatched."

"No more than humans and Vulcans," Offenhouse said. "Or humans and Klingons, humans and Romulans, humans and Betazoids, humans and Bajorans—oh, never mind." He rubbed the black stubble on his chin. "You're serious?"

"Certainly. I wanted to ask you—" Picard stopped and stifled a yawn. A restless night had left him fatigued. "Excuse me. The Ferengi are one of the most mysterious races in the galaxy, yet you have made some remarkable deductions about them."

"I like to call them 'guesses,'" Offenhouse said. "That reminds me I could be wrong; I don't have enough facts to support all of my ideas. But if you want my best guess as to why they like alien women, it's simple. What do *you* look for in a woman?"

"In a word? Companionship," the captain said.

"Same here," Offenhouse said. "Everyone needs someone they can share their feelings and dreams with. We're what biology makes us, so we look for that someone in a lover. But the Ferengi—does the phrase 'battle of the sexes' mean anything to you?"

The captain smiled despite himself. "I do believe I've heard the term somewhere."

"Well, I figure that on Ferengal it's open warfare," Offenhouse said. "The Ferengi act as if they have two separate societies, one male and one female, and the only thing they have in common is the little matter of producing children. The separation may be so extreme that the women won't even raise the boys—

they give them to their fathers, who take their sons into—into the family business—"

This is no time for him to have a problem, Picard thought, hearing the man's voice catch. "It doesn't sound emotionally satisfying."

"It wouldn't be," Offenhouse said. "Maybe that's why Ferengi men are so outgoing with alien females. Ferengi men and women don't get any companionship from one another, so they look for it in aliens."

Picard nodded thoughtfully. "I see. I had wondered if it was the same cause which attracts humans to aliens."

"No. Ferengi are lonely, but humans just like the exotic. Look at Shrev and Peter—I mean Wesley."

He needs to talk, Picard thought. Something in the man was pressuring him to raise his past. Picard decided he would have to risk an explosion. "Wesley Crusher is much like your son, isn't he?"

Offenhouse sighed. "In more ways than I can describe."

"For the little it's worth," Picard said, "your son's death had meaning. He helped to destroy Khan Singh's empire—"

"I know that," Offenhouse said. "And I know how little it was worth."

Picard was baffled. The destruction of the Great Khanate had started the process that led to Earth's unification and the abolition of war. "I don't understand."

The ambassador sat in silence for a long moment. "Let me tell you something that isn't in the history books," he said at last. "Do you know where Khan's super-race came from?"

"That's hard to answer," Picard said. "Their progenitors were an international group of scientists; they had labs in Haiti and Pakistan during the nineteen-sixties and seventies—"

"They also had a lab in Chad," Offenhouse said, "and headquarters in North Yemen. They worked in the poorest countries on Earth because it was easy to bribe officials into silence and hire human guinea pigs—"

Picard felt a chill. "How do you know?"

"Because I supplied a lot of their equipment," Offenhouse said, his voice thick with self-disgust. "Electron microscopes, computers, drugs, chemicals, name it. Everything they wanted, and no questions asked, not even when I had to break export regulations and smuggling laws. They couldn't have done it without me. I'm as much Khan Singh's godfather as anyone."

No wonder Counselor Troi sensed guilt in him, Picard thought. "You couldn't have known what they planned," he said. "You were no scientist. Even if you had known what to ask—"

Offenhouse shook his head. "I didn't *want* to ask. I knew something was fishy, but I was making too much money to care. If I'd reported them to Interpol—well, I didn't. My son paid the price. So did the world. And what happened to me? I died rich, and I died right before I had to face the consequences. Then I got a second chance at life, an important job, respect—when I *deserve* to burn in Hell." He sighed. "You people should have left me where you found me—dead and lost."

"You made a mistake," Picard said. "We've all done that—"

"You've never done anything as big as this," Offenhouse told him.

"My conscience doesn't take a tape measure to my errors," the captain replied. "It only asks me what I will do to make amends."

"I've been looking for a way to do that, Picard," he said. "Ever since I talked to your counselor. Maybe even before that—sometimes I don't understand what's going on inside my head. Only, what can I do to make up for bringing the Khans into the world? *Nothing* is enough—"

Offenhouse stopped speaking at the sound of voices outside the hut. Picard listened intently, but without his Universal Translator he could extract no sense from the words.

The door opened and Odovil Pardi, the woman with whom Picard had talked at the castle, entered the hut. She wore an ugly gray coverall in place of the dress she had sported earlier. Odovil was unarmed, but the large man who stood in the doorway carried a scimitar, which compensated for that. The woman approached Picard and said something in her own language; her nervous voice had a questioning tone.

Picard sighed. "I'm afraid I don't understand."

Odovil frowned, then drew a folded paper and a pencil from her coverall pocket. She sketched something on the paper and showed it to the humans. "Meh-gah-rah," she said carefully. "Feh-ren-gee."

Picard looked at the sketch. It showed two stellar systems, one accompanied by a crude human face and one by a Ferengi. *Is she asking us to choose sides?* Picard wondered as Odovil handed him the pencil. She and the guard were giving him some intense looks. . . .

Offenhouse took matters into his own hands. "Ferengi!" he said emphatically, drawing a thumb across his throat.

That brought a smile to Odovil's face. "Ferengi!" she repeated, and matched the throat-slashing gesture. She looked at Picard and waited.

I hope I'm not cutting my own throat, Picard thought as he pulled a thumb across his throat. "Ferengi!"

That made Odovil smile again. "See, Picard?" Offenhouse asked cheerily. "It pays to speak a second language!"

Neanderthal? Picard wondered, looking at the paper. There was a good deal of open space on it, and that gave him an idea. He took the paper and borrowed Odovil's pencil. He sketched a dozen stellar systems, then drew the heads of a human, a Vulcan and a Zhuik, whom the woman might have heard described in the away teams.

The ambassador looked over his shoulder as he sketched. "Not bad," he said in admiration.

"Art is a mandatory Academy subject," Picard said. "I hope to convey the idea that the Federation is larger and more powerful than the Ferengi. And—" He added a Klingon head. "—if I know Commander Riker, he'll send Worf to look for us. Let's make sure she knows he's a friend."

"Good idea," Offenhouse said. "Add a few more people, Picard."

Picard drew a Tellarite and a Saurian before the pencil became too blunt for use. "Federation," he told Odovil, pointing to his sketch.

"Federation," she repeated, looking at the paper. She seemed impressed by the Federation's implied size. Odovil took the paper from Picard, then fished a second scrap of paper from her pocket. She showed it to Offenhouse and Picard.

The ambassador peered at it. "That's money," he said.

"I believe you're correct," Picard agreed. He watched Odovil move the currency back and forth across the sketch, between Megara and the Federation. "Trade," he said as Odovil gave him an inquiring look. "Mr. Ambassador, I believe she wants to do business."

"Well, now," Offenhouse said, smacking his lips. "Things are finally looking up."

Data had programmed himself to understand Ulathic, the local Megaran language, before he left the *Enterprise.* This was more efficient than using a Universal Translator, a device that his creator had incorporated into his circuitry. The translator had several limitations: it could not always distinguish the subtle differences among words of similar meanings, and such vital features as idioms and emotional overtones were lost in the translation process. It could only handle one voice channel at a time, and two or more speakers could overload the device.

Anit led Data and Worf through a string of narrow, twisted alleys. Most of the buildings that abutted the alleys were brick, but their doors were thin and their windows were glassless holes covered only by shutters. As he walked along, his sensitive ears picked up a string of conversation fragments, one after the other. The topics seemed appropriate to the early-morning activities of diurnal creatures: the rousing of late sleepers, the preparing and eating of breakfasts, dressing, the saying of farewells for the day. In this respect the Megarans seemed no different from humanoids throughout the galaxy.

Data also heard references to yesterday's riots. The statements blamed the disturbances on the Ferengi, who on several occasions were identified by a word that meant "outworlders." The word was related to a term that meant "demons," a point he would have missed if he had relied on a translator.

Data did not like the implication. *It appears that the Megarans view "Ferengi," "alien," and "evil" as identical concepts,* he thought. *This is unfortunate, but it could explain why our crew members were attacked. Their language forces the Megarans to regard all aliens as enemies.* At least none of the voices had a high emotional loading, which suggested that the local population had grown calm. A second riot seemed unlikely.

The trio walked down an alley that finally opened into a crowded public square. "Dung on this I hurl," Anit said to Worf and Data. "Empty in the morning often this place is."

Worf growled inside his robe's hood. "There is trouble?"

"Here trouble quickly could grow," Anit said. "The Prophet Against the Dark here speaks."

"We this crowd must go around?" Data asked. He believed he understood the Ulathic syntax; as with Russian and Latin, proper grammar put the verb at the end of the sentence. Placement of subjects and objects seemed to depend upon poetic requirements of scansion and meter, with suffixes to differentiate among the cases.

"Correct you are," Anit said. He scowled at the knot of people who blocked the alley mouth. Data noted that several of the people wore alt-robes, while one man wore a garment similar to a toga. All others dressed in gray coveralls.

"The crowd a problem is not," Anit said at last. "Trouble I expect, if you the Prophet should see. Outworlders accursed you are."

"We are enemies of the rat-eyes," Worf said, his voice sour with irony. "Perhaps the Prophet will forgive us for that."

"Perhaps," Anit said. "The edge of the crowd behind we shall circle. Caution we must exercise. Come."

The square was a sea of heads and a murmur of voices. There was little space between the crowd and the line of shopfronts, and it took a quarter of an hour for the three men to make their way to the next alley entrance. During this time Data tried to observe the Prophet. At first he heard only the voice, loud and strident, which he analyzed as having a seventy-five percent probability of being female and a ninety-nine-point-three percent probability (approaching certainty) of being artificial. This was such an unusual observation that Data stopped, found a ledge mounted in a wall and climbed onto it.

The precarious perch let him observe the Prophet. She stood in the center of the square, her arms upraised and her hood thrown back to expose a head of long, straight gray hair. During the five seconds in which Data remained on the ledge, he adjusted his optical sensors several times. The Prophet was not entirely opaque to visible light; she transmitted approximately one ten-thousandth of the ambient light that fell upon her, making her translucent to Data's enhanced vision. In addition, she was invisible when viewed in the infrared and ultraviolet portions of the spectrum. Her gaze turned toward Data, but she did not react to his presence.

Remarkable, Data thought as he hopped off the ledge. *The Prophet is a hologram.*

He hurried after the others, who had not noticed his absence. Anit and Worf turned down another alley, and Data followed them. He had traveled approximately ten meters when a small, solid object impacted between his shoulder blades. He estimated that the blow would have caused severe injury in a human.

"Outworlder!" Data turned around at the shout. A trio of young Megaran males stood in the opening of the alley. One hurled a cobblestone, which Data easily ducked. They ran down the alley toward Data, and two of them brandished knives. "Outworlder, demon, monster!" they shouted.

"Get down!" Worf roared, while Anit cursed. Data

assumed that Worf was giving him an order appropriate to the situation. He rapidly lowered himself to the ground and lay in a facedown posture, after which he heard the shriek of a phaser set for heavy stun. Data raised his head and saw his three assailants fall to the alley's muddy surface.

Worf and Anit were already running down the alley. Data found this a well-advised action; he ran after them. They slowed only after they had rounded a corner. "Alive we remain," Anit gasped. "Followed we are not."

"Indeed." Worf glowered at Data from inside his hood. "We must exercise *more* caution, Commander, not less."

"I shall endeavor to do so," Data said. The Megarans' xenophobic reaction had surprised him. Anit seemed a reasonable being, and Data saw how that had led him to discount the experience of the other crew members. He reminded himself that Anit had an economic interest in helping the aliens, while the other Megarans saw outworlders as a threat.

Anit found a doorway and knocked at it. After a moment it opened and the trio entered a brick-walled room that reminded Data of Anit's dwelling-place. There were straw pallets, a crude table and a small fire pit, where embers now smoldered.

A man in gray coveralls greeted Anit. "My old captain!" he exclaimed, hugging him with two sound arms. "We not often enough one another see. Old days we must discuss."

"*Gold* we must discuss, Sergeant Taygar," Anit said, throwing back his hood. "And blood of rat-eyes. Still much rat-eye blood you would shed?"

"Much and much," Taygar said. The young man's eyes gleamed, then turned on Worf and Data. "With *them?*" Data heard the suspicion in his voice.

"Reliable they are," Anit said. "They the rat-eyes with a passion hate, and they with gold pay. The old company you can find?"

"I can," Taygar said. "Today no work is. Closed the factories are, and the power grid in a tangle lies. The company by noon here you will see. But who your friends are?"

"*Good* outworlders," Anit said. "Outworlders who the rat-eyes hate. Worf, Data, your faces my sergeant must see."

"Certainly," Data said, and pulled his hood back. He noted that Taygar did not appear disturbed by the alien faces. This implied that his xenophobia was not deeply rooted.

Anit nodded at them. "Rat-eyes they are not, Taygar. Soldiers for them we can be, honor we can have."

"Honor again," Taygar said. "But what if us they betray?"

Anit shrugged, a gesture made lopsided by his missing arm. "Then as betrayed soldiers we die. Or forever you as a rat-eye slave would live?"

"Good your question is," Taygar admitted. He looked Worf over, then pointed at his mace. "That you can use?"

"Easily," Worf rumbled. "How many men can you summon?"

"Two handfuls," the sergeant said. "Good men, good weapons."

Worf grunted in approval, then reached into his robe. "Good soldiers deserve good gold," he said, and handed his money pouch to Taygar. "Bring them and we will talk battle."

Taygar opened the bag and stared into it. For a moment he seemed transfixed by the coins. Then Anit nudged him. "More they will give," Anit said. "Much more."

Taygar left, and Anit sat down in the room's only chair. "Not all our men now I would trust," he said, "but so long as the gold lasts, they last."

"We have much gold," Worf said. He carefully turned off his Universal Translator, turned to Data and spoke in Klingonese. "I heard the Prophet speak. Her words were sweet with hate, but she did not sing like a native."

Data reviewed the Prophet's speech, then answered in the same tongue. "Yes, her syntax was wrong. I also noted that the Prophet was a hologram."

Worf looked puzzled. "A mere seeming?"

"Correct. I cannot explain why the Ferengi desire to create rage, but they are doing so."

Anit watched impatiently as Worf and Data spoke a language he could not understand. "Of what you do speak?" he asked.

Worf dodged the truth as he reactivated his translator. "We wonder how you will find our captain."

The Megaran rubbed his chin. "No details I have. Where last he was seen?"

"In the castle of the Vo Gatyn," Worf said. "We believe he escaped into the woods north of the castle, but if he did, he has not contacted us."

"Fregav Woods," Anit murmured. "Much thought must I give."

"Give, then," Worf suggested.

Data had his own thoughts. In Ulathic, "good outworlders" was almost a contradiction in terms, yet Anit had used the words and Taygar had accepted them without hesitation. It appeared that these people had a great deal of mental flexibility. *Yet they do not always exercise it,* he thought, reflecting on the attack. That did not bode well for the future.

I could use more sleep, Wesley thought as he studied the helm display. He'd grabbed a few hours of downtime during the night, but he didn't feel fully operational. Well, he'd gone into final exams at the Academy with no sleep, and that hadn't hurt his performance.

A light blinked on his display. "Sir, the Ferengi ship is hailing us," Wesley told Commander Riker.

"Ignore them," Riker said. "We'll talk when *I* am ready. And keep trying that neutrino detector."

"Yes, sir." Wesley returned his attention to his instruments. A short while later, Shrev came onto the bridge and joined Wesley at the helm. "I am extremely pleased to see you are well," Wesley whispered to her.

Her chuckle sounded like the rustle of dry leaves. "I am equally pleased to be well," the Zhuik said. "Your estimable mother is satisfied with my recovery. Could I now trouble you to inform me on the situation?"

Wesley did so, quickly, and Shrev shook her head when he described how Worf had ordered him to return to the *Enterprise*. "This seems a waste of a talented junior officer," Shrev said. "Did Lieutenant Worf explain this decision?"

"Mr. Worf *never* explains orders," Wesley said, although he thought he could guess Worf's reasons. Wesley was inexperienced in this sort of operation— and there was the incident at the Academy. Worf had never said so, but he had to feel displeased by Wesley's soiled honor.

Wesley shrugged off his thoughts. "I've been doing what I can up here," he told Shrev, "looking at our sensor readings."

"That is a useful function," Shrev said. "Have you found anything yet?"

"I don't know," Wesley said. He keyed in one of the records and put it on the helm display. White dots drifted around the screen; the display was speeded up at a rate of fifty to one. "Here's a record of the activity outside the castle, starting an hour after our last contact with the captain. The searchers are circling in the woods, all except this one group of six or seven people. We don't know what to make of them."

"Travelers, perhaps," Shrev said. She studied the display. "How odd. I intend no slight, but for humans all of these people move quickly in the dark, as though it does not handicap them."

"The Ferengi or Cardassians must have given them infrared viewers," Wesley said.

"Including these travelers?" she wondered.

"They were probably following a road," Wesley said. "That would have made travel easier . . . wait. It was *still* dark for them. They weren't carrying lights or torches or anything; we'd have spotted that. So how could they have seen the road?"

"Unusual acts bear investigation," Shrev said. Her antennae twitched eagerly. "Let us see which flowers line this road."

"Good idea," Wesley said. He turned on the mapping sensors.

Chapter Twelve

UBINEW LOOKED up from his console in the command room. "The *Fatal Arrow* will arrive in four hours," the Cardassian intelligence officer told Verden. "The ship is maneuvering to keep itself on a line between the neutron stars and the *Enterprise.*"

That pleased Verden. The binary neutron star's radiation would mask the *Fatal Arrow*'s approach, if the commander kept his vessel precisely between the star and the Federation craft. "What of the Federation ship?" Verden asked.

"Agents have beamed down from the *Enterprise* into the city. We are keeping tensions high in the city, to hamper their activities. Chudak is back on his ship and attempting to communicate with the human vessel."

"'Attempting'?" Verden repeated.

"The *Enterprise* has not yet responded," Ubinew told his commander. "My estimate is that they desire to annoy the Ferengi by delaying their response."

"That is typical human behavior," Verden said. "Inform me when they open communications."

"I obey," Ubinew said.

With that, Verden sat down in his chair to ponder the situation. *Fatal Arrow* would destroy both the human and Ferengi ships, making it appear that the two craft had destroyed one another. Verden would have to create evidence to support this, as the Federation would inevitably send a vessel to investigate the loss. He would also have to prepare to deal with a heightened Federation interest in Megara.

That would not be a problem. The plan was almost complete, and the Federation could do little to interfere—their preposterous ethics would keep them from doing anything effective. Verden could have used the Ferengi for a while longer, but he could cope with their loss, and the plan had always called for their elimination. Sacrificing them now would protect the plan.

It is a pity that Chudak will die cleanly in space, Verden thought. Once the Ferengi had finished building Megara's industries, the plan called for the Megarans to regain control of their world. That would be done in the guise of a revolt; the Cardassian team would have instigated uprisings all over the planet—after beaming a fusion bomb onto Chudak's ship. Verden had been looking forward to the revolt. Its violence would have confirmed the success of the plan, the final transformation of these tribal apes into something resembling warriors . . . and he had wanted to see Chudak die at the hands of a mob.

That was not to be. At least Chudak and his Ferengi would all die, which was also important; dead, they could not sell their secrets to the Federation. Verden drew some consolation from the fact that Chudak would never see the billion credits he had been promised for helping to destroy the *Enterprise*. He hoped Chudak would live long enough to understand that he had been cheated.

Other problems remained. The two human spies had escaped. Sensors indicated that they had neither signaled the *Enterprise* nor transported back aboard her, but so long as they remained loose their knowledge threatened the plan—and several Federation personnel had beamed down into the city, against Verden's expectations. In addition, all of the Vo Gatyn's guards had returned from their search empty-handed—all but one squad, and their sergeant had been found in the woods, stabbed to death.

The desertion perplexed Verden. Like humans, Ferengi, Vulcans and so many other inferior races, the Megarans had evolved from tribal apes. That heritage gave them a strong, instinctive loyalty to their own groups and leaders. The guards had clearly betrayed that loyalty.

Or had they? Their loyalty was an instinct, but it remained the instinct of intelligent minds. Perhaps the guards had not run off on their own; perhaps they had given their loyalty to someone other than Gatyn —or given it to themselves? Sometimes humanoid groups split into smaller groups after a disagreement. And sometimes they could be subverted by a strong and clever leader—such as a starship captain like Picard—

Verden stood up. "Give me a map which charts the path taken by the deserters," he said to Ubinew.

"I obey." Within seconds a sheet of paper materialized in the printer.

Verden took the map and turned toward the exit before training caught up with him. "I believe that the human spies have joined forces with the deserters," he told Ubinew. "I owe you a full explanation of my new plans, but time is short and I must ask you to wait for the explanation."

"You have never betrayed my trust," Ubinew said.

"I thank you for your trust," Verden said. He left

the room and went upstairs into the castle. He strode quickly into the Vo Gatyn's audience chamber, where the Vo conferred over a map with her guard captain. Tattered battle pennants hung on the dark stone walls around them.

The powerless ruler of Megara gave her master a bitter look. "You with your Vo an audience crave?" she asked.

Verden ignored her sarcasm. "I believe your missing guards have joined forces with the Federation spies. One of the spies is a ship-leader, and your lost soldiers may have found him too strong a leader to resist. You will send your guards after them and kill them."

"I will?" she asked in disdain.

Verden turned away from her and thought. Gatyn had a pride to match a Cardassian, and that made using her difficult. Although only a figurehead, she demanded that everyone treat her as though she were the true power on Megara.

Verden looked back to her. "My Vo," he said in a formal voice. "It is my sad duty to say that there may be treachery among some of your forces. I believe your missing guards have given their loyalty to your enemies. At least I can tell you where to locate the traitors."

"Tell," Gatyn said.

Verden spread the map on the table. Gatyn and her guard-captain studied the print. "They a hunter's trail follow," the captain said. "My Vo, to follow them my forces you do command?"

"Follow," Gatyn ordered. "But kill them you may not."

"They must all die!" Verden snapped.

Gatyn glared at him, then looked to the captain once more. "Living prisoners I wish. Your company I will join, so that live prisoners I may see taken."

"Combat is dangerous," Verden said. "You're too valuable for me to risk."

Her gaze turned haughty. "A *tool* I am not, for you the costs and risks to measure. Leave."

Verden strode out of the audience chamber. *My own training betrayed me here,* he thought. Among Cardassians, anyone whose discipline was so weak that he would betray his friends was destroyed. His demand that the traitors be killed had been almost a reflex—and it had made him forget Gatyn's vanity, her wish to feel that she commanded here. She had decided to let the traitors and spies live merely to spite Verden.

Verden closed his eyes as the elevator took him down to the intelligence room. *It does not matter if the spies and traitors live or die,* he thought. *Their capture is the important thing.*

Worf wanted to *move,* to find his captain, to fight his enemies with phaser in one hand and mace in the other. Waiting was torture, and the answers that Anit had given to his questions did not convince the Klingon that fruitful action was imminent.

Data had not been idle, but neither had he spent the past hour in a useful pursuit. His first act had been to read the half-dozen books that Taygar had kept on a shelf. After he had assimilated the texts, Data had described them to Worf as disgustingly violent—a combination of words that disgusted Worf. The android had then drawn Anit into a discussion of pre-Ferengi life on Megara, a display of idle chatter that had further annoyed the Klingon's warrior instincts.

"Traditional Megaran society contained a remarkable division of authority," Data said to Worf, as though sharing an important observation. "Males and females shared economic power. However, diplomacy and warfare were male domains, while females controlled politics and religion."

"This the rat-eyes have attacked," Anit said angrily. "But the will of the Elder Gods? No evil creature this can change." The look he gave Worf suggested he found all outworlders evil.

The alley door opened, and a young girl looked into the dingy room. She spoke rapidly to Anit, who sighed as he got out of his chair. "Soon I return," he promised Worf and Data, and left.

Worf took the chair, and sat with his back to the brick wall as he faced the door. He did not expect Anit to betray him, but Worf did not discount the possibility. Meanwhile, there was another problem. "We are in a *tactical* situation, Commander," Worf told Data. "I do not see how your talk with Anit aided us."

"You had already asked Mr. Anit all questions which seem relevant to our position," Data said. "I therefore took the opportunity to fill in other gaps in my knowledge."

Worf grunted. "Do you have any other gaps to fill?"

Data, as always, took his sarcasm literally. "Yes. I would like your comments on Commander Riker's personal behavior."

Worf felt suspicious. "What of it?"

"Although human, he seeks to emulate Klingonese attitudes," Data said. "As a Klingon, would you describe his emulation as a success?"

Worf's temper rose. "Must you ask such a *personal* question?"

"I must," Data said. "I wish to develop human characteristics in myself, but my efforts have met with minimal success. However, if Commander Riker *has* adapted himself to Klingon standards, I might study his example and use it to find a way to become more human."

Worf mulled that over as he watched the room's

door. As always, Data's wish to become human annoyed him, and at the moment Worf's toleration had dipped to a new low. "I wonder why you seek to become human," he said. "It would seem more *logical* for an android to copy Vulcans."

Data absorbed the barb as though it had been nothing more than a reasonable suggestion. "I find a certain merit in that concept," he said. "I *am* a creature of logic, and my creator programmed me so I would not behave in too human a fashion. However, I believe that when Dr. Soong programmed me he felt a subconscious desire to give me human behavior, and my programming mirrors this desire."

"Instinct," Worf said.

Data nodded. "Whether by evolution or by engineering, we are all molded by the forces which created us."

Worf felt stirred by an odd emotion. He had been orphaned after a Romulan attack on the Klingon colony of Khitomer, and he had been adopted by his human rescuers. The Roshenkos had tried to raise him as a true Klingon, but they had not fully succeeded. In consequence Worf had labored to develop Klingon virtues in himself, even though they sometimes felt alien: the indifference to others' pain, the use of treachery, the joy of seeing a friend die in glorious combat. It had been difficult, but by and large he had succeeded. *And if that is so,* he thought, *it is because I have always had it within me to become fully Klingon—and because I need to do so, to fulfill myself. This need makes Data and myself . . . brothers.*

Worf could not express that aloud. "Do you think you can become human?" he asked gruffly.

"I believe I have the capacity to grow into humanity," Data said. "And I seek to make this transition in the least possible time."

"Unfortunate," Worf said. "Why would you wish to hasten this change?"

Data puzzled over that statement. "Because . . . I find delay . . . undesirable."

"You are impatient," Worf said. "Impatience is a *human* failing."

The android looked intrigued. "Fascinating. Although I cannot correctly describe this as a feeling, it seems I may have developed a human trait without realizing it. I must investigate this when the opportunity arises. Thank you for bringing this to my attention."

"My pleasure," Worf said sarcastically—but, to his surprise, he *did* feel pleasure.

"Riker to Worf," Riker's voice said. "Lieutenant, we may have some information on the captain's location. We're downloading a map projection into your tricorder."

Worf activated his tricorder. The display showed a map of the region north of the castle, including several local cities. There was a wavy line that made a broad arc from the castle. It looped around this city and ended in the woods. The scale said the line was some thirty kilometers long. "Do you have more precise information?" Worf asked.

"No. This is the best Ensign Shrev and Cadet Crusher could do. The captain is probably hidden somewhere along the marked route. Our best guess is that somebody down there is playing a double game."

"Excellent," Worf said, almost purring. There was nothing like a little betrayal to enliven the day. It also pleased him to learn that Crusher had not gone into a sulk after being ordered to return to the ship. By doing his duty the youth helped to earn his way out of the disgrace he had brought upon himself after the disaster at the Academy. It was a pity he lacked a warrior's training; this mission would have given him the perfect chance to earn honor.

Anit returned a moment later, accompanied by two men. "More soon will arrive," he told Worf. "Two handfuls, as promised."

Worf grunted in approval. He assumed that referred to the six-fingered Megaran hand, which would mean twelve more men. A total of eighteen soldiers, counting himself, Data, Anit and his sergeant. That should make a respectable force for this mission. The new men wore gray coveralls, but carried short swords and daggers belted to their waists. They looked at Worf with the expressions of soldiers, and he knew they were sizing him up, either as a potential enemy or a potential leader. Respectable, indeed.

Worf returned their looks, then showed his tricorder map to Anit. "Let us discuss how we will find my captain," he said.

After a few hours Picard would have given a great deal for a Universal Translator. Even so, he and Offenhouse had made progress with Odovil Pardi. The Megaran woman was intelligent and eager to communicate, which aided the process of learning her language.

"It also helps that I know what she wants to talk about," Offenhouse said, when Pardi stepped out of the stone hut for a moment. "Business. Profits. She's a woman after my own heart."

"With a scalpel," Picard said.

Offenhouse grinned. "She *is* a sharp operator, isn't she?"

"I'd call her ruthless," Picard said. "She arranged our abduction—"

"—and her henchman killed his leader," Offenhouse finished. "I know. We can still use her here, once we give the Ferengi the heave-ho."

Odovil reentered the stone hut. She was accompanied by a gust of wind, and the forest odors only heightened Picard's awareness of the hut's fetid air. "More talk," she said. She stayed close to the door, and her nervous eyes gave Picard the impression that she thought the humans might attack her. "Ral'feh, some factories a thing make, I what not know."

"Describe thing," the ambassador said in his pidgin Megaran.

Odovil gestured with her hands. "A metal box it is, more big than this hut. Inside the box, many coils of cable, strange rock, comp'ter, pipes like this—" Her hands made a zigzag pattern in the air.

Picard found something familiar in that description. "This strange rock," he said. "When it touch—" His hands mimed a lightning strike while he imitated the sound of thunder.

"Lightning," Odovil said, and nodded. "When lightning the strange rock hits, it goes—" She flung her arms wide. *"Whoomp!"*

"Dilithium," Picard said. "Mr. Ambassador, she's describing an antimatter generator."

Offenhouse nodded. "Chudak said they were making things like that for him. I wonder—" He switched to his Megaran pidgin. "Odovil, how many factory this box make?"

"This many." She held up both hands and wiggled her fingers five times. "To full production already they go."

"Sixty factories," Picard said. "There aren't that many on Earth. Chudak couldn't possibly hope to sell so many generators."

"I know," Offenhouse said. "And I don't see how his employers could use that many, either. So who could?"

Picard tried to think. Back in the castle—twelve hours ago?—she had described the enormous amounts of tritanium produced by her foundries. "Odovil," he said. "Factory on Megara is, make—" He struggled to describe a phaser coil. Odovil agreed that many factories were producing such items, although she was at a loss to describe their purpose.

Picard knew their purpose. "Odovil, is one place, all make-things bring together?" he asked.

The woman pursed her lips. "Tritanium to five places we send," she said. "And . . . to these places also other things are sent."

Picard nodded. "Up to ship, do Ferengi take things?"

"No," she said. "Things in large buildings are kept, why I do not know."

Things fell into place. "Starships," Picard said. "They're going to build starships here."

"A whole thundering lot of them," Offenhouse said. "And with all those phaser coils—Picard, somebody is arming for war."

I can't put it off forever, Riker thought. "Hail the Ferengi ship," he said.

"Aye, sir." Ensign Anna Novotny, one of Worf's subordinates, stood at the Klingon's usual post. The tall, muscular woman—*A human designed to Klingon specifications,* Riker thought in admiration—opened a channel, and the Daimon Chudak appeared on the bridge's main viewer. To Riker's surprise, the man did not look annoyed to see him.

"All right," Riker began. "Where are Captain Picard and the ambassador?"

"I don't know," Chudak said. "I haven't seen them since last night, at the castle. But let's deal, Riker. Several of *my* crew members are missing. Maybe they were grabbed by the same people, and if that's true, we have a common enemy."

192

"You have nothing *but* enemies," Riker said. "What do you propose to do about this?"

"I propose that we join forces," Chudak said. "Share information, discuss ideas, search the planet."

Riker snorted. "What's your price?"

"No price," the Ferengi said. "My profit is what I get out of this arrangement. That's your profit, too. Let's trust one another."

Hell will freeze first, Riker thought. "Close channel."

Seated at his side, Deanna Troi touched his elbow as a starfield replaced Chudak's image on the screen. "He didn't actually *lie* about anything, but he's hiding something," she said. "It's obvious."

Riker nodded. Deanna couldn't sense Ferengi minds, but she was still a shrewd judge of character. "He acted wrong," he said. "Every Daimon I've seen has been either arrogant or fawning, depending on the situation."

"He tried to appear cooperative," Deanna agreed. "But I'd say he's stalling for time."

Shrev and Wesley Crusher were seated at the helm stations. Now Shrev turned in her seat and faced Riker, her head bowed to focus her antennae on him. "Commander Riker," she said, raising her voice to a near-normal level, "if I interpret the neutrino detector's readings correctly, a starship is entering the Megaran system at bearing seventeen-mark-eight."

Novotny was busy with her own instruments. "I don't have anything, sir," she said. "Weber Five-Twelve is at that bearing. The radiation is saturating the sensors."

"I see," Riker said. That sort of maneuver was practically a Cardassian trademark. He stroked his beard as though he could extract an idea or two from it. *This is like that silly movie I showed Worf,* he reflected. *We face more and more enemies at every turn. Too bad I'm not laughing.* "Counselor, do you suppose Chudak is stalling until this ship arrives?" he asked.

"That seems likely," Deanna said. "I suggest that you press him as hard as you can."

"I will," Riker said. "Novotny, sound red alert. Lock all weapons on the Ferengi ship, then open a channel."

"I didn't mean to press Chudak *that* hard," Deanna said.

Riker smiled tightly. "This gives me a reason to put the *Enterprise* on alert without alarming that Cardassian ship. Chudak!"

The Daimon was back on the viewer. "What is going on?" he demanded. "Why have you—"

"Here's *my* proposition," Riker said. He slipped into the arrogant, commanding slouch of a Klingon captain. *"You* are going to answer all of *my* questions, *now."*

Chudak spluttered. "This is—"

"Chudak, I trust you as far as I can throw you." Riker smiled again, showing his teeth. "Shall we find out how far that is? Now, *dammit,* where was the last place you saw Captain Picard?"

"In the Vo Gatyn's castle!" Chudak snapped.

"Exactly where?" Riker roared, rising to his feet. "Who was he with, was he well, what was happening? I'll have the *truth!"*

Chudak's image vanished from the screen.

Deanna raised an eyebrow. "I could almost sense how scared he was."

Riker chuckled like a Klingon. "His Cardassian masters must want him to keep us occupied," he said. "They won't thank him for botching the job."

Riker noticed that Shrev and Wesley were whispering to one another. He stepped up behind them and cleared his throat. "If Worf heard you two whispering like this," he said, "he'd suspect a conspiracy."

"I would assure him that there is nothing but polite conversation, sir," Shrev said. "We were merely discussing the sensor readings on the Cardassian ship."

"Do you have something?" Riker asked.

"Yes, sir," Wesley said. "From the size of the neutrino flux I'd say that the Cardassian ship has a reactor system even more powerful than ours. That would make it a Liburnian-class warship—one of their largest. It's on course for Megara, and it will arrive in twenty minutes."

Chapter Thirteen

THE MERCENARY BAND moved quickly, and within an hour it was out of the city and deep inside the woods marked on the tricorder map. Data scanned constantly for a human presence. Because humans and Megarans were so similar, he realized that even a small amount of interference would confuse the tricorder; a few centimeters of stone or dirt would blur the readings enough to mask the human parameters. Consequently he expanded the search to locate caves and dwellings.

He found something. "Lieutenant," he said to Worf, "there is a stone building, range three hundred meters, bearing thirty-seven degrees. I detect at least one being who probably is not a Megaran."

"Human?" Worf asked, signaling the band to stop.

"Sensor readings are indeterminate," Data said, "but that would be my . . . best guess. I detect five Megarans in the immediate vicinity. The building is in the center of a clearing some twenty meters in diameter."

"Excellent." Worf conferred with Anit while Data

scanned the area. The tricorder found a small path that branched off from the trail and led to the clearing. That was the only way to approach the building; it would have taken hours to pass through the dense forest underbrush, and Worf did not think it could be done quietly.

"We outnumber them," Worf said.

"Not for long," Anit said. "Crossbows, darts they may use."

"I shall lead," Worf said, drawing his phaser.

Data verified that his own phaser was set on stun, then followed Worf down the path. It was narrow and winding. As the mercenaries neared the clearing, Data held up a hand, halting the group. "There are people on the main trail," he whispered to Worf, holding out his tricorder. "They are moving quickly."

Worf looked at the readings. "More soldiers," he said.

Anit glanced back down the trail. "Cork in a bottle," he whispered in dismay, seeing a trap.

"The situation is not bad," Worf said.

Data realized that Worf was attempting to keep the mercenary in good spirits. The android recalled a phrase which seemed appropriate to that task. "Things have never been better," he stated.

Worf stared at him for a moment, then made an odd grinding, wheezing noise, as though he was having trouble breathing. When he had regained control of his respiration he gestured for Data to follow him.

As they reached the clearing Data saw a small stone hut. Three Megarans squatted on the ground in front of it, warming their hands over a campfire. Two more men strolled around, crossbows in their hands. The similarity of their dress suggested they were soldiers. As Data raised his phaser, one of the men spotted him, took aim and fired his weapon. The bolt missed him, but its impact shattered a tree trunk at his side.

Data stunned the man before he could reload; Worf shot the other crossbow-wielder as he fired. The bolt sailed off into the woods.

The men around the campfire were on their feet, swords in hands. Worf and Data stunned them. Data heard shouts behind him, and knew that the mercenaries were under attack from the rear. "Get the captain!" Worf ordered, and plunged back down the trail. The sounds of combat grew louder.

Data went to the stone building. He opened the door and saw three people inside; Picard and Offenhouse blinked in the morning light while a local woman gaped at Data. "Hello, Captain, Mr. Ambassador," Data said. *"Enterprise,* beam us up."

Transporter room three solidified around Data and the others. Worf stumbled as he materialized; he held the mace above his head. *"No!"* he roared at De Shay. *"Send me back!"*

De Shay stood at his controls, frozen by surprise and indecision. Worf turned to Picard. "Captain! Please!" he said.

Picard nodded. "Quickly."

Looking like a man who knows he is making a terrible mistake, De Shay returned Worf to the surface.

Picard's jaw clenched. "Report," he ordered Data.

"There is only one significant fact to report, sir," Data said, while he, Picard, Offenhouse and the Megaran woman stepped off the transporter stage. "We have found that the Cardassians are conducting a clandestine operation on Megara."

"Understood," Picard said. "Picard to Riker. Number One, Mr. Worf has returned to a battle on the surface. Take an away team and assist him."

"We can't, sir," Riker answered from the bridge. "There's a Cardassian warship entering orbit. We took enough of a risk lowering our shields to beam you back."

The captain hesitated, then nodded as he accepted that. "I'm on my way to the bridge," Picard said. "Mr. Data, see to the ambassador and our guest."

"Yes, sir." As Picard left the transporter room, Data realized that the captain was uncertain of his actions. Data himself was not certain that sending Worf back to Megara had been correct. While Klingon ethics demanded such a move, beaming into the middle of a battle had placed Worf in enormous danger. He would require a few seconds to assess his new situation, and during that pause he would be exposed and vulnerable.

The ambassador was scratching the coarse stubble on his chin. "Cardassians, eh?" he asked Data.

"Yes, sir," Data said. "I have reports from our away teams."

"Good, I'll want to look at them. Oh, yeah—Odovil needs one of those translator gizmos."

"That is an excellent suggestion." Data removed his communicator badge. The Megaran woman stepped back as the android approached her, then made a visible effort to stand her ground. Data pinned the translator to her coverall. "You should be able to understand me now," Data said.

"You I understand," she said, and fingered the badge. "How this works?"

"The Universal Translator works—" Data verged on explaining linguacode theory, neuroinduction techniques and recursive computer processing, then thought better of it. "—quite well," he finished.

The ambassador laughed and clapped Data on the shoulder. "I couldn't have put it any better myself. Let's see those reports now."

* * *

"They're waiting for us to lower our shields," Riker said as Picard studied the tactical display on the bridge's main viewer. The numbers and stylized symbols showed the positions of three starships. The Ferengi vessel held a position only a hundred kilometers from the *Enterprise,* while the Cardassian ship carefully maneuvered to stay in the cover provided by Weber 512; the Cardassian had slowed to sublight speed, and it would be in phaser range in a matter of minutes. Wesley Crusher and Shrev sat at the helm, ready to move the *Enterprise* out of danger. They had listened quietly while Riker had briefed the captain on the situation. "Chudak has been trying to sweet-talk us into standing down from our alert," Riker added.

"He expects us to be destroyed," Deanna Troi said.

"I'm afraid we'll have to disappoint him," Picard said. He noticed that Troi, seated in the chair at his left side, was leaning away from him; the captain decided that his stay in the hut had given him a certain aroma. *A pity I can't take the time to clean up,* Picard thought ruefully, and nodded at the tactical display. "Number One, can you imagine an innocent reason for a Cardassian ship to approach us in this manner?"

"A friendly little ambush, perhaps," Riker said. At last the Cardassian ship came close enough for the optical sensors to scan it despite the background interference. The image on the main viewer reminded Picard of a lance: long and narrow, a shape that exposed the smallest possible area when the ship was making a frontal attack. Its forward end bristled with weaponry. "Captain, their presence here is an act of war," Riker said.

"I'm aware of that, Number One," Picard said. "I'm also aware that a Liburnian-class starship outguns us. But perhaps we can dissuade them. Ensign

Novotny, lock all weapons on to the Cardassians and hail them."

"Channel open, sir," Novotny reported.

"Cardassian warship!" Picard called. "I *assume* that you're here through a slight navigational error. Return to your territory at once."

There was a prolonged silence as the Cardassian ship made its final approach. For a moment Picard could hope that the Cardassians would decide to avoid trouble. Then the bridge lights dimmed and the artificial gravity wavered as phaser beams raked the *Enterprise.* "Return fire!" Picard ordered.

Picard heard the screech of phasers and the hollow roar of photon torpedoes blasting from their tubes. "Shields holding!" Novotny reported. *Enterprise* shuddered from more hits.

"Maintain firing rate," Picard called, and checked the tactical display. "Come to course fifty-two mark eighty, ahead one-half impulse." *Enterprise* was more maneuverable than her attacker, and that advantage might save her now. A Liburnian's long, thin shape made it clumsy, and the bulk of its weapons were concentrated in its bow. A Liburnian could not concentrate all of its firepower on its flanks.

On the tactical display, the Ferengi ship turned and began to accelerate away from the battle. As Picard watched, a torpedo spread leaped from the Cardassian ship and speared into the Ferengi vessel. As it slowly pitched over, Picard saw that its warp drive had been crippled. It could not escape.

With the Ferengi ship crippled, the Cardassians returned their full attention to the *Enterprise.* The Liburnian's attack weakened as the Federation ship maneuvered around the attacker, but the battering continued at an intolerable level. "We're losing the port shields," Novotny shouted over the din.

Wesley had news of his own. "Sir, the Ferengi are hailing the Cardassians—" he began.

Novotny interrupted him. "Cardassian shields are dropping," she said. "Down to fifty percent . . . ten percent . . . they're firming up, back to twenty percent . . ."

The shields never recovered, and the image on the main viewer told the story. The *Enterprise's* phasers sliced through the faltering shields, and raw plasma vented into space as photon torpedoes slammed into its engineering section, demolishing reactors and leaving the ship powerless. A sputtering pink glow around the sensor arrays spoke of the fading strength of the ship's emergency power supply.

"Cease fire," Picard ordered. He rose from his chair and took two steps toward the main screen, a perplexed look on his face. How could the Cardassian shields have failed so quickly? "What happened?"

"The Ferengi, sir," Wesley said. "They transmitted a computer worm into the Cardassian comm system. It brought their computers down for a few seconds, before their countermeasures could erase it."

Saved by the Ferengi, Picard thought, shaking his head. He wondered if Chudak would present him with a bill for his services.

On the main viewer the lance-shaped Liburnian tumbled slowly, revealing blackened gouges in its hull. Metal glowed white-hot inside the gaping holes, and plumes of gas sprayed from fissures in the metal skin. The damage to the Ferengi ship appeared less dramatic, but it was equally fatal. The ship's warp drive had become a red-hot pit, and as Picard watched, sequential explosions rippled down the ship's port side, tearing open the cargo holds.

Murder, Picard thought in disgust, suddenly understanding the Cardassian plan. Had it worked, it would have seemed as if the *Enterprise* and the Ferengi had destroyed one another . . . and the Ferengi would have taken their secrets to the grave. The Cardassians might have managed to conceal their own presence here.

Shrev scanned the Cardassian ship. "All of their weapons are out, sir," she reported, in what was for her a virtual shout. "They retain emergency power and one impulse engine. I read thirty-one survivors."

"Stand by to pick them up," Picard said. "Open a channel—"

On the viewer, the tumbling Liburnian stabilized itself and began to accelerate toward the *Enterprise*. "Captain," Wesley said, "they've activated their self-destruct system. Estimate twenty seconds to detonation."

Picard nodded curtly. "Ensign Novotny, put a tractor beam on the Cardassian ship," he ordered. "Helm, come to course eight-six mark twelve, ahead warp factor two."

"Captain, a Cardassian self-destruct system—" Riker began as the *Enterprise* maneuvered.

"—is equivalent to a hundred-gigaton fusion bomb," Picard finished. The Federation had paid dearly for its knowledge of Cardassian suicide bombs; several ships had been destroyed by them while attempting to rescue the survivors of defeated Cardassian warships. "If it detonates this close to Megara, the blast and radiation will disrupt the atmosphere and magnetosphere. That will render Megara uninhabitable. We need to draw that ship away from the planet."

"Understood," Riker said grimly. "Captain, I recommend that we disengage and go to warp eight at five seconds before detonation. That will take us clear of the explosion and still protect Megara."

"Make it so," Picard said. *And hope we're right about the time factor,* he thought. The Cardassian ship would destroy itself by building up an overload in its reactors. Under ordinary circumstances that was a straightforward catastrophe, but combat damage would only make the reactors more likely to explode without warning.

At eight times the speed of light, they saw Megara swiftly shrink from a world to a small disk on the main viewer. *Enterprise's* engines labored as they towed the massive derelict, but the Cardassian ship remained firmly caught in the tractor beam. "Estimate five seconds to detonation," Wesley reported.

"Disengage tractor beam," Riker ordered. "Ahead warp eight." The tractor beam cut loose, and the wrecked ship vanished astern as the *Enterprise* accelerated away from it. The Federation ship was as far from its attacker as the moon is from the Earth when the Cardassian vessel exploded.

The emergency blowers were losing their battle to clear the smoke from the bridge. Chudak's leg throbbed from where he had been slammed to the deck, but nothing felt broken. The Daimon picked himself up and limped to the helm. Oshal sat at the controls, dead, the top of his skull sheared away. Chudak pushed the blank-eyed corpse out of the seat and sat down.

His ship was dead. Weapons out, shields inoperative, life support on emergency power . . . emergency power itself at thirty-one percent and falling. Warp drive down. Artificial gravity down to fifteen percent. Fires out of control in the shuttle dock and cargo holds. No response from engineering.

Chudak saw an image on the central viewscreen: the Cardassian ship, badly damaged but wallowing toward the *Enterprise* on impulse power, still game for a fight.

At least they're ignoring us now, Chudak thought.

He had always known that the Cardassians might betray him someday; they double-crossed people as enthusiastically as the Romulans did. Warlike idiots that they were, they could not imagine that a simple, peace-loving merchant would prepare to meet treachery with treachery. The software weapons he had acquired from an Orion trader had served their purpose. Survival was always profitable.

Nyenyor staggered to Chudak's side. "Daimon," he gasped in a voice thickened by shock, "the Cardassians . . . sensors say they have . . . initiated self-destruct."

"Debt!" Chudak snarled. There went any chance of salvaging his ship; the Cardassian would glimmer out of existence as a small star, destroying everything nearby. "Abandon ship," Chudak ordered.

Portals slid open in the deck and bulkheads, and survivors of the bridge crew climbed into the emergency teleports. Chudak and Nyenyor picked up a wounded man and carried him into a chamber. The dirt-simple controls said that the emergency battery had a full charge. Chudak pulled the survival kit from its container, then yanked the power handle.

The teleport set the three men down in the middle of a Megaran forest. Chudak looked at his two companions and saw their injuries. Nyenyor's left arm was a mess of shredded skin and violet blood. The other man had jagged metal shards poking out of his chest and belly.

Chudak opened the kit and got out the medical tools. "The others shouldn't be too far away," he said as he set to work on Nyenyor's arm. "We'll be fine once we link up."

"Yes, Daimon," Nyenyor said without conviction. With his uninjured arm, he drew the communicator from the kit and switched it on. Despite his best efforts, he received no answer to his calls.

My crew could be scattered all over the place, Chudak realized. Emergency teleports weren't fussy about where they sent people; they locked on to safe spots at random.

Something snapped in the woods, as if a careless foot had trod on a dry twig. Chudak looked around at the trees and brush, and heard a second snap, followed by a third.

Natives, he thought, seeing the raw fear on Nyenyor's face. Chudak reached into the emergency kit and pulled out its phaser. Its power cell held enough charge for five shots. Chudak searched the kit for spare cells but found none. Five shots it was, then . . . against a world of vengeful barbarians.

The sounds drew closer in the lonely forest.

Worf's head hurt. Something had bashed him over the head as he materialized, and when he awoke it was to find his hands bound behind his back. He, Anit and three other mercenaries were being marched back toward Gatyn's castle. A dozen of Gatyn's soldiers had survived the fight, but several were wounded and all seemed worn out by a forced march. One man carried Worf's equipment; he puzzled over the tricorder as he followed the trail. He had tucked the phaser into his belt.

Worf tested his bonds and decided he could break them when he wished. He began to edge closer to the man with his equipment. That would take a while; he could not risk being too obvious.

Anit stumbled closer to Worf. His one hand was roped to his waist. "Back you came," he said in disbelief.

"I did." Worf tried not to bridle at the man's tone. Anit had come to expect nothing but dishonor from outworlders.

He did not seem impressed by Worf's action. "A fool you are," he said. "Kill you they shall."

Worf grunted. "The company is honorable—"

Light filled the sky; grew brighter. The tree branches above the trail cast sharp shadows on the forest floor. Worf squeezed his eyes shut and ducked his head against the glare. The light grew brighter still, and he could *see* through his eyelids and nictitating membranes. Frightened cries filled the air around him. A blinded man staggered into the Klingon and fell with a thud. *A ship has died,* Worf thought, feeling the intense glare on his back.

The light faded. Worf strained his arms and snapped the cord around his wrists. He raised his face to the sky and howled at the dying glare, warning all in the afterlife to beware; the souls of warriors were coming. *Cardassian warriors,* he thought. *My son lives. I feel it!* Enterprise *was not destroyed. Alexander* must *live!*

His eyesight blurred by the glare, Worf pushed toward the man who had his equipment. The blinded soldier clutched a tree, paralyzed by fear. Worf searched him, flinging aside a knife and worthless baubles until he found his communicator badge. "Worf to *Enterprise,*" he bellowed. "Answer, you tribble-loving *taHgeg!*"

"Good to hear you, too, Mr. Worf." Radiation static roughened Picard's voice, but the captain sounded amused. Filled with relief, Worf did not feel bothered by Picard's tone. "Report your status."

Worf regained his composure. He took his phaser from the soldier. "I have captured the Vo Gatyn and her soldiers," he said. "Medical assistance will be required."

"We'll have a medical team on the way shortly," Picard said. *"Enterprise* is undamaged, but the Cardassian and Ferengi ships have been destroyed. Survivors may have beamed into your area."

"I shall capture any I see," Worf promised. He smiled at the sky. *My son lives,* he thought.

Picard closed the channel, and Worf walked over to Anit. "Now both eyes I have lost," he said bleakly, as Worf untied his one hand from his waist.

"You will see again," Worf said. He gave the man's shoulder a reassuring squeeze. "Have no fear."

Radiation flooded the base's sensors, but enough data filtered through to reveal the extent of the disaster. *Fatal Arrow* was destroyed, along with the Ferengi ship—and the Federation vessel was unscathed. It would not be long before the humans came to Gatyn's castle and probed its secrets. That might give them the means to defeat the plan, if they had not done so already.

Verden sat in the intelligence room and studied his orders. The men who had devised this project had known that Federation interference was a possibility, and they had taken that into account. The orders filed in his electronic book suggested ways to salvage the plan even now. The orders were imaginative and filled the leader with admiration. It could be done. He summoned his team.

"We have not lost," Verden told his men as they joined him. "Not while we live. We are superior to our enemies. We shall defeat them."

"You have a plan?" Ubinew asked.

"I do," Verden said. "Prepare to evacuate. We will go to our outpost in Metari Leeg."

"The shipyard," Ubinew noted. He hesitated. "Sir, we have fifteen shipyards on Megara. Would it not be better to occupy a more distant yard?"

"Yes," Verden said. "Unfortunately, the teleport limits our choices. The farther we transport, the more power we must use, and the greater the chance that we will be detected. Metari Leeg is closest to us, and minimizes that chance. Now set the coordinates for Metari Leeg."

"I obey," Ubinew said, and sat down at a control station.

Verden and the rest of his unit went to the arsenal, where they strapped on weapons belts. A moment later Ubinew joined them and armed himself. "The coordinates are set," he told Verden as he wrapped himself in an alt-robe. "I have found a cave outside Metari Leeg. We can transport into it without attracting the attention of the *Enterprise's* sensors, or of the natives. I have already transported emergency supplies into the cave."

"Excellent," Verden said. He felt proud to have such a follower. "You obey orders with imagination. I have one more order. If the Federation captures the Vo Gatyn, she will keep no secrets from them."

"She does not know the plan," Ubinew said.

"True, but she is observant. You must find her and kill her."

"I obey," Ubinew said at once. Then he looked thoughtful. "She and her troops will still be in the forest. Finding them may not be easy, especially if they scatter. I will require two men to aid me."

Verden nodded. "Choose your men. Do not allow yourself to be captured."

"I obey," Ubinew said without hesitation. He gestured to two men and took them away. A moment later Verden heard the transporter hum.

Verden led the rest of his men to the transporter. Before he stepped onto the stage he paused to arm the base's self-destruct unit. It was far smaller than the one that had taken care of the *Fatal Arrow,* but it was powerful enough for its job. The humans would find nothing here but a glowing crater.

A pity I cannot leave it as a booby trap, he thought as he crowded onto the transporter stage with his men. It would have pleased him to kill a few humans as they entered the base . . . but booby traps were unreliable, and humans might have defused such a device. No, it was better to make sure that the base and its secrets were destroyed.

The transporter surged and placed the Cardassians inside a dank, reeking cave. A native carnivore snarled to life as it sensed intruders in its home. Almost offhandedly, Verden shot it as it jumped at him. The creature tumbled to the cave's muddy floor and lay still, its lips still pulled back to bare its fangs.

Verden looked at his men. "We will split into small groups and enter Metari Leeg separately. We will meet at the spaceport."

"What are we to do there?" Hrakin asked.

"Regroup and blend in," Verden said. "There are several ships in Metari Leeg which are ready for flight. We shall see to it that the natives use them as we planned. They are a cocked pistol with a hair trigger; it will not take much to set them off."

"And strike the Federation in the heart," Bwolst said.

Hrakin saw further than the hope of victory. "The Federation will interfere," he said.

"That is possible," Verden agreed. "But if they send agents to Metari Leeg, we will kill them."

The Cardassian leader assured himself that the plan could still succeed. The chances were poor that the Federation would turn its back on Megara—but their bizarre concept of morality would keep them from destroying Megara to protect themselves. And while they dithered, he could launch the Megarans onto the proper course. Give these people one taste of the easy wealth piracy could bring, and there would be no stopping them.

Verden found himself looking at the cave beast he had killed. It had been a solitary creature, proud and independent, in many ways like a Cardassian. *Yet not too much like us,* he thought. It had attacked without thought, and it had died for that. It had not known how to make combat serve its needs, to create by destroying.

Light glared in the cave's mouth as the castle blew up.

Chapter Fourteen

A FEW SECONDS at warp eight had flicked the *Enterprise* halfway across the Megaran system, and the starship was still maneuvering back toward a standard orbit around the planet. Wesley had gone to the science officer's station to scan the planet. There was a lot of radiation from the Cardassian ship's explosion, but the readings looked good. "Megara is all right, Captain," he reported. "There's no damage to the atmosphere, and the magnetosphere has stabilized. The radiation levels are high throughout the inner system, but they're dropping."

"Excellent," Picard said. Wesley saw him smile slightly, but he could not tell if the captain was happy or relieved that his gamble had succeeded. "When will it be safe to use the transporter?"

"Not for another hour, sir," Wesley said.

"That could be a problem," Riker said to Picard. "There are a lot of Ferengi down there, not to mention the Cardassians. I don't like leaving Worf alone in a spot like that."

"I'm certain that Mr. Worf won't hurt them too badly," Picard said thoughtfully. "Mr. Crusher, can you locate any Ferengi or Cardassians near Lieutenant Worf's position?"

Wesley shook his head over the display. "No, sir. There's too much radiation for a high-resolution scan. We'll have to get closer to Megara—" He stopped as the readings surged on his instruments. "Captain, there's been an explosion at the Vo Gatyn's castle."

"That's where the Cardassians had their base," Riker said. "How big was the explosion?"

"Less than a kiloton, sir," Wesley said. The numbers on the display made the situation obvious. "It's a simple antimatter explosion. There's no residual radiation or fallout."

"We can be grateful for small favors," Riker said. Unlike fission and fusion bombs, antimatter weapons did not leave any lingering radiation. There would have been a swift pulse of heat and gamma radiation, and then nothing but a charred crater.

"I cannot imagine a smaller favor," Picard said. "Mr. Crusher, scan the area around the castle for survivors. There are bound to be injuries; inform the chief medical officer when you find them, so she can plan relief activities."

The radiation from the destroyed ships still fogged the sensors, but as the *Enterprise* drew closer to Megara Wesley began to get some reliable data. He barely noticed when Ambassador Offenhouse called the captain away from the bridge; he was too wrapped up in the intricate problem of winnowing data from the haze of radiation surrounding Megara. Wesley located fifty or so Megarans within a five-kilometer radius of the castle, although the data wasn't good enough to tell him if they had been injured in the blast. He spotted several clusters of Ferengi, and as he widened the search area he found Worf's distinctive trace in the readings.

A certain absence struck him at once. "No Cardassians," he said quietly.

"How's that, Mr. Crusher?" Riker asked.

"I can't find any Cardassians, sir," Wesley said, looking up from the display. "Even with all the interference, they should stick out like a sore thumb, but they don't show."

"Perhaps they were all in their base when it blew up," Counselor Troi suggested. "Suicide would let them avoid capture."

"And keep us from interrogating them," Riker said. He shook his head. "I don't believe it. It's too unlikely that all of them would be in the base when it blew up. Besides, Cardassians are warriors. They'd go down fighting."

"If I may comment," Shrev said quietly, "they could have a hiding place down there, a second base."

"My thoughts exactly," Riker said. "Keep searching."

Data had been in the conference room during the battle, and in his own way he was glad to have missed the engagement. This had given him the chance to observe the ambassador and Odovil Pardi. The Megaran woman had seemed distressed by the dramatic changes in artificial gravity and lighting, but not unduly so; considering that this was her first experience with spaceflight, much less space combat, Data found her poise quite impressive.

Ralph Offenhouse's reaction perplexed him. The man had looked annoyed by the battle, as if it were a mere nuisance. He had studied the reports made by the away teams, and while phaser blasts rocked the ship he had asked Data to expand upon his observations of the counterfeit money. All in all, the most appropriate word for his behavior might have been "monomaniacal."

Offenhouse summoned Picard to the conference room a half-hour after the battle. "Pull up a chair, Picard," Offenhouse said as he entered the room. "Are you done slamming us around?"

"For the moment," Picard said, sitting down at the table. His tone suggested that he found the ambassador's attitude inoffensive, perhaps even amusing. "Incidentally, we won."

"That would explain why we're still alive," Offenhouse said. "But I've got a hunch that our problems are just starting on Megara. Our tourists dug up a real mystery down there."

"This sounds promising," Picard said. He idly rubbed at a soiled spot on his uniform sleeve. The captain was a fastidious man, and Data believed he was unhappy that he had not had the chance to clean up after last night. "What's the mystery?"

"It's just that nothing makes sense," Offenhouse said. "At first glance, it looks like the Cardassians hired the Ferengi to turn Megara into an industrial world with a lot of shipyards."

"To build ships for the Cardassian fleet," Picard concluded. "I see. For a fifty-billion-credit investment, the Cardassians get a fleet and base worth trillions. And Megara would make an excellent jumping-off point for an assault into the Federation. Our border is lightly defended here. All the Cardassians have to do is to bring in people to fly the ships . . . no."

"You see the difficulty with that theory, Captain," Data said. "The Cardassians would have to bring tens of thousands of personnel to Megara. It is improbable that they could hide the movement of such a large number of soldiers."

"Perhaps to their world the ships they would take," Odovil suggested.

"Perhaps—no," Picard said, shaking his head. "We would spot such ship movements. Furthermore, that does not explain why they're building them so close to the Federation."

Offenhouse nodded. "Megara's strategic location must be the key to what's happening here. But there're other mysteries. One is the way the Ferengi have bungled with Megaran society. You'd think they want an efficient industrial organization here, but everything they've done undercuts that. Take the poverty. No matter how hard a Megaran works, he can't get ahead. That kills initiative and encourages corruption."

"Because people see that honest work is inadequate to their survival?" Data asked. Corruption was a human failing that had always eluded his understanding, and he was glad for any insight into it. "Perhaps this explains the widespread occurrence of counterfeiting."

"Printing funny money is easier than earning the real thing," Offenhouse agreed. "And poverty gives people a good reason to take bribes—"

"Lucky for you that is," Odovil said. "A corporal I bribed, so that you to me he would bring. If he the bribe had refused, you to the rat-eyes he would have given. Dead you would be."

The ambassador nodded as though her twisted syntax made perfect sense to him. "And that corporal knifed a man to earn his bribe," he said. "Life doesn't mean much on Megara—"

"Much it means," Odovil said uneasily. As she tapped her fingers on the tabletop, Data noted that her nails appeared ragged, as though she chewed them. This suggested a nervous personality. "But many lives the rat-eyes destroy," Odovil continued.

"The Ferengi have been doing something clever here," Offenhouse told Picard. "A Megaran can't get a job without a work permit. When a Megaran displeases the little monsters, they make his boss take away his permit. That's nastier than an execution, because it forces the victims to turn to crime or take degrading jobs, *and* it forces the boss to participate in the brutality, *and* it shows other people the prolonged suffering of anyone who crosses the Ferengi."

"That seems excessive, even for the Ferengi," Picard said. "What's more, it's wasteful. These outcasts become a drag on society. Such waste is not typical of the Ferengi."

"There is an error in your logic, sir," Data said in a regretful tone. "While the Ferengi have carried out these actions, they are done at the behest of the Cardassians. We must assume that the Cardassians find these actions productive."

"It's hard to see a purpose," Picard said.

"I agree, sir," Data said. "Cadet Crusher remarked that the Ferengi appeared to be destroying the Megaran culture. It does seem a pointless act."

"As pointless as the Prophet," Offenhouse said to Picard. "Someone has been using a holographic projector. A device that creates images out of pure light," he explained to Odovil.

"About holographs I know, Ral'feh," she said mildly. "And one of these the Prophet Against the Dark is?"

"That is correct," Data said.

"So a rat-eye fraud the Prophet is," Odovil said to herself. "Surprised I am not. Always wrong her words are."

"It is not surprising that the Prophet's operators would have trouble with the grammar of the Ulathic language," Data said. "While pleasing to the ear, the correct placement of words is difficult for non-native speakers."

Odovil looked impatient. "Of jumbled words I do not speak," she said. *"Evil* the Prophet is. To her once I listened, and hate she praised. In such a way no true priestess would speak—yet people to her listen, when to hate outworlders she commands. *All* outworlders," she added, in a wondering tone which told Data she had just noticed something odd, "not just rat-eyes."

"Teaching the Megarans to hate aliens seems insane," Picard said. "How could anyone expect them to supply starships to their enemies? The situation on Megara would be so unstable that they wouldn't make a reliable source."

"There's more," Offenhouse said. "The Ferengi pay the Megarans in scrip, paper money that isn't backed up by any intrinsic value. You can buy food and clothing with it, but it has nothing to do with the industrial economy. Just the same, the Ferengi take a lot of it back as taxes."

"Taxes?" Picard looked thoughtful. "As I recall from history, heavy taxes often helped to provoke revolutions. That would only add to the instability here."

Data listened to the discussion with less than one percent of his information-processing capacity. He devoted the rest of his attention to an intriguing perspective: destruction could be the first step in a process of replacement. The process on Megara seemed baffling only because it was incomplete. Given the parameters, could he define the process and predict its outcome?

He could. "Captain," he said, "I have arrived at a hypothesis which I desire to explore."

Odovil looked puzzled. "Always like this he speaks, Ral'feh?" she asked Offenhouse.

"He needs subtitles." Offenhouse rested an elbow

on the conference table and cupped his chin in his palm. "What have you got, Data?"

"I require the answer to one question," Data said. "Miss Pardi, do you know if the Ferengi planned to train any Megarans to fly in space?"

"Of this a rumor I heard," Odovil said. Data noted that her pulse and respiration increased, while both hands clenched into fists. He found it curious that she would appear more frightened now than she had during the battle. "A school they have built in Metari Leeg, about starships people to teach."

"This fits my hypothesis," Data said, looking to Picard. "Captain, the Cardassians would find it useful to have a hostile, spacefaring world here, to threaten the Federation. To that end, I believe they are *creating* such a society on Megara."

"You're calling this an example of social engineering?" Picard asked.

"Yes, sir," Data said. "The first step was to destroy the old culture, which cleared the ground for the construction of a new society. As with individuals, societies are shaped by what they see and experience, and conditions have been arranged so that Megarans know nothing but the law of the jungle. It is a well-established principle that constant exposure to violence and brutality causes most people to become brutal and violent.

"I believe the most important piece of evidence in favor of my hypothesis is the holographic prophet. This entity serves no function except to sanction hatred of aliens. In addition, someone has been supplying Megaran children with pornographic novels which glorify war and robbery. This is useful only if one assumes the Cardassians wish to instill xenophobia in the Megarans. Xenophobia is useful only in a warlike society.

"The precise aim remains unclear," Data continued. "Perhaps the Megarans are meant to become conquerors. A more limited goal of piracy would be equally useful to the Cardassians. In either case, it would be necessary to give the Megarans the ability to construct and fly their own starships. This has now been done."

For a long moment the only sound in the conference room was the hiss of the ventilators. The silence of the three humans made Data wonder if his suggestion was foolish. His theory depended on an analysis of emotional factors and responses, and he knew he had only a sketchy understanding of such matters.

"I dunno," Offenhouse said at last. "If the Cardassians are trying to make the Megarans hate all aliens, how could the Cardassians use them as allies?"

"It does seem paradoxical," Picard said. Data heard a rising note of interest in his voice. "But perhaps they do not need a formal alliance. If a hostile force arose on Megara, the Federation would be required to respond to it, whether or not it had a treaty with the Cardassians. We would have to reinforce our border and station warships here."

"Which would tie up some of our forces," Offenhouse said slowly. "We wouldn't be able to use them against the Cardassians when they attack. That would give the Cardassians an advantage, kinda like taking a rook off a chessboard before a game starts."

Odovil's face had clouded. "My people as weapons they use?"

"That's how it looks," Offenhouse told her. He rubbed at his eyes, and Data noticed the fatigue on his face and in the slump of his shoulders. "It's the same sort of crap the superpowers used to pull back in the Cold War. We'd give a small country a gazillion dollars' worth of weapons and turn 'em loose. Cuba, Libya, Iran, contras, mujahideen, Palestinians—it was a great way to wage war. You could attack somebody, or threaten their interests, and not put your own country at risk."

"And the Cardassians have expanded upon this concept," Picard said, leaning back in his chair. "They've gambled a great deal on this operation—but it seems they've lost this wager."

"Also my world has lost," Odovil said bitterly. She stood up and walked over to the ready room's window. She looked down on the cloudy expanse of her homeworld. Radiation-induced aurorae flickered over the crescent of night at the horizon as though a cold fire were slowly consuming the world. "Into monsters we are made, for the good of others to fight and die."

"I know," Offenhouse said. He brushed at a smear of dried mud on his jacket. "We've stopped the Cardassians before they could pull it off, but the mess they left down there stinks worse than me and Picard put together. Straightening it out—" Offenhouse fought down a yawn. "Odovil, right now we could all use a meal, a bath and sleep. Picard, could you get Counselor Troi to fix up a cabin for the lady?"

The meeting ended then, and Data left the conference room for the bridge. Although both the captain and the ambassador had accepted his hypothesis as correct, Data felt dissatisfied with his work. Somehow his theory did not seem complete, as if he had overlooked a factor.

Of course. Megara was close to the Federation border, and the Cardassians must have known that discovery of this project was always a possibility. They would have planned for that eventuality, and while Data could not yet deduce their plans, he knew they could only work to the detriment of the Federation.

* * *

Geordi was halfway buried in the access hole as he worked on the shield generator. "Okay, Al, give me the readings on the polyphase coupler," he said.

Alexander looked at the readout on the unit he held. "Five-point-four . . . four-point-six . . . four-point-one . . ." The numbers dropped steadily as Geordi adjusted the shield generator. "Zero-point-zero," Alexander said at last. "It's in phase now."

"Great." Geordi squirmed out of the access hole and sat on the crawlway decking. "La Forge to bridge. The forward shield is back at one hundred percent now."

"Is everything fixed now?" Alexander asked, as Geordi closed the hole's cover plate.

Geordi nodded. "Thanks for lending a hand, Al. You helped me get everything done faster."

"I like doing this," Alexander said. He knew that Geordi hadn't really needed his help; the engineer had wanted to keep him busy so he wouldn't worry about his father. On the other hand, Geordi had let him do some real work on the ship's systems, as if he were a trainee instead of a nuisance. That was something he liked about the engineer. Most adults seemed annoyed by kids, as if they were a life-form that hadn't quite evolved intelligence, but Geordi always took him seriously.

Alexander watched him put his tools back into his repair kit. "Geordi? Why does my father do all these crazy Klingon things?"

Geordi seemed unsurprised by the question. "You mean, like beaming back into a fight? A lot of humans would do that, too, for their friends."

Alexander shook his head. "Humans would stop to think of a better way to help their friends. Father just charged in there."

"Well . . ." Geordi sat down and rested his back

against the bulkhead. "I think he's trying to prove that he's really a Klingon."

"Why would he have to do that?" Alexander asked. "He *is* a Klingon."

"I mean he's trying to prove it to himself," Geordi said. "He was raised by humans, and sometimes he must feel confused about what he is."

"Oh." Alexander could understand that. Most of the time he wasn't sure whether he was human or Klingon, and his emotions often grappled like a pair of Triskelion gladiators. Even now, when he *knew* he had to talk about his problems, he still felt like he should go off by himself and brood. At least the need to talk was winning out now. "I guess that's why he wants me to act like a Klingon. He can't stand to see a Klingon act human."

Geordi rubbed his chin thoughtfully. "I don't think that's it, Al," he said. "I know he feels mixed up sometimes because of how he was raised. Maybe he thinks that if he raises you like a Klingon, you'll have an easier time than he did."

Alexander thought that over. "It won't work," he said. "I'm part human."

"I know," Geordi said. "I guess he can give you a hard time over it."

"No," Alexander said quickly. "Well, not on purpose. He's just got this way of acting when I do anything too human . . . like he's trying real hard not to let it upset him. He doesn't even know he does it. Counselor Troi's talked with us about it, but . . ." He shrugged, unsure of just what to say.

"But she can't help as much as you'd like," Geordi said. "I guess it isn't easy for Klingons to take emotional advice."

"What do you mean?" Alexander bristled. "We can take it when we have to."

"I know," Geordi said. "Maybe the trick is to get your dad to take it without knowing he's taking it."

Alexander felt blank. "Huh?"

"Strategy," Geordi said. "When one approach doesn't work, try something else. You've been acting human around him. Maybe you should try acting Klingonese. *Really* Klingonese."

"You mean, overdo it?" Alexander asked.

Geordi nodded. "It won't seem right, so maybe that'll show him it's okay for you to act part-human."

Alexander thought it over. It might take a while for that to work . . . but it could be fun. He'd have to check the computer library and see how a Klingon kid was supposed to act—and that might give him some ideas. "Thanks, Geordi," he said as they stood up. "You know, for a human, you really know a lot about strategy."

Geordi chuckled as he picked up his toolbox. "Thank your dad for that. He's a good influence."

"I'll say this one more time," Beverly Crusher told the people gathered in transporter room three. Wesley was among them, adjusting the medical kit belted to his waist. "None of you are doctors, so don't try anything fancy. When you find an injured person, just stabilize them and call for help. Okay, De Shay, they're all yours."

The relief team beamed down in groups of six. *I'll have my work cut out for me in an hour,* Beverly thought as she hefted her field kit. As the radiation from the battle cleared, the ship's sensors had located over a hundred injured people in the area around the destroyed castle. She knew that many of them would need surgery to survive. The explosion would have insulted their bodies with radiation, heat and blast effects—burns, fractures, shock, marrow damage, retinal scarring and Hiroshima eyes, weakened immune systems—plus surprises, of course; battles always seemed to create novel kinds of hurts—

One problem at a time, Bev, the doctor thought as she stepped onto the transporter stage. That was the key to handling a disaster: concentrate on the problem in front of you, and don't think about the scale of the problem. Relief workers who tried to think about the big picture usually became emotionally overwhelmed.

She beamed down onto a forest trail. Worf stood two meters from her, and a number of Megarans sat on the ground. Beverly scanned Worf at once with her tricorder, although his most serious injury was obvious to the naked eye. Several of his scalp ridges had been crushed, and drying violet blood clotted the flesh. Other than that he was fine; the armorlike Klingon skull had done an admirable job of protecting his brain from damage. "I'll have you fixed up in no time," the doctor promised.

"The others are more severely injured," Worf said as she worked on his head. "My injury is minor."

"Sure, it's just a head wound," Beverly said in annoyance. She started to mend his injury with a protoplaser. "Hold *still,* Lieutenant. If you want to enjoy pain, do it while you're off-duty." She looked around as he growled at the joke. "What happened to the others?" she asked.

"They were flash-blinded," he said.

"That should be a temporary condition," Beverly said. She had a sudden, shuddering thought that half the planet might have been blinded—no, haze and dust in the atmosphere would have filtered out much of the light from the explosion, even under cloudless skies. Even so, many people would have had the bad luck to have been looking straight at the Cardassian ship when it blew up, barely a million kilometers from Megara. She might have to treat thousands of blinded people—

One thing at a time, she reminded herself. "It looks like some of these people have other injuries," she said.

"I met them with enthusiasm," Worf rumbled. "You must tend to the one-armed man first. He is a valuable ally."

"Whatever you say." She finished with Worf's scalp and gave him a final scan with her tricorder. "You're fine now, Lieutenant. Just stay off your head for a few days."

Beverly moved on to treat the nearest person on the trail, the man with one arm and one eye. "You must be Kardel Anit," she said as she scanned him. The tricorder found some inflammation in his retina and elevated pressure in the vitreous humor, along with several dietary deficiencies. "My son Wesley mentioned meeting you yesterday."

"Him I remember," Anit said. "He much gold spent."

The man sounded tense. *Xenophobia,* Beverly guessed, *plus the shock of going blind.* "Your sight should return to normal in a moment," she said as she gave him an injection. "Replacing your arm and other eye will have to wait awhile." She gave him a second injection to make up for his lack of assorted minerals and vitamins.

"'Replacing'?" Anit repeated. "Understand this I do not."

"We can probably restore what you've lost," she said. "But it's going to be a few days before I can start on that."

Anit looked impatient, as though he felt she had misunderstood him. *"Why* this you would do?"

"Why not?" she replied, and then recalled some of the horror stories Wesley had told her about Megara last night. The man must have thought there would be strings attached to the offer. "Worf can explain it better than I can," she said.

Worf, however, was not ready to offer explanations. As Beverly approached her next patient, she noticed that the Klingon had dropped into a crouch, his phaser in his hand as he peered into the woods around the trail. The doctor was about to say something when a pair of phaser beams lanced out of the woods. They struck two of the blinded men sitting on the trail; their bodies exploded as the high-intensity beams tore into them.

"Down!" Beverly shouted. "Everyone down!" She heard Worf crash off into the woods as she flattened herself against the dirt trail. She heard frightened cries from the men around her; if there was anything worse than being in a battle, she thought grimly, it was to be blind and helpless during an attack. *"Enterprise,"* she called, "send down a security detail!"

Beverly drew her phaser, checked its stun setting and looked around. The blasts had touched off several small fires in the foliage, but over the crackle of flames she heard other noises. Lying flat on the ground, she could see almost nothing. She didn't mind. She wasn't about to draw attention—and a shot, perhaps—by standing up for a look.

She heard the whine of phaser shots, and then a Megaran stumbled onto the trail from among the trees. When Beverly saw him she hesitated until she saw the phaser in his hand. She stunned him and felt grim satisfaction as he dropped. *That'll teach you to kill* my *patients, you son of a bitch,* she thought.

A second Megaran charged out of the woods,

stopped on the trail and looked at the stunned man. He killed the man before Beverly could stun him, and then Worf's phaser beam caught him and sent him sprawling.

Worf stepped onto the trail as a security team materialized. Beverly joined them around the fallen man. Worf was already busy stripping the man of weapons and other equipment. "He's a Cardassian," she said as she scanned him. "He isn't hurt."

"Regrettable," Worf said, and gestured to one of his ensigns. "Take him back to the ship and place him in a security cell. The rest of you will form a defensive perimeter."

Beverly watched as the ensign and prisoner dematerialized. "He killed his own man," she said in surprise.

"And another as well," Worf said. "Cardassians do not allow themselves to be captured."

"You sound like you approve," she said.

Worf scowled. "It is an—honorable inconvenience. I have questions which demand answers."

"At least you have one prisoner," Beverly said. She looked at the people waiting on the trail. "And I still have patients."

"Yes." Worf's scowl turned thoughtful. "Treat the woman next, Doctor—"

"*I'll* set the medical priorities here, Lieutenant," Beverly said sharply.

"You will treat her first," Worf rumbled. "She is the Vo Gatyn."

"You think—" Beverly began.

"I do not think the Cardassians found us by accident," Worf said. He looked at the woman, who sat on a fallen tree trunk, despair heavy on her face. "I believe they wished to assassinate her."

"And you want to get her to safety before they can

228

take another shot at her," Beverly said. Put that way, the Klingon's request made sense.

Worf nodded. "If they seek to kill her, it must mean she could be useful to us."

"Of course," Beverly said with a sigh. *And I thought he was getting soft.* She went to take care of Gatyn.

Chapter Fifteen

MEGARA WAS a fat crescent outside Ten-Forward's viewpoint. Radiation from the battle still flooded its magnetosphere, and the ionized particles painted the night sky below the starship with eerie aurorae. Although Deanna Troi's people had no legends about ghosts and goblins—strange lights and bumps in the night could not trick their empathic sense—the eldritch light somehow made the Betazoid woman think of lost souls.

Guinan brought a chocolate sundae to Deanna's table and sat down facing her. "You look melancholy," the hostess said.

"I *feel* melancholy," Deanna said. She stared idly at the sundae. "We have a Megaran woman on board. I've just spent some time with her, and . . ."

". . . and she has a lot of problems," Guinan concluded.

"Problems which are beyond me," Deanna said.

"I doubt there's such a thing," Guinan said. "You have a knack for finding answers, Counselor."

"Odovil Pardi suffered a bad mental hurt some ten years ago," Deanna said. "Have you ever seen a tree that was bent as a sapling? It grows into a distorted shape. Odovil's hurt has shaped her personality in much the same way."

"I can guess what Data would say if he heard that," Guinan said. " 'Your analogy is erroneous, Counselor. People are not trees.' "

Deanna smiled wanly at the hostess's imitation of Data's speech pattern. "I know, Guinan. The trouble is that helping her could, *will,* take years, and I'm not even sure where to begin."

Guinan looked up as someone entered the lounge. Deanna had her back to the door, but she sensed Ralph Offenhouse's presence as he approached her table. "Mind if I sit down?" he asked as he slid into a chair. He had bathed and put on clean clothes, although Deanna sensed he was still tired and hungry. She decided that he had something important on his mind if he would postpone his meal and sleep. "I wanted to ask you about Odovil."

"Did you have a particular question, or is this idle curiosity?" she asked.

"I want your professional opinion," he said. "I know something's wrong with her; she's as tense as a politician on a polygraph, and I can't figure out why."

"And that's important to you?" Guinan asked him.

"Yeah, because I need to know how it could affect her judgment," Offenhouse said. He looked needled by the sly amusement in her voice. "I'm the ambassador to Megara. She runs a major industry down there, and she has a lot of connections, so I'm going to have to work with her. Any idea what's eating her?"

"It has to do with her education," Deanna said. "The Ferengi needed a high literacy rate to create a technological society, but most Megarans were illiterate when they took over. Under normal circumstances it can take years to educate an adult. When hundreds of millions of people are involved, the job can require a million teachers."

"The Ferengi never brought that many people to Megara," Offenhouse said thoughtfully. "Did Odovil tell you how they did it?"

Deanna nodded. "Her condition gave me a few clues, and I asked the right questions. They used neural imprinting. Do you know much about that?"

"Never heard of it," Offenhouse said. "I musta slept through a class, or a century. What is it?"

"It's illegal now," Deanna told him. "Neural imprinting was an experimental educational technique developed some fifty years ago. In theory, it can impart the equivalent of a college education in a matter of hours. In practice, it damages two percent of the people who undergo it. The damage can range from a few minor personality quirks to schizophrenia or catatonia."

Deanna sensed a protective anger roil inside Offenhouse. "And Odovil—"

"—was subjected to neural imprinting," Deanna said. "It gave her a thorough education, but it also left her agoraphobic and introverted. Part of her wants to crawl into a hole and hide. She works hard because that's easier for her than dealing with people. She can also be quite ruthless, because she's afraid of the consequences of failure."

To Deanna's surprise, that left Offenhouse speechless.

"I suppose the Ferengi would punish her for failure," Guinan suggested.

Deanna shook her head. "She's terrified that they might decide to improve her skills by giving her a second 'lesson.' That's one reason why she wanted to deal with the Federation—she saw a chance to escape from Ferengi control, and she was desperate enough to take it."

The ambassador's mouth opened and closed several times before any words came out. "Can you do anything for her?"

"I've been thinking about that," Deanna said vaguely. "Her biggest problem has been the Ferengi, and they're gone now."

"Yeah, they won't be around to give her another cram course at Imprint U.," he said. "Although—do imprinted lessons fade with time?"

"No," Deanna said. "They're permanent."

Offenhouse shook his head in bewilderment. "Then why would she think they'd do that to her a second time? It doesn't make any sense."

"Fears are seldom rational," Deanna said.

"No, but Odovil is," Offenhouse said. "If she's scared of something, it's real."

"Well, they wouldn't repeat a lesson," Deanna assured him. "That would cause some very confusing interference. You might call it a type of mental double vision, something which would make it impossible for the victim to function."

"Then maybe she's scared they'd give her a *different* lesson," Offenhouse mused. His scowl reflected the churning power of his thoughts. "Maybe they'd have a new job for her—God, yes. *That's* how they'd train astronauts."

"Astronauts?" Deanna asked, before she could place the archaic word. "Oh, you mean starcrew. But what does that have to do with Odovil?"

"Plenty," he said. "God, I'm an idiot. No wonder

she's scared—of *course* they'd draft the brightest people. And . . ." Suddenly oblivious to everything around him, Offenhouse got up and left the lounge.

Guinan watched him depart. "What got into *him?*" she wondered.

Deanna shook her head. "I don't know."

"Does it involve a certain Megaran?" Guinan asked.

"You might say that." His thoughts had been a confusing whirl . . . but Odovil Pardi had featured prominently in them. "It would kill him to admit it, but he's attracted to Odovil Pardi, and it's not just sexual. It's not surprising, either."

"Because he's lonely, and he has things in common with her?" Guinan asked. *"That* has a familiar sound."

"Doesn't it, though?" Deanna asked, smiling despite herself. She suddenly remembered her chocolate sundae. She carefully spooned up a taste of whipped cream and chocolate sauce. "My mother has a favorite saying: 'Men are so predictable, bless their weaselly little hearts.' But if anything comes of this, I think it could be good for both of them."

"Well, now, Counselor," Guinan said. "You really do have a way of finding answers, don't you?"

"A Cardassian prisoner could prove useful," Picard said after Riker had described events on the surface. He leaned back in his bridge chair and stifled a yawn. Riker had called him back to the bridge just as he was crawling into bed. He consoled himself that it would not be much longer before he could rest. "Where is he?"

"He's in the brig," Riker said. "Worf is interrogating him now. We've got a security detail on Megara, stamping out some fires and looking for anything the Cardassians may have left."

"While keeping their eyes open for more Cardassians, I trust," Picard said.

"Yes, sir," Riker said. "There may be a few more wandering around down there. I'm convinced that the castle explosion was a diversion."

"Perhaps," Picard mused. "Once we had learned of their base's presence, it was no longer useful to them. Have you found anything yet?"

Riker shook his head. "With all the radiation, we couldn't even spot the ones who attacked Worf."

Data gave the helm instruments a puzzled look, then turned in his seat to look at Picard. "Captain, I have noted a development on the surface. Fifty-seven minutes ago there were six hundred and seventeen Ferengi on Megara. The number has dropped to five hundred and eighty-two."

"Some of them may be dying from injuries," Riker said. "Catching a brace of photon torpedoes is unhealthy."

"I do not believe this entirely relates to the battle," Data said. "There are Megarans in all of the locations where Ferengi have died. I conjecture that they are taking revenge."

"That seems almost inevitable," Riker said. "Captain, we'd better move before we have a bloodbath."

"I agree, Number One," Picard said. He spent a moment marshaling his thoughts. He had no love for the Ferengi, not since their wanton attack on the *Stargazer* . . . but Federation law and morality alike demanded that he rescue them. "Clear out cargo bay two; we'll use it as a holding area. Ensign Novotny, take a security detail to cargo bay two and prepare to receive prisoners. Mr. Data, give Chief De Shay the coordinates of all the Ferengi you can locate. Inform Dr. Crusher that some of our prisoners may require medical attention."

"Sir," Data said, "if we are to hold the Ferengi as prisoners, regulations demand that we specify the charges on which they are detained."

"They've violated the Prime Directive," Riker said. "That's good enough for me."

Picard sighed. "The Prime Directive does not apply to non-Federation members," he said.

"We can't take them on as passengers!" Riker protested.

"Ferengi passengers *would* form an unacceptable security risk," Data said. He looked thoughtful. "Captain, as the Ferengi are in danger from the Megarans, I suggest that we take them into protective custody."

"Make it so," Picard said.

"And let's protect the daylights out of them," Riker added.

Picard handed command of the ship over to Riker and went to his quarters. He felt thoughts chase one another through his mind, as though he were a computer trapped in an endless programming loop. *A few too many unpleasant experiences today,* he told himself in deliberate understatement. He had risked the safety of his crew and ship; he had brought them within seconds of obliteration. It had been an unavoidable risk, taken to pull the Cardassian warship away from Megara and save that planet, but it had still been a gamble. And now he had to rescue the Ferengi, the same creatures who had helped to devastate Megaran society.

Picard changed into his bedclothes and ordered a cup of Earl Grey tea from the replicator. As he sipped the steaming beverage, he found himself recalling the conversation he'd had with Offenhouse on the holodeck—not even a week ago? A conversation in which the ambassador had criticized the design of the *Enterprise* for taking civilians into harm's way. Picard wondered if the man's criticisms had been justified. One reason civilians were here was to keep the ship's captain from taking undue risks that might jeopardize galactic peace. Perhaps that was nothing but a cynical exercise in social engineering, using people to accomplish a goal—

No, Jean-Luc, Picard told himself. The goal was to help maintain the peace. The method was no secret, and the civilians on the *Enterprise* had freely chosen to accept the risks. This was nothing like Megara, where the Ferengi and Cardassians had manipulated a world for a purpose its people would never know, a purpose that could only harm them.

And that purpose was an overture to war.

Picard climbed into bed and closed his eyes, but sleep eluded him. He reminded himself that the war had not yet begun. The Federation's diplomats would work to preserve the peace despite this provocation. Equally important, the Cardassians' plan had failed, and the Federation would be on the alert. The Cardassians were bold, but not reckless enough to attack a prepared enemy. The peace would hold a while longer.

That was enough to let the captain sleep.

He does not look defeated, Worf thought as he stared at the prisoner. The man on the other side of the forcefield sat on his bunk and ignored the Klingon. His shoulders retained a firm set, and his head did not droop. He had kept silent during the interrogation, revealing nothing. The only certainty was that a slow poison would deprive the Klingon of his prisoner in a few more hours.

The sight of the man filled Worf with melancholy.

The Cardassian presence on Megara meant that there would be another Cardassian war . . . and Worf did not want that. *There is glory in combat,* he thought, *and I hunger for that . . . but not for the danger it would bring to my son. When Alexander dies, let it be as a warrior, not a victim.*

The man gave Worf a disdainful look. "What do you want of me now?" he demanded.

"Tell me why you would fight the Federation," Worf said. *Tell me why you would endanger my son.*

The prisoner laughed bitterly. "A Klingon must ask that?"

"We have *reasons* when we fight," Worf said. "What are yours? Has the Federation harmed you?"

"We *must* fight," the Cardassian said. "We are alike in that, Klingon. War holds our peoples together."

"That is not true!" Worf said.

"It is," the prisoner said. "Our peoples are lone wolves, Klingon, yours and mine alike. We *need* war to hold us together. Without enemies to unite us, we would divide against one another. Is that good?"

Disgusted, Worf turned away without answering. War was good, but Klingons did not use it as a tool to hold society together. That was dishonorable . . . even if combat seemed like the foundation of Klingon society, even if war seemed like the Klingon Empire's first answer to all its problems.

But we are not like the Cardassians! he thought angrily. *We do not make war for such cynical reasons. We avoid it when it is dishonorable!* Yet even as Worf reassured himself, he felt uncertainty. There was just enough truth in the Cardassian's words to sting.

Worf was about to enter the turbolift when he realized that he had let the prisoner distract him. *I should wonder why he did not seem defeated,* he thought in chagrin. *He behaves as a man who expects to win. It must be that other Cardassians survived the castle's destruction, to continue the battle for him. That is reasonable. But where would I look for them?*

Worf thought that over as he went to the bridge. Cardassians often took advantage of natural camouflage—or other forms of interference. The native cities were filled with crude electronic systems that degraded sensor readings. Perhaps the Cardassians were hiding in one of the native cities—or many of them.

The turbolift deposited Worf on the bridge, where he took over his duties from one of his ensigns. A quick study of the security instruments revealed that everything was normal; the minor damage the *Enterprise* had sustained during the battle was already repaired. Cargo bay two was slowly filling with rescued Ferengi. On the surface, relief parties were still searching for injured survivors of the castle explosion.

Wesley Crusher had volunteered to join the relief effort. To Worf's annoyance, Picard had deliberately assigned the young human to a group that operated in an area far from any likely danger. It baffled Worf that Picard would deny Wesley a chance to face danger and prove his honor . . . wait. It could have had something to do with human empathy. It was no secret that Picard felt responsible for the death of Wesley's father, a Starfleet officer. Perhaps Picard now felt responsible for the dead man's son; a human would seek to preserve his son's life, just as a Klingon would raise his son to be a fierce warrior.

It was not the Klingon way to understand aliens and their feelings. Worf shook his head as if to clear it of such thoughts, but he could not entirely dismiss them.

Riker, who was in command at the moment, got out of his seat and walked around to Worf's station. "I hear you had an interesting time down there," Riker said.

Worf grunted. "It was diverting. I think more diversions await us."

"More Cardassians?" Riker nodded. "I've had the same thought. It may be a while before we can look for them, though. The radiation and the native electronics are making a hash of sensor readings."

Worf grunted again. "They will have a second base, a fallback position. That should be easier to find."

"I've thought of that," Riker said. "We've scanned for signs of a second base, but we haven't found one." He smiled grimly. "Ensign Shrev can recognize Cardassians, but we can't expect her to search the entire planet."

"There should be more efficient ways to find them," Worf said. "We are superior to them."

Riker looked surprised at Worf's vehemence. "I'm not going to disagree," the human said, "but you sound like you take this personally."

Worf scowled. "The Cardassians lack honor."

Riker nodded, accepting that explanation. As Riker walked to the helm to confer with Data, Worf realized that this *was* a matter of honor. The prisoner had compared Worf's people to the Cardassians, and there was just enough truth in that to sting.

We are not alike, Worf told himself. *I shall prove it.*

A voice spoke from nowhere. "Lieutenant Worf, report to transporter room three."

Worf growled at the computer's aggressively cheerful tone. "Why am I wanted?" he demanded.

"Ambassador Offenhouse has requested that you accompany him to the surface," the machine answered.

Worf snarled at the computer. "It could be worse, Lieutenant," Riker called out as he went to the turbolift.

"How?" Worf rumbled.

Riker scratched his head. "Well, he could have asked for me instead."

Worf growled again and left the bridge.

Picard had fallen into a fitful sleep, and he did not feel unduly upset when the ambassador's call summoned him to the planet. Picard made his way to the nearest transporter room, where he found Data waiting for him. "The ambassador has requested my presence in Metari Leeg," the android explained as Picard checked out a phaser. "He also asked me to familiarize myself with all the available information on neural-imprinting techniques."

"Did he, now?" Picard asked as they stepped onto the transporter stage. The captain nodded to the duty technician, and in a matter of seconds they had materialized on the surface.

It was night, and brilliant aurorae flickered in the Megaran sky. The multicolored glow showed Picard that he and Data had landed in the heart of an industrial zone. Towering buildings rose all around them. Broad, paved avenues separated the structures. Several vehicles, including a large floating platform, cluttered the roadways as though abandoned. In the distance, Picard heard noises that might have been a riot, a celebration, or both.

Data scanned the area with his tricorder. "The ambassador is inside the building to our left, sir," he reported. "He is in the company of Lieutenant Worf, but he is otherwise alone."

"I hope we're alone as well," Picard said, hearing the burr of a sonic stunner echo down the street. He looked at the looming bulk of a building. "These structures are far too large to be factories. What is your analysis, Mr. Data?"

"This is a shipyard, sir," Data said, consulting his tricorder. "I detect at least five starships which are ready for flight. Each is armed with ten phaser banks and carries shielding equivalent to that of a Constellation-class starship. Their cargo bays have a volume of approximately two hundred thousand cubic meters. I would estimate their peak velocity at warp nine."

"Remarkable," Picard said. "A pirate could not ask for a better ship. It would appear your theory is correct, Mr. Data."

Data tilted his head. "This discovery does tend to support my hypothesis, sir."

Picard smiled at Data's caution. His smile faded as he saw a dead Ferengi. The man hung by his heels from a lamppost, and by all appearances he had not died quickly. *Monstrous,* Picard thought, looking away. The captain had known that the Megarans were taking revenge on their enemies, yet the reality still revolted him.

Picard and Data entered the training facility. It was a fairly small structure, a two-story rectangle with no windows. The tricorder led Data and Picard to a small room. The brightly lit room reminded Picard of a medical examination room, although at second glance he saw that the chamber did not hold enough equipment for that role. There were only a few chairs, a simple biomonitor, and a set of silvery helmets on a shelf. The walls were blank white plastic.

Offenhouse was in the room with Worf. The Klingon did not look as though he enjoyed the ambassador's company. "Glad to see you, Picard," Offenhouse said cheerily. "Welcome to the party."

Worf turned his back on Offenhouse and reported

to Picard. "The ambassador *insisted* on coming here, sir," Worf said. "There has been no trouble. The rioters have avoided this building."

"Rioting's an outdoor sport," Offenhouse said. "We're safe as long as nobody spots us, and we couldn't wait for the riots to end before we examined this place."

"What *is* this place?" Picard asked.

"It is a training facility, sir," Worf said. "It is equipped with a large number of starship simulators."

"Sorta like Starfleet Academy," Offenhouse said. "Only I figure that this is the warp-speed version of the Academy."

Data was inspecting one of the metallic helmets. "This is a neural-imprint helmet," he said.

Offenhouse nodded. "That's why I asked you to brush up on the field, Data. The Ferengi used neural imprinting to teach adult Megarans how to read and write, and it figures they'd use the same technique for astronaut training. Can you tell exactly what it teaches?"

Data peered at the electrodes inside the helmet. "I believe I can access its software."

"Good," Offenhouse said. "I need to know—hey, *stop!*"

Data had placed the helmet over his head. Lights pulsed across its shell. "You are correct, Mr. Ambassador," he said. "This unit—"

"Take it *off!*" the ambassador said in horror.

Data removed the helmet. "As I was saying, this device is intended to imprint humanoid minds with instructions relating to the operation and maintenance of starships—"

"Data," Offenhouse said in a weak voice, "don't you know what a chance you just took?" He sank onto a chair as though his legs had turned to water.

" 'Chance'?" The android looked puzzled. "Ah. You

243

refer to potential damage. You need not concern yourself, sir, as neural imprinting can have no effect upon my positronic brain."

"Mr. Data," Picard said, "just how extensive are its instructions?"

"The device can impart a variety of lessons," Data said. "The technical level is equivalent to that of an advanced course at Starfleet Academy. The list of specialties includes piloting, navigation and engineering. There are also numerous programs relating to combat, as well as to espionage, reconnaissance and the financial evaluation of targets."

"Pirates would need such knowledge," Worf said. Picard thought the Klingon sounded a bit wistful.

"I agree, Lieutenant—odd." Data looked puzzled. "There are no instructions on communication devices or linguistics."

"That figures," Offenhouse said. "The Cardassians wanted these people to fight, not talk. Data, how long would it take someone who used that gimmick to get the hang of flying a ship?"

Data looked thoughtful. "A period of familiarization with an actual starship would be mandatory," he said, "as neural imprinting imparts knowledge, but not experience. However, given the sophistication of this"—he hefted the helmet, which glittered under the room's intense light—" 'gimmick,' the familiarization would require only a matter of hours."

"They could use the simulators in this building," Worf said.

"So a crew could be ready for space almost at once," Picard concluded.

"That's what I was afraid of," Offenhouse said, standing up. "Picard, we unconsciously assumed that the Ferengi would take years to train their crews. After all, that's how long it takes at Starfleet Academy, right?"

"And they've only recently begun to train starcrew here," Picard said grimly.

Worf growled thoughtfully. "This suggests that the Megarans are ready to take the offensive now."

"Exactly," Offenhouse said. "This is an efficient operation. It'd be inefficient to build a bunch of ships, then have them sit idle while the crews were trained. I'm surprised that the Megarans aren't already using their ships."

"The danger of that is over," Picard said. "We've defeated the Cardassians."

"That may not be relevant, sir," Data said, as he placed the helmet back on its shelf. He paused, and the look on his face told Picard he was considering a new idea. "Our actions may have fitted into their plans. Once Megara was ready to play its role, it would have been necessary for the Cardassians to remove the Ferengi, to return control of their world to the Megarans."

"And we've just removed the Ferengi," Offenhouse concluded. "We don't control this planet; nobody does. There's nothing to restrain the Megarans now."

"Nor is there anything to provoke them," Picard answered.

Offenhouse gestured at the silvery helmets on the shelf. "With the sort of training they've had, they may not need a provocation. They've literally had their heads filled with ideas of piracy."

"There are also the Cardassians," Data said. "It is probable that any survivors will continue their clandestine activities. If a provocation is needed here, they can supply it."

" 'Here'?" Worf repeated, a look of curiosity on his face.

"I meant on Megara in general," Data said. "However, if their goal is to subvert the Megarans into a career of piracy, then they would have to operate within a spaceport."

"Indeed," Worf said, almost purring. "And this is the closest spaceport to their last known location. Captain, I suggest that you and the ambassador return to the ship now."

Picard felt grimly amused by the Klingon's tone. "Do you expect trouble, Lieutenant?"

"I have my hopes, sir," Worf rumbled.

Chapter Sixteen

ODOVIL PARDI entered transporter room three as Picard and Offenhouse materialized. The captain thought she looked tense. The Megaran woman had traded her drab coverall for a long-skirted dress—Picard imagined that Troi had helped her select it; the flowing style reflected the Betazoid counselor's tastes—and her fingers plucked nervously at a sleeve. "Ral'feh," she said, as soon as the transport process had ended, "rat-eyes on this ship there are. *M-many* rat-eyes."

"What the hell?" the ambassador asked. "Picard, what are Ferengi doing here?"

"We rescued them," Picard said. "The Megarans were lynching them. We're holding the survivors in protective custody."

The ambassador's jaw twitched. "Put them back where you found them," he said in a voice as cold as space.

"No," Picard said, shocked. "That would be murder."

Offenhouse glanced at De Shay, whose jaw had

sagged in surprise, then looked back to Picard. "We need to talk—in private."

There was a conference room down the corridor from the transporter room. Picard led Offenhouse and Odovil into it and sat down facing them across the table. "I will not allow the Ferengi to be slaughtered," Picard said.

"Hear me out," Offenhouse said. "Have you thought about how we're going to straighten out the mess down there?"

"Frankly, no," Picard said. "I haven't had the time."

"You should take it," Offenhouse said. *"Think,* Picard. I have to convince the Megarans that we're the good guys, that we *aren't* evil outworlders. How in *hell* am I supposed to do that if they see us rescuing the Ferengi?"

"True this is," Odovil said. "If the rat-eyes you help, our enemies you are."

"And if we're the enemy," Offenhouse said, "we can forget about fixing things down there. Know what that means? We won't have a chance in hell of keeping the Megarans from becoming pirates. Sure, Starfleet can beat them, but we'll kill thousands of them in the process—and we'll be doing exactly what the Cardassians planned all along. Or are you ready to bombard their brand-new spaceports and factories, *now,* to keep them out of space?"

"Certainly not," Picard said in annoyance. "I shall not commit an act of war on the assumption that these people *might* cause trouble."

Offenhouse snorted in disgust. "But you're willing to help their worst enemies. Saving the Ferengi could be the thing that provokes them into hitting the warpath."

"So what you propose," Picard said, "is that we

gain the friendship of Megara by allowing them to kill the Ferengi."

"Think of it as justice," Offenhouse said.

"I think of it as something uncomfortably close to human sacrifice," Picard answered. "And it is not for us to decide where justice lies here."

"No, it's for the Megarans," Offenhouse said. He nodded at Odovil. "The Ferengi used neural imprinting to give her an education. Any idea of what that was like for her?"

Picard looked at the woman. *Is this why she always seems so apprehensive?* he wondered. Her nervous state might well be a pathological by-product of neural imprinting—and the Ferengi would have done far worse things to many other people. "I doubt that I can imagine the full extent of the crimes the Ferengi have committed here," Picard said, "but that does not matter. I will not hand over the Ferengi to mob violence."

Offenhouse stared at him across the table. "Even though it means blowing our chance here?"

"Yes," Picard said. "If we deny justice to anyone, then we deny the very concept of justice. And consider this," Picard continued, raising his voice before the ambassador could interrupt him. "The Cardassians sought to turn Megara into a hellhole of violence. If we hand over the Ferengi, it will only encourage more bloodshed, not end it—"

"Dammit!" Offenhouse slammed a fist down onto the table. *"Listen,* Picard—"

"Ral'feh," Odovil said quietly. "Too much evil I have seen. Somewhere it must stop."

"Dammit—" The ambassador stopped as the woman flinched at his anger. He took a deep breath. "I'm sorry, Odovil, but I don't want the Ferengi to get away with what they've done."

"Justice I would see," Odovil said. "But like a rat-eyes I would not act, even if justice they escape."

"They won't," Offenhouse promised, looking to Picard. "I'll find a way to make them pay."

"If you can find a way to bring the Ferengi to *justice,*" Picard said, emphasizing the word, "I shall be the first to congratulate you. But there is another matter here, Mr. Ambassador—the Prime Directive. You speak of 'straightening out' the situation on Megara. I find that a laudable goal—but precisely how do you intend to do that?"

"Well . . . well, I'm not sure," he admitted. "Not yet."

"Yet you're willing to send the Ferengi to their deaths," Picard noted, "without considering the effect this slaughter might have on your unformed plans. Mr. Ambassador, this is precisely why we abide by the Prime Directive. Well-intended blunders are as destructive as deliberate malice."

"So what are you saying, Picard?" Offenhouse demanded. "Are we just going to walk away from Megara, then come back and blow them to hell if they make trouble?"

"I have said nothing about 'walking away,'" Picard said in irritation, "although we shall, if the only option is to cause further harm here. Mr. Ambassador, you may *not* simply impose your solutions on the Megarans. That is what the Ferengi and Cardassians have done. We may offer them advice, we may offer lessons from our own mistakes, but it must be the Megarans who choose their own course."

"To mistakes you admit?" Odovil asked in surprise.

Offenhouse sighed. "Yeah . . . and when we make 'em, we don't do it by halves. Odovil, let me tell you about Khan Singh. Then you can decide just how much help you want from me." He took her hand

and helped her out of her chair, and they left the room.

Picard leaned back in his chair. *It's too much to expect that man to serve justice,* he thought sadly. Offenhouse's first impulse had been to throw away the lives of the Ferengi in the name of expediency. For all his intelligence, the ambassador was a product of the twentieth century, and justice had not been a concern of that era.

Shrev checked her phaser's charge as she stepped onto the transporter stage with the security detail. *You must think of this abomination as a tool,* she thought in disgust. *You will use it to carry out your orders.* While her people had no qualms about war and violence—Zhuik hives had been invading and conquering one another since before humans had evolved —they fought with honor. It was ignoble to use a weapon that struck down an enemy at a distance, or to kill without first identifying oneself to an enemy. That was the way most mammalian races fought, and their anonymous style of combat often had led to millions of anonymous dead.

De Shay worked his control console, and the transporter set Shrev and five other people in the middle of a street in Metari Leeg. It was night, but the heat from buildings and pavement gave her antennae enough infrared light to show her the scene. This part of the town was nothing like the city she and Wesley Crusher had visited. There were no old buildings here, no cobbled roads or alleys. Everything was stark and modern.

Lieutenant Worf and Commander Data came out of a building. "Cardassians may be present in this area," Worf said, coming right to the point as he always did. "They are disguised as Megarans. We will find them and defeat them."

251

"Sir, how many are there?" one of the men on the security detail asked.

"That is uncertain, Ensign," Data answered. "It is possible that there are no Cardassians present in Metari Leeg—" Worf growled at that. "—but there are logical reasons to assume that we shall encounter them," Data added hastily.

"Indeed," Worf said. "Ensign Shrev."

"Yes, sir?" Shrev whispered.

"You are able to recognize Cardassians," the Klingon said. "When you see them, commence fire at once. We will fire at your targets with you."

"Yes, sir." Shrev set her phaser for heavy stun, then looked to the Klingon. "Sir, would it not be possible to identify a Cardassian with a tricorder?"

"There is too much electronic interference in this area," Data explained. "However, it is known that your senses are reliable."

"Let us begin," Worf said. The Klingon began walking down the street. At a gesture from him, Shrev fell into step at Data's side. Worf and the rest of the detail spread out, screening them.

The city was not deserted. Shrev heard the sound of a riot in the distance, and hot smoke glowed in the sky. There was something odd about the sky itself, but it was not until she heard one of the human security agents mention aurorae that she realized what it was. The woman called the sight glorious, but Shrev's color-blind eyes could detect only vague smears of light.

Concentrate on your duty, she ordered herself. From time to time she saw Megarans, but they seemed intent on avoiding the heavily armed away team, running off the moment they saw the aliens. On this occasion Shrev did not mind the rudeness; it proved that they wished to avoid trouble.

Without warning a phaser beam flicked out of a

building and killed a man. "Take cover!" Worf called. As Shrev dashed behind a parked truck she saw Data fire a rapid, precise string of shots into each window, covering the rest of the team.

Worf landed behind the truck alongside her. "Are they Cardassians?" the Klingon asked.

Shrev peeked around the truck's cab. She had a brief glimpse of someone in a window, but she could not decide if she had viewed a Megaran or a Cardassian. "I regret that I cannot give a confident answer, sir," she said.

Worf grunted. "A pity you cannot see through walls."

"I share your admirable sentiment, sir," Shrev whispered. Then an idea struck her. "Perhaps we can remove the walls."

Worf shook his head. "Our phasers lack the energy for—"

A phaser beam carved into the truck, which thumped to the pavement as its suspensors died. "There may be another way, sir," Shrev said. "Shrev to De Shay. Could I trouble you for some technical advice?"

"That's why I'm here," De Shay's voice answered.

"We are being attacked from a building to our immediate north," Shrev said. "Exposing our assailants would be of great help. Could you use the transporter to remove sections of the building's walls?"

"I think so," De Shay said in a distracted tone. "I'll have to override the safety parameters—"

"I urge haste," Worf said.

"Give me a minute, Lieutenant," De Shay grumbled. "Beaming up *part* of an object is considered poor form. This machine isn't designed for it."

Worf snarled something in what Shrev presumed

253

was an obscure Klingonese dialect. He adjusted his phaser to a high setting and fired several shots at the building. Shrev saw no effect from his assault; whoever was in the building continued to shoot back.

A ten-meter section of wall shimmered and vanished, exposing several people. Deprived of cover, they fell within seconds as the away team stunned them. More sections of wall vanished, along with slabs of roof and floor; Shrev saw that De Shay was methodically demolishing the building with the transporter.

Shrev watched a man tumble to the ground. "That is a Cardassian, sir," she told Worf.

"Good," Worf said.

Another section of wall vanished. Shrev saw a Cardassian with a phaser rifle. She stunned him, then felt her antennae writhe in shame at her dishonorable act. At least he had lived; she could apologize to him for her shameful behavior later.

After what seemed an eternity the building was reduced to a few tottering walls. A trio of Cardassians had gathered with their backs to one wall. They looked at the humans and stopped shooting. Shrev wondered if they were going to surrender.

"Down!" Worf bellowed. "Everyone take cover!" Shrev hesitated, then heard the rising whine of a phaser set on overload. She pressed herself against the pavement as the roar of an explosion boomed over her.

Worf walked over the rubble while the others scanned it with their tricorders. The remains of bodies lay amid smoking, ruined equipment. *Cardassian military equipment,* he thought, recognizing bits and pieces he had seen in intelligence reports. Some of the debris came from nonportable equipment, including a short-range holographic projector, which when activated produced the ghostly image of a cruel-faced woman in a robe. It was his opinion that this building had been some sort of outpost, pressed into use as an emergency base.

"Scan complete, Lieutenant," Data reported, crossing a debris pile to reach the Klingon. "No sign of survivors."

Worf nodded. "And no sign of an escape route."

"That is correct," Data said. The android tilted his head thoughtfully. "When the Cardassians realize how thoroughly we have defeated them here, they will surely hesitate to attack us. It appears that your victory is complete."

More complete than you can know, Worf thought. By fighting here, he had prevented a larger war. *I have proven that my people are not like the Cardassians. I have fought to preserve honor, not to create war.*

And I have won because I am a Klingon.

The Klingon smiled up at the night sky, where aurorae shimmered like a hero's spirit.

It was a coincidence that Picard was in the same transporter room that brought Wesley Crusher's team back to the ship; Picard had been waiting for Worf's return. De Shay wrinkled his nose as Wesley and three other relief workers materialized. They were wet and filthy, and carried the odors of organic substances in assorted states of decay. "Apparently I should have given your assignment more thought," Picard said as Wesley stepped off the platform.

Wesley smiled sheepishly as he glanced at his uniform. "It was a bit messy, sir," he admitted, "but we got through our search area all right."

"Too bad we didn't find anything," one of the men said. "The whole thing was a waste of time."

The team's leader, a medical orderly, nodded ruefully. "All of our sensor contacts were either interference artifacts or false alarms. They've got some kind of swamp-ape down there that reads a lot like a person—and hides a lot better. Right, Wes?"

"It kept me busy," Wesley said.

"You'll want to get cleaned up now," Picard said, noting the young man's attitude. He did not seem dejected by his "failure" to rescue any Megarans, or by the rest of the team's low spirits. "Well done, Wesley."

"Thank you, sir," Wesley said. As he left he seemed puzzled by Picard's praise. *He will understand,* Picard assured himself, thinking of the new maturity he had just seen in the cadet. He would have liked to have said something about it to Wesley, but the best thing he could do for the cadet was to let Wesley make this discovery for himself.

Worf beamed up a moment later. He had stayed on the surface after the rest of his away team returned, and Picard thought he had been savoring the battlefield. If so, the Klingon had earned that, and Picard thought he looked satisfied. "Your report, Mr. Worf?" Picard asked.

"No Cardassians survived, sir," Worf said.

"Can you offer any evidence of this?" Picard asked. The Cardassians had proven themselves canny and determined opponents, and he did not want to underestimate them.

"The ones we fought did not try to escape," Worf said. "Instead they fought to the death."

"That's typical of the Cardassians, Captain," De Shay said. He had served as weapons officer aboard another starship, and he had fought in the Cardassian War. "They're calculating devils. They would have tried to escape if they thought they had a chance to continue the fight later. When they go down fighting like that, it means they know everything is over for them."

"I see," Picard said. "Well, Mr. Worf, now that we've disposed of all our enemies—"

The door hissed open and Offenhouse looked into the transporter room. "Hey, Picard, you busy? I need you at cargo bay two."

Holding back a sigh, Picard joined Offenhouse in the corridor. "Is there a problem, Mr. Ambassador?" he asked.

"No, we're just going to take the Ferengi off your hands." Offenhouse looked at the captain as they walked down the corridor. "Picard, keeping the Ferengi alive was the right thing to do."

Picard felt an eyebrow rise. "What caused you to change your mind?"

"Mainly it was Odovil," the ambassador said. "She can be persuasive. But I also realized something. The Megarans still need to see that justice is done. Killing the Ferengi looked like the best way to do that—but I've thought of something better."

Picard raised an eyebrow. "I trust it's something legal."

"It is, according to your ship's computer," Offenhouse said. "Gatyn is still in the sickbay— Crusher won't send her home; she's afraid the Megarans will lynch her. Anyway, I had a long talk with Gatyn about her Ferengi contract, and it turns out that, technically, the Ferengi are working for her."

"Is that important?" Picard asked.

Offenhouse nodded. "Very important. Worf did us all a big favor when he saved Gatyn's neck."

There was a momentary pause. "You're being very mysterious," Picard said in exasperation.

The ambassador showed a wicked grin. "I thought you liked mysteries."

Picard sighed. "Only in my spare time, Mr. Ambassador. I would appreciate an explanation."

"Well, the Megaran economy is a lopsided mess," he said. "Everything is geared toward building starships, while providing the people with the bare essentials of life. We have to reorganize the factories and the economy so people get what they need. The Ferengi understand the technology involved here, so we can use them as advisors, to convert old factories to new production and to design new plants and services. Gatyn is going to set herself up as a consultant, hiring out Ferengi services."

"Gatyn has formally accepted the Federation's presence on Megara?" Picard asked.

"She's planning to do that at a public ceremony in a few days," Offenhouse said. "Technically she's the only government Megara has, but now that the Ferengi are gone her position is shaky. She needs a Federation alliance to help prop her up, and Megara needs her to keep things stable. She may have been a Ferengi puppet," he added with a shrug, "but she never was a wholehearted quisling. We can work with her—and she knows she needs us to help straighten out the mess down there."

They entered a turbolift, and the ambassador directed it to cargo bay two. "Tell me something," Picard said as the lift slid along the shaft. "You may have Odovil Pardi and the Vo Gatyn on your side, but they're special cases. Given the xenophobia of the Megarans, do you think they'll accept Federation aid?"

"Things will be a bit rough at first," Offenhouse admitted. "But we've got our foot in the door, which is always the toughest part when you're doing business. Your people are responsible for that," he added. "You've handled everything right."

"Getting rid of the Ferengi was bound to make a favorable impression," Picard said.

"It's more than that," Offenhouse said. "Everything we've done here has made a good impression on the Megarans, whether it's the away teams buying things for a fair price, or Worf beaming back to rescue what's-his-name, or you towing that Cardassian kamikaze away from the planet. It all adds up."

The turbolift came to a halt and released its passengers near the entrance to cargo bay two. Four members of Worf's security department stood guard in the corridor outside the bay's massive sliding doors. "Fetch Chudak," Offenhouse told the senior guard.

Picard nodded to the woman, who spoke into the intercom. A small secondary door opened a moment later, and Chudak stepped into the corridor. His clothing was soiled and scorched, and dust streaked his hairless scalp, but he maintained his innate dignity as he looked up at Offenhouse. "Oh, it's *you,* you hairy horror. What in hell do you want?"

"I want to talk about that contract you signed with the Vo Gatyn," Offenhouse said. "It seems the whole thing is still perfectly legal, ironclad and valid—"

"Of course!" Chudak sneered. "Are you looking for some loophole to prosecute me, bug-eyes? That contract made everything I did on Megara legal."

"I know," the ambassador said. "In fact, I want to see you fulfill your contract."

Chudak looked puzzled. "What trick is this, you blunt-tooth freak?"

"It's no trick," Offenhouse said. "Listen up, butt-head—"

" 'Butthead'?" Chudak demanded. "Do you expect me to butt heads with you? Is this some perverted human sex-ritual?"

"Listen," Offenhouse snarled. He grabbed Chudak by his tattered lapels, picked him up and shoved him against the corridor bulkhead. "You signed a contract to industrialize Megara. The Megarans are waiting for you to finish your work. They want you to get down there and—"

"Are you insane?" Chudak demanded. Picard saw him squirm in fright as Offenhouse held him against the wall. "Those filthy debtors will kill us!"

"Guess again." Offenhouse released Chudak and let him drop to the deck. "You'll have guards to make sure nobody harms a hair on your head—as long as you're working for us. And, if you decide you don't like the arrangement, you'll be free to leave."

"We will?" Chudak asked suspiciously.

"Sure!" Offenhouse said. "Of course, once you quit we'll withdraw your guards, but maybe you won't mind being alone and unarmed on Megara while you wait for a ride home—"

"Picard!" Chudak said. "I demand asylum for my crew and myself. You *must* grant it."

"I must?" Picard asked. Despite himself he felt a slight increase in his respect for Chudak; the man had thought of his crew's safety before his own. "On what grounds do you request asylum?"

"On—on—on whatever grounds will keep us alive!" the Daimon sputtered.

"You'll have to do better than *that,"* Offenhouse said. "The Megarans will take every possible step to keep you alive. Your only reason for requesting asylum is to break your contract—"

"—and we can't grant asylum merely to allow you to escape a legal obligation," Picard finished.

Chudak glared at Picard. "We've already fulfilled our contract."

"Then where are the hospitals, the houses, the libraries, the universities, the mass-transit networks, the municipal water systems?" Offenhouse snickered at the Daimon. "You can't claim that you've finished your work just because you've built a few shipyards here. When the Vo Gatyn talks to you later, she'll—"

"The Vo Gatyn?" Chudak repeated in a fading voice. The color drained from his face.

Offenhouse beamed at Chudak. "She's your boss."

"You can't do this!" Chudak squeaked. The Daimon's obvious terror astonished Picard. He actually cowered against the cargo-bay door. "Gatyn is insane! She'll kill me!"

"No, she won't," Offenhouse said with a smile. He patted Chudak on the head. "Don't worry, little fellow. She's looking forward to working with you for a *looong* time."

Geordi was having a drink with Worf in the Ten-Forward lounge when Riker strode up to their table. "Okay, mister," Riker said to Worf, his arms crossed over his chest, *"explain."*

Geordi's VISOR showed him that the Klingon was genuinely puzzled; his bioelectric fields rippled in confusion. "Sir?" Worf asked, setting his glass of prune juice down on the table.

"I've talked to Data," Riker said. "He heard you *laugh,* mister. It's not much of a laugh, from what he says, but it *is* a laugh. What brought this on?"

"It was Megara," the Klingon said.

"You found something funny down *there?"* Riker asked in an incredulous voice.

Worf nodded. "It was something Commander Data said."

"Data finally told an effective joke?" Riker asked. Geordi watched the man's bioelectric field intensify with his disbelief. *"Data?* What did he say?"

"It happened moments before we rescued the captain," Worf said, picking up his glass. "The tactical situation was not good. The odds did not favor us. Victory appeared uncertain." Worf paused to take a slow, maddeningly deliberate sip of prune juice.

"Okay, so things were black and getting darker," Riker said impatiently. "What in hell did Data *say?*"

Worf toyed with his glass. "'Things have never been better.'"

"That made you laugh?" *Enterprise's* first officer demanded. *"That?* Worf, you hardly even smiled when you saw that movie. I said the exact same words to you on the bridge, and you barely growled at them. So why did you laugh on Megara?"

"I cannot explain, sir," Worf said, and sipped more prune juice. "You had to be there."

He's got a pretty good sense of timing, Geordi thought as Riker neared the boiling point. "Commander, we're both on duty in a few minutes," Geordi said, getting up. "We'd better go."

Riker left the Ten-Forward lounge with Geordi. "It isn't fair," Riker complained, once they were out in the corridor. "I bent over backward to find a way to make Worf laugh, and Data finally made him crack. *Data!*"

"Look on the bright side," Geordi consoled him. "The real joke is on Worf."

"Oh, really?" Riker asked sourly. "How's that?"

"You know how Data is always looking for advice on how to become human, develop emotions, and all that?" Geordi watched Riker nod. "Well, now that Worf has started laughing, Data is spending every free moment he has studying him to learn how Worf did it. Data won't leave him alone, and it's driving Worf nuts."

The corridor boomed with Riker's sudden laughter.

* * *

Wesley rarely drank synthehol; by his reckoning, this was only the third time in his life that he'd ever had any. It was part of the celebration. The relief workers had found over a hundred people who had been injured when the Cardassians blew up their base; sensor scans said that they had found every single survivor, and the word from sickbay was that the workers had saved at least a score of Megarans from otherwise certain death. After they had returned to the *Enterprise,* Wesley and the rest of the workers had congregated in Ten-Forward, to rehash their adventures and congratulate one another on their accomplishments.

Wesley would have liked to spend a little time alone, to unravel what the captain had said to him . . . or the way he had said it, he reflected. It was good to have the captain's approval again, but he wished he knew what the man had seen that mattered so much.

Wesley saw Shrev enter the lounge. He excused himself from the group and went to join her. "I hear that Mr. Worf gave you a commendation for original thinking," he said quietly. "Congratulations."

"Thank you," she said, and looked him over. He had bathed and changed his uniform, but he knew he still looked a bit ragged. "I believe you have been busy, yourself."

"It's been a long day," Wesley agreed. They ordered snacks at the bar—a bowl of nectar for Shrev, a milk shake for Wesley—and sat down at a table. Wesley had a difficult time persuading Shrev to tell him about her experience. He decided that this went beyond modesty; Zhuiks saw nothing wrong with a little justified boasting, but she seemed troubled. "I guess that being in a firefight is a lot rougher than a knife duel," he said.

"Yes, in ways I had not imagined." Shrev toyed with

her spatula as she stared down at her nectar. Wesley noted that she had fixed neither her eyes nor her antennae on him. "It was all remote, distant. My actions led to the deaths of many people, and I never knew their names or saw their faces."

And now she feels guilty, Wesley realized. "It's strange," Wesley said. "The most upsetting thing a human can do is kill someone you know. We fight our wars at a distance; a human soldier hardly ever sees his enemy when he kills him. The way our minds work, keeping a distance between ourselves and a victim keeps us from feeling guilty. It makes killing a lot easier."

"I have heard of this," Shrev whispered.

Wesley nodded. "And I guess you know our wars are a lot bloodier than yours ever were. Maybe humans would be better off if we were a bit more like Zhuiks."

"That is an interesting thought," Shrev said, raising her head slightly to look at Wesley. He thought she had taken some solace from his words. "I have talked much of what I have done and felt, without doing you the courtesy of hearing your story."

"I haven't really done much," Wesley said. "Most of my search zone was a swamp. The ship's sensors thought they'd spotted some people down there, but I didn't find anyone."

"So your efforts were wasted?" Shrev asked in sympathy.

"I wouldn't say that," Wesley said. "Someone *could* have been down there, and someone had to check it out. That was me."

"I am delighted that you took pleasure in your task," Shrev said.

"I did," Wesley said, and meant it. He talked with Shrev as they ate their snacks, but the feeling of satisfaction remained with him when he finally left

Ten-Forward. He had spent endless hours slogging through a swamp, several times holding his tricorder and medical kit above his head to keep them safe while he sank chest-deep in green water and chased after swamp-apes that *might* have been terrified Megarans. He was worn out, he stank, and he had not felt this good since . . . since the incident at the Academy, he decided.

Wesley thought he understood the reason—and the reason Captain Picard had shown approval even though he had accomplished nothing. *After Josh died I had all these heroic fantasies about how I'd make up for what I did,* he thought. *Save the ship, rescue the captain, win a battle—do one big thing to balance the books. But it doesn't work that way, does it?* Redemption would only come through a lifetime of small acts—doing his duty, telling the truth, obeying orders and playing straight with everyone.

He realized he had been doing that all along, without a second thought, and the captain had understood that before he had. Wesley decided that he had made a good start on making amends for his mistakes.

It was unseemly for a warrior to skulk, to glance over his shoulder and peek around corners . . . but it was unacceptable for a Federation officer to assassinate a superior, and Data's persistent questions about humor inspired heartwarming thoughts about knives in the dark and accidents with airlocks. Worf knew it was better to avoid the android.

Worf sighed. If only Data would develop the emotion of *discouragement* . . .

Alexander sat at the table, doing his homework as Worf entered their quarters. He stood up, but instead of delivering one of those embarrassing human hugs the boy gave a proper bow of respect to his father.

Worf felt vaguely disappointed. "I heard that you won a battle today, Father," Alexander said.

"A small battle," Worf said.

"Did you kill all of your enemies?"

Worf shook his head. "There was no need to kill."

Alexander scowled. "Not even once?"

"No," Worf said.

Alexander growled at that and returned his attention to his homework. Somehow disgruntled, Worf took his *bat'telh* sword from its wall mount, sat down with it and began to hone its edges. He thought about humor, and laughter. He reasoned that it was like needlepoint, or cooking, or swimming—useful talents in other people, but not worth developing in himself. Childish, really. He would gladly leave this undignified humor-stuff to Data . . . although it *had* been interesting to needle Riker with it . . . and it was important to Alexander.

From time to time Worf heard his son growl as he battled an especially tough question. *Alexander is in one of his moods,* Worf assured himself. This mood caused him to act, well, Klingonese, but in an exaggerated style. That would stop when the boy's mood passed—which was not a displeasing notion. *Alexander should act like Alexander,* Worf thought. Troi had said so on several occasions, but until now Worf had never understood that. He wondered how he could tell that to the boy.

Worf finished sharpening his *bat'telh* and put it back in its place. He stood behind Alexander and looked at his homework. "What are you studying?" he asked.

"It's my Earth-history assignment, Father." He twisted the computer pad so Worf could see it. There was text, and an animated image of humans dressed in costumes similar to the one Ambassador Offenhouse had affected on Megara—black coats, pin-striped pants, stovepipe hats and sashes. "It's about a human called Theodore Roosevelt. There was this big, stupid war between Russia and Japan, and he was asked to help end it. That was hard because the two enemies really hated one another, and if either side saw any sign that he wasn't being fair to them, they'd leave and the war would go on."

"That is natural," Worf said. "What did this Roosevelt do?"

"Well, custom said that he had to invite both sides to a feast," Alexander said. "Humans are like us, they eat together to show they're friendly. Only at human feasts like this one you bring in one group at a time, announce who they are and let them sit down. Coming in first is important, so it was going to look like whoever sat down first had Roosevelt's favor. Everyone was scared that the dishonor would start the war again.

"So Roosevelt changed the custom. He had all the chairs taken out of a feast hall. Then he told everyone that the feast would start at a certain time, and each side would come in through a different door. They arrived at the same time, and because there weren't any chairs nobody was dishonored by sitting down second."

"Clever," Worf rumbled. He heard the enthusiasm in his son's voice; his human side was filled with admiration for this war-ending Roosevelt. Worf was both pleased and puzzled to discover that this did not trouble him. "And did Roosevelt make a peace?"

Alexander nodded vigorously. "The humans gave him something called a peace prize, too. His people felt honored because he was the first of their line to win that."

"Interesting." Worf wondered how he could tell his son that he could accept the human side of Alexander's nature. "There are *some* things to be learned from humans," he said at last.

The intercom signaled. "Riker to Worf. Lieutenant, Data is tied up in his lab. Let's talk battle over dinner."

"Understood," Worf answered. He decided that Riker's reference to Data and his lab was figurative, and not literal. *Pity,* he thought. "Come," he told Alexander.

"Okay." Alexander switched off his computer and got up. "I guess Commander Riker wants to hear about your battle, too."

Too? Worf thought, and smiled. "Commander Riker is a human of many interests," he said as they left their quarters.

"He's okay, but . . ." Alexander's voice took on a conspiratorial tone. "I hear he *likes* tribbles."

"Nobody's perfect," Worf said. He found it good to hear his son laugh at that.

Dazed with fatigue, Beverly Crusher stumbled down the corridor toward her cabin. She had lost count of the number of operations she had performed in the past dozen hours, and one of her staff had sent her off to rest before she could start blundering. At least the worst of it was over, but her mind was crowded with memories of melted eyeballs and irradiated tissues; how could any rational being use weapons that did such things?

The same way we use knives and clubs, she thought, recalling Kardel Anit's injuries. He'd lost an arm and an eye the old-fashioned way. His injuries had been repaired easily enough—although he had been a difficult patient, as uncooperative and suspicious as a Romulan with an engraved invitation to a Klingon banquet. Well, he might not like aliens, but every time he used his new arm or opened his new eye he would be reminded that he owed them a debt. That might temper his xenophobia, and that of anyone who knew him.

Just the same, she was sorry she'd gone to so much trouble to make sure his new eye matched the old one.

Beverly reached her quarters. The door slid halfway open and jammed. Tired and annoyed, she banged the activator panel with her fist, then gave up and eased through the crack. Her foot caught on something, and it was all she could do to keep from sprawling on the deck.

She gaped at the junk heaped in her quarters: bolts of cloth, intricate metal devices, leather bags, a set of grotesquely ornate chairs, artwork, scrolls, clothing, a loom and sundry devices unknown to Beverly. *Wesley said he'd bought a few gifts for his friends,* she thought as she picked her way toward her bedroom. *He must be on good terms with everyone in Starfleet!* "Crusher to De Shay," she said. "What's all this junk doing in my quarters?"

"Junk?" De Shay repeated. "Oh. Sorry, Doctor. We had to clear everything out of cargo bay two, and the only option—"

"—was to give it back to its owners," she concluded. "Okay, just beam it all into space, or something."

The transporter chief gave an apologetic cough. "I'm sorry, Doctor, but that would violate waste-disposal regulations."

I'd like to prescribe something for whoever cooked up that regulation, Beverly thought as she broke the connection. *Maybe a good antipsychotic drug or two . . . maybe a pacemaker for a feeble bureaucratic brain.*

She couldn't reach her bed over the mounds of rubbish. Too weary to fight on, she grabbed a bolt of quilted fabric, unrolled it on one of the floor's few open spots, and curled up on the deck. "Wesley Crusher," she muttered, "when you get home, you're going to wish you were *back* in that swamp."

"You should not have patted Chudak on the head," Picard told Offenhouse. The ambassador was seated on a biobed in sickbay while a Vulcan doctor ministered to his bloodied, mangled hand. "He was bound to take offense."

"I know, but I didn't think the jerk would *bite* me." Offenhouse looked at the doctor. "Are Ferengi allergic to human flesh and blood?" he demanded.

"There are certain metabolic incompatibilities," the doctor told him as she adjusted her protoplaser.

"Good!" Offenhouse raged. Anger had turned his face as red as a Martian sunset. "I hope I gave him food poisoning! I hope he has the dry heaves for a week! I hope he swells up like a dead fish and starts foaming at the mouth!"

"That's quite possible, Mr. Ambassador," Picard said. "You *do* have a remarkable effect on people. Now, would you explain why Chudak is so terrified of the Vo?"

"He raped her," Offenhouse said, slowly calming down. "Now the little space-sleazoid is scared stiff that Gatyn plans to get even—which she does. She's going to work his fanny off for the next thirty or forty years. I'm going to enjoy watching *that,*" he added, glancing at his injured hand.

"Thirty or forty years?" Picard repeated, nonplussed. "It sounds as though you're keeping the Ferengi as slaves."

"Who, me?" Offenhouse affected an innocent look. "Picard, Chudak's contract says that he has to industrialize Megara, *and* that the Vo Gatyn decides when he's done—"

"And I doubt she'll ever feel satisfied," Picard said in suspicion. "You suggested this arrangement, didn't you?"

"I wish I had, but Odovil and Gatyn worked out most of it," Offenhouse said. "Don't feel sorry for Chudak, Picard. That contract was meant as a sham; there's justice in making the Ferengi live up to its terms."

The doctor finished working on the ambassador's hand. She wasted no time in speaking with Offenhouse; there were other patients in sickbay, Megarans waiting to have their injuries treated, and the doctor went at once to tend to her next patient. Picard and Offenhouse left the sickbay.

They walked down the corridor. "What will happen on Megara now?" Picard asked. "I've heard your talk about reconstruction and justice, but what do you really have in mind?"

"I want to help undo everything the Ferengi did to these people," the ambassador said. He flexed his hand and nodded at its supple motions. "The poverty, the crime, the violence—we have to help get this society back on its feet."

"And you think you can do that?" Picard asked.

"Me? No," he said. "All I can do is offer a few ideas and call in some help from the Federation. But the Megarans can do it."

"You sound quite confident," Picard said.

Offenhouse nodded. "Despite everything the Ferengi did to drag them down, they're still decent people. There's a lot of violence down there, but most of the Megarans are peaceful and hardworking. If they weren't, Megara would be a lot worse . . . and Odovil wouldn't have drawn the line at killing the Ferengi. They'll make things improve because that's what they want. Give them a few years, and they'll have their world back in order."

"I'm sure they will," Picard said thoughtfully. "But for the present, the Megarans still pose a serious threat to the Federation."

"Because they have ships and an attitude." Offenhouse waved a hand, dismissing the point. "We've taken care of that. Odovil plans to hire all of the astronauts the Ferengi trained here—"

"—and keep them away from their ships?" Picard nodded. "That's a most elegant and straightforward solution to our problem, Mr. Ambassador. Well done."

The ambassador cleared his throat. "Well, we won't ground *all* of them," he said. "Only the ones we don't trust. The others—see, Odovil's going into the shipping business. I told her she could sell tritanium to the Federation, and we could contract out to supply warp generators and other goodies to folks all over the quadrant. We'll turn a profit doing this—"

"Why am I not surprised?" Picard muttered, addressing himself to the corridor ceiling.

"—and we'll use the cash to finance Megara's reconstruction," Offenhouse finished.

"Even so, allowing the Megarans into space seems risky," Picard said as they came to a turbolift door.

"Everything worthwhile is risky," Offenhouse said, leaning against the bulkhead. "This'll give the Megarans contact with people on other worlds, and that's the best way to cure their xenophobia. They'll see for themselves that outworlders aren't as monstrous as they've heard.

"And think about this," Offenhouse went on. "The Cardassians wanted to destabilize this part of the galaxy and threaten the Federation. Well, I'm turning the tables on them, using their ships and factories for *our* purposes. Not only is Megara going to be the key to developing this sector, but some day soon it'll join the Federation. Don't be surprised if we're selling you starships in a few years."

"At a profit, no doubt," Picard said.

"You wouldn't want the Megarans to feel cheated, would you?" The turbolift door opened, and the two men entered the elevator. "Transporter room three," Offenhouse said, and glanced at Picard. "It's time for me to beam down and get to work."

"You seem to have a lot of plans for Megara," Picard said as the lift slid into motion.

"Oh, I do," Offenhouse agreed. "Megara has unlimited potential. It's going to be the most important world in this sector, count on it. And if you think *I'm* ambitious, you should hear Odovil's plans. Talk about your irresistible forces! Give us a few decades, and Megara will rival Earth."

Picard smiled at the man's optimism, but something occurred to him. *A few decades?* he wondered. By twentieth-century standards Offenhouse was already middle-aged, and even with modern medical technology to keep him healthy his remaining lifespan probably would amount to no more than forty or fifty years. "It sounds like the work of a lifetime."

"Well, I've *got* a lifetime," Offenhouse said. He became oddly subdued as he looked at the captain. "I never thanked you people, did I?"

"For helping you on Megara?" Picard asked.

"For bringing me back to life," Offenhouse said. "I made a lot of mistakes the last time around, and now I've got a chance to make up for them. Maybe there's even some justice in this. I used my talents to bring Khan Singh into the world, and now I can use those talents to help another world. Thanks."

"Not at all," Picard said. The prospect of saying good-bye to Offenhouse made him magnanimous. "Working with you has been a unique experience."

"Ain't I something?" he asked, recovering his normal cockiness. The turbolift stopped and opened its door. "So long, Picard," Offenhouse said as he stepped into the corridor. "I've got a world to save."